THE CORNISH MIDWIFE

JO BARTLETT

Boldwood

First published in Great Britain in 2021 by Boldwood Books Ltd.

Every effort has been made to obtain the necessary permissions with reference to copyright material, both illustrative and quoted. We apologise for any omissions in this respect and will be pleased to make the appropriate acknowledgements in any future edition.

A CIP catalogue record for this book is available from the British Library.

Paperback ISBN 978-1-80048-942-4

Large Print ISBN 978-1-80048-938-7

Hardback ISBN 978-1-80048-937-0

Ebook ISBN 978-1-80048-935-6

Kindle ISBN 978-1-80048-936-3

Audio CD ISBN 978-1-80048-943-1

MP3 CD ISBN 978-1-80048-940-0

Digital audio download ISBN 978-1-80048-934-9

Boldwood Books Ltd
23 Bowerdean Street
London SW6 3TN
www.boldwoodbooks.com

To Lloyd, who taught me that second chances are the best ones of all xx

1

Ella's attempts at breathing in and out slowly were being seriously curtailed by the hold-it-all-in underwear she was wearing. She had no idea how she was going to manage a glass of champagne at the reception, let alone eat anything. All she'd had the day before was a bowl of soup, so maybe a glass of champagne would be a bad idea anyway. It would all be worth it in the end, though, and Weller would get the wedding he'd always dreamed of. So what if it was usually the bride who was supposed to plan every last detail and it wasn't the wedding she'd have chosen? Their relationship had been different from the start and she'd been glad not to have to do all the organising. Okay, maybe the sixties wedding dress he'd bought from a vintage shop in Camden – without her even seeing it, let alone trying it on – might have been a bit on the snug side, but it was a small price to pay.

'Are you decent, Ysella?' her dad called out from the other side of the door.

'I hope so, if I'm not now then I never will be.' Turning, she smiled as he pushed the door open and mirrored her expression.

'Will I do, do you think?'

'Oh, my love, you look amazing. I hope Weller realises what a lucky man he is.' Her father held out his arms. 'I can't believe I'm losing my little girl.'

'You're not losing me, Dad.' Ella leant her head against his chest, not even caring if her shoulder-length veil got knocked skew-whiff in the process. In a weird sort of way she was doing this for her dad – for both her parents. They'd made it clear they couldn't wait to be grandparents, a wish only Ella could grant, and getting married first was the right thing to do. In their eyes anyway. None of that changed the fact that Weller probably wasn't their first choice of son-in-law, though.

'You'll be hundreds of miles away though, won't you?'

'I've been hundreds of miles away since uni, Dad, but as long as you and Mum are there, Port Agnes will always be home.' Ella sniffed, determined not to cry and ruin the eyeliner that had taken her weeks of trial and error to perfect. She might have been able to keep a steady hand in a life-or-death situation at work, but when it came to creating the perfect sixties flick with a liquid eyeliner brush she might as well have been wearing boxing gloves.

'I know you're doing the right thing, making a career for yourself that you wouldn't be able to do back in Port Agnes, but I still can't help hoping you'll come back one day, when you've got every promotion possible under your belt.'

'Maybe one day—' They both knew she was lying, and Ella fought to hold in a sigh. Maybe if she hadn't been an only child, it wouldn't have been so difficult. There might have been at least one brother or sister among the babies her parents had tried so hard to conceive through years of IVF before Ella was born, who wanted to take over the family bakery and never feel they had to leave Port Agnes to make their parents proud. Relationships were all about compromise, though, and Weller's life was in London. If she wanted to be with him, then Port Agnes was never really going to be home again. London was better for both of their careers, which was why she'd been so willing to make it their permanent home. It was the only way she could envisage earning enough to help her parents out when they retired, if they needed it.

She was a senior midwife in a busy city-centre hospital and Weller's career as an indie record producer was just starting to take off. They were achieving things they never could if they settled down in Cornwall and, whatever her father might say, deep down she knew he was proud. The last time she'd been home for a weekend, he'd told everyone who'd come into the bakery about Ella's latest promotion and her degree certificate was still on display behind the counter.

'Just as long as he promises to look after you.' Her dad took a step back and nodded slowly. 'He might not be my cup of tea, but if he makes you happy that's all that matters.'

'He will. My biggest worry right now is that the registrar will make a pig's ear of pronouncing my name. Sometimes I wonder if I should have shortened it to Ella on an official basis.' She smiled at the look that crossed her father's face. Jago Mehenick was a dyed-in-the-wool Cornishman, who at one point had even considered campaigning for local office with a manifesto of pursuing Cornish independence. So his only daughter's decision to move to London for university must have been baffling at first.

'Ysella is a beautiful name and any registrar worth their salt would make the effort to learn how to pronounce it. Ellas are ten a penny in comparison and, if you are going to insist on short-ening it, then Yssy would be a far better option.' Her father folded his arms daring her to argue and she couldn't help but smile again.

'Ella works for me. At least it did until I got engaged... Having a name that rhymes with my husband's is a bit... I don't know. Ella and Weller, it just doesn't sound right.'

'Hmm.' Jago shook his head. 'What kind of name is Weller anyway?'

'We must have had this conversation a hundred times. You know Jim and Karen named him after Paul Weller, and you know why. They met at one of The Jam's concerts.' She raised an eyebrow, but her father just shrugged.

'I don't get it, the whole Mods thing. Fancy turning up to your wedding on a Lambretta!'

'You don't have to get it, Dad. It's something their family are into, not to mention the fact it's the reason Weller's got a career in music. If theming a wedding around that makes him happy, then I can live with it. Even if it does sometimes feel like a bit of an obsession.' Ella shrugged. 'Anyway, getting to the wedding on a Lambretta is a good decision given where we're having it. At least he'll be able to weave through the traffic.'

'But that's another thing, isn't it?' Jago was like a dog with a bone when he got onto his favourite subject, which was anything that extolled the virtues of Cornwall over everywhere else on the planet. 'You could have been getting married in St Jude's church. I told you it was in *Cornwall Life* as one of the ten prettiest churches in the county, didn't I? And that's saying something in a county as beautiful as ours.'

'Dad—'

'Go on, tell me you didn't grow up dreaming of getting married there? Like me and your mother, and your nana and grandpa before you?'

'Okay, I might have imagined it once or twice, when I was still young enough to fantasise about wearing a princess dress on the big day, but Weller has always wanted to get married at The Old Marylebone Town Hall. His grandparents copied Paul McCartney, then his mum and dad got married there in the late nineties. Weller was already a teenager at the time, and he remembers it really clearly. It was the first thing we talked about after he proposed. It might not be your idea of tradition, but it means just as much to them as St Jude's does to us.'

'I s'pose you're right.' His response was grudging all the same. 'But I would never forgive myself if I didn't ask this and I know your grandpa asked your mother when she married me.'

'What is it, Dad?'

'I just want to make sure that you really want to do this and you're not just going through with it because you think it's all too late. I need to know that he's really the man you want to marry, without even a hint of a doubt, because it's not just one day this marriage lark you know and sometimes it's hard.'

'You and Mum have always made it look so easy.'

'That's because your mother's a saint!' Jago laughed. 'But your grandpa wanted to make sure she wasn't just settling for me because they didn't let her take that job singing on the cruise ships when she left school. I think sometimes they regretted it as much as she did, keeping her tied to Port Agnes and bound to marry a local lad from the very small pool available, just because that was all the choice she had.'

'You don't really think that's the only reason she chose you, do you?' Ella had heard about her mother's dreams of singing for a living when she was younger and she'd known Ruth had never been given the choice to pursue those dreams. But it had never crossed her mind that her father had been the consolation prize.

'I like to think not.' Jago grinned. 'But we're not talking about your mum and me, I think we've been married long enough now to prove our doubters wrong. Just tell me you're sure he's the right one for you, because you can't change people.'

'I'm sure, Dad. I love—' Ella caught herself just before she'd been about to utter the name that definitely didn't belong to her fiancé, and shook her head hard. '*Weller*. I love Weller, I really do.'

'You sound like you're trying to convince yourself.' Her father gave her an appraising stare. If he'd realised she'd been about to say someone else's name instead of Weller's, it was all his fault anyway. She'd only done it because her father had mentioned her dream of getting married at St Jude's; when she'd been young enough to feel like a church wedding and a big princess dress mattered. Back then, when she pictured walking down the aisle, the one person she imagined waiting at the other end was the boy she'd dated all through sixth form. Dan Ferguson. That was the thing about first loves, though. They were all fantasy, unrealistic expectations and oversized love hearts with initials and arrows running through them, doodled on the back of exercise books. She'd been hauled up in front of the headmistress for that one and Ella could still picture the look on the teacher's face, as she'd delivered a stark warning.

'You'll have to cut out that sort of thing, Miss Mehenick, if you want to be a good enough role model to be worthy of being Head Girl.'

So, Ella *had* cut it out – as least the part about doodling on the back of her exercise books. No one could police her thoughts, though, and the fantasies about marrying Dan had been hers alone. They hadn't diminished in the two years they'd dated, and she'd even held on to them when she'd first headed off to university in London. But she hadn't thought about any of that in years, not until her dad started talking about how much better it would have been to get married at St Jude's. It was all down to that, and maybe the fact she'd barely eaten for the last forty-eight hours. It didn't mean anything.

'Well, my love, that's all I needed to hear and even if you change your mind on the way over there, I want you to know that it wouldn't be too late.'

Something about the way he said it gave Ella goosebumps. Was it really not too late? If she changed her mind, could she still walk away from all this? Straining against the dress in another attempt to take a deep breath, she shook the feeling off. Last minute jitters; that was all this was. The best thing she could do was just get on with it, the way she always did.

'We'd better get across the road then. I don't think the bride's usual prerogative of being late is an option, there's a ceremony booked in straight after ours.'

'Like a conveyor belt, then?' Her dad couldn't stop the veiled comparison with St Jude's and she forced another smile.

'It doesn't matter; as long as you're the one walking me down the aisle and Weller is the one waiting for me at the end of it, it could be anywhere.'

'Okay then, my little Ysella, let's show London what we're made of.' Jago crooked his arm and she linked hers through it. It was a short walk from the Dorset Square Hotel to The Old Marylebone Town Hall. The hotel might have been budget-busting, but it was the perfect venue for the wedding breakfast. And with such a small guest list, choosing the Soho Room for the ceremony, which had a maximum capacity of twenty guests, seemed a perfect fit too. Weller had wanted to keep it low-key and it was sensible to save as much as they could for the three-bedroomed flat they were moving to, in preparation for starting a family. It would allow Weller to have a studio at home too. Getting on the property ladder in central London had been a hard-won dream and hopefully it would give her parents another reason to feel proud of her. Not to mention giving Weller a few much-needed brownie points.

'At least it isn't windy.' Ella dipped her head as they walked the last hundred metres or so to the steps of The Old Town Hall. She hated being the centre of attention and she'd seen a few passers-by look in her direction. So keeping her gaze firmly fixed on the pavement to avoid eye contact seemed like the best option.

'Your mother's standing on the steps.' Jago said the words with an upward inflection at the end, as if he was asking a question, and Ella finally raised her gaze from the pavement.

'She should be inside by now.'

'I know.' Her father quickened his pace and Ella had to half-run to keep up. 'She's got that look she only ever gets when something's worrying the hell out of her.'

'What's wrong?' Ella beat her father to the question, as they met her mother on the steps.

'I've had a call from Weller, the Lambretta has broken down.' Ruth Mehenick furrowed her brow as she looked from her husband to her daughter and back again. 'But it's okay, they're on their way in a taxi, so they should be here soon.'

'*Should?*' Jago bellowed the word, making a city-confident pigeon fly up from the step beside him. 'If he ruins this wedding with his silly themed antics, I swear to God—'

'Dad, it's fine, I'm sure they'll make it in time.' Despite her words, Ella's stomach dropped. The registrar had been quite clear that lateness wasn't an option. If Weller didn't get here in the next ten minutes, they'd almost certainly lose their slot, and her parents would have to go back to Port Agnes and tell everyone that there had been no wedding after all. It would be so embarrassing.

'Let's all go and have a chat with some of the guests. It'll pass the time and it might help take your mind off the stress of waiting.' Ruth already had hold of her husband's arm, but Ella shook her head.

'You and Dad go in. I'll wait out here, so I can see when Weller turns up.'

'It's bad luck for the bride to see the groom before the ceremony.' Her mother gave her a pleading look, but she shook her head again.

'I'll be more stressed if I'm inside.'

'We'll stay out here with you then.' Her father still looked as if he might land a blow on Weller's nose the moment he turned up, and she didn't want her wedding day to kick off with an argument. That would definitely make her the centre of unwanted attention.

'I'd rather wait by myself. Anyway, I need you two to see if you can charm the registrar into giving us as long as possible.'

'We'll speak to her, but then we're coming straight back out.' Her dad's tone was insistent. 'I'm not leaving my daughter standing out here like the last oggie in the bakery that no one wants to take home.'

'Thanks, Dad!' Ella laughed despite herself. He was partial to a baking analogy if he could think of one, having run the family bakery business since he left school. The comparison might not be exactly flattering, but she found it strangely comforting. And if anyone could persuade the registrar to give them a bit more time, it was Jago Mehenick.

Watching her parents walk up the steps hand in hand, Ella breathed out. At least negotiating with the registrar would keep them busy and stop them worrying about her so much. She hated it when they did that. If she'd been uncomfortable about sticking out like a sore thumb in her wedding dress, standing alone on the steps outside The Old Town Hall wearing one was a whole other level of attention she could do without.

'Come on, Weller.' Whispering the words under her breath, she attempted to blend in with a pillar at the top of the stairs; all the time scanning the road in front of the building, willing a black cab to pull up and for Weller and his best man, Ste, to get out. Her father had had even more to say about Ste's name than he did about Weller's the first time he heard it. *'Can't that boy even be bothered to finish the name Steve?'* was about the gist of it. Ella liked Ste, though, which was just as well, seeing that he came as a package with Weller. They'd been best mates since sixth-form college, and he shared Weller's passion for all things Mod. Ste was the sound technician at Weller's start-up record label and the fact that they got on so well, when they spent as much time together as they did, said a lot about their friendship. Their shared love of the same music let Ella off the hook, and she didn't have to pretend to enjoy camping at the Stone Valley music festivals, or use her annual leave up to go and keep Weller company. They were the times when she got the chance to head back to Port Agnes and give her parents her undivided attention. After all, she'd had theirs all her life.

Looking towards the road again, a crowd of what appeared to be mostly teenage girls had congregated at the bottom of the steps and they seemed to be on an even higher level of alert than Ella. Every time a black cab looked like it might be about to stop, they surged forward with their mobile phones held aloft to capture the perfect shot of whoever it was they were expecting. In the end curiosity, and a desperate desire to distract herself from how late it was getting, got the better of Ella.

'Excuse me.' Approaching a young girl on the edge of the crowd, she cleared her throat to be heard over the excited chatter. 'But can I ask who it is you're waiting for?'

'Jed Harris and Petra Alexia.' The girl looked her up and down, but she clearly wasn't curious enough about Ella to ask why she was hanging around on the steps of The Old Town Hall in a wedding dress.

'Thank you.' She might be turning thirty on her next birthday, but even she knew who Jed Harris and Petra Alexia were. He was a YouTube sensation who'd made a substantial fortune from a string of appearances on reality shows. And Petra was a former *Love Island* contestant and something the press called *'an influ-*

encer' which apparently meant she was paid to advertise products on Instagram. At least no one would be looking at Ella any more.

'Ysella!' She looked up as her mother called her name, trying to read her expression.

'Have you heard from Weller?' She called out as she headed back up the steps towards her mum.

'No, he's not answering his phone now, so he must be somewhere without a signal.' Even Ruth didn't look convinced. 'But the registrar says if he's not here in the next few minutes, then you'll have to rebook for another time. Apparently, there's a wedding straight after yours and the rumour is it's someone famous.'

'That's who they're all waiting for.' Ella gestured towards the ever-growing crowd at the foot of the steps. 'But I don't think it's anyone you'll have heard of.'

'I don't care if it's Prince Charles and Camilla renewing their vows. I just want Weller to get his behind in gear and get here in time. Your father's about to burst a blood vessel as it is. I've banned him from coming out, so he doesn't make a scene. You know what he's like when he gets a bee in his bonnet about something.'

'At least there aren't a hundred and fifty people filling the pews at St Jude's, waiting for a wedding that might not happen.' Ella bit her lip. If the worst came to the worst and they had to postpone the wedding, it might be embarrassing, but at least they'd only be inconveniencing a handful of people. She hadn't been able to invite even her closest friends from the hospital, or her childhood friends from Port Agnes. But now that seemed like a good thing. Having old friends travel for a non-wedding would have been a disaster. 'You don't think he's having second thoughts, do you, Mum?'

'No, of course not!' The crease between Ruth's eyebrows could have clamped a fifty pence piece in place. 'Why? Are you?'

'No. Just a few pre-wedding jitters, that's all.' Ella shrugged, feeling anything but casual. 'And all this waiting around really isn't helping.'

'Ooh, there's a cab now!' Ruth was halfway down the stairs before Ella could stop her, but the roar from the crowd nearly knocked them both backwards. It definitely wasn't Weller.

'That's the celebrity wedding booked in after us. If they're here already—' Ella didn't even have the chance to finish the sentence before someone tapped her on the shoulder.

'Miss Mehenick, I'm really sorry, but unless your fiancé shows up in the next five minutes, we'll have to move on to the wedding after yours. We're pushing it as it is, and we really can't keep the next couple waiting.' The registrar, who was wearing a dark fitted skirt suit and an air of impatience, looked at her watch. 'We've really been as generous as we can.'

'What if the next couple were prepared to wait a bit longer?' Ruth turned to the registrar, who shook her head.

'It doesn't work like that, and we really couldn't ask someone to push their own wedding back, just because you've had a bit of a hitch.'

'Well, you might not be able to ask, but I can!' Ruth was down the steps and pushing her way through the crowd of celeb spotters before the registrar could even respond.

'She wouldn't actually have the gall to ask them to delay their wedding, would she?' The registrar looked at Ella.

'I wouldn't put it past her.' It would only make things worse if Ella tried to stop her mother. Jed and Petra would tell her there was no way they were postponing their wedding and that would be that, but at least Ruth would feel like she'd done her bit. Except that wasn't it. And seconds later Ruth was heading back up the stairs, with Jed and Petra trailing in her wake, the crowd still ebbing and flowing behind them.

'Ysella, right?' Jed pronounced her name perfectly and stuck out his hand. He had brilliantly white teeth and a smile that showed off his expensive dental work. 'Your mum tells us you've had a bit of disaster this morning with a missing groom?'

'Hi, yes, but he's not missing, he's just broken down en route.' Ella was only too aware of the crowd hanging on their every word.

'Nightmare!' Petra had the long legs and wide-eyed look of a startled foal.

'Either way, it's delayed the wedding, right?' Jed waited until she nodded. 'Your mum asked if we'd mind holding on for a bit, before I finally make an honest woman of this gorgeous girl. I'm sure we can keep ourselves busy with our friends here for a bit longer, can't we, babe? A bit of live streaming on Insta never goes amiss!' He looked at Petra, who nodded in agreement and the crowd let out another roar of approval.

'I love you, Jed!' One young girl at the front of the crowd, with train track braces and dot-to-dot spots, looked like she might be about to pass out. The Old Marylebone Town Hall might have had to cope with Beatlemania back in the sixties, but these days a YouTuber could have much the same impact on a young fan. If he'd been there, Weller would have been horrified.

'I'm assuming that's okay with you...' Jed peered at the registrar's name badge, 'Fiona?'

'Of course. As long as the two of you are happy?' She smiled, suddenly only too willing to oblige, and Jed handed his phone to a man standing to the right of him.

'Get all of this, will you, Jimmy? Like I said, this will make a great Insta story while we're waiting for the main event. Let's get a couple of shots first, before we start live streaming.' Jed put one arm around Petra and the other around the registrar. Whether they liked it or not, Ella and Ruth were marshalled into the photo too. It was a small price to pay for the celebrity couple delaying their wedding.

The next ten minutes passed with Jed and Petra taking a series of shots and posing with fans, while the registrar continued to drum her fingers on the notebook she was holding. Glancing back at the road, Ella made a pact with herself. If Weller didn't step out of one of the next ten cars that passed, then she was calling the wedding off; even if Jed and Petra were still willing to wait. As stressed as all this was making Ella, it would be even worse for her parents and there was her dad's blood pressure to think about.

One, two, three, four, five... they all drove straight past and then a black cab came into view. Her heart had already lurched at least thirty times at the sight of a black cab, so she wasn't expecting it to stop. Even when it did, she was almost beyond believing that Weller would be the person to step out. And then he did. He'd made it, in the nick of time.

'We were just about to give up on you!' Ella didn't know whether to hug him or slap him when he bounded up the steps with Ste following hot on his heels.

'I know, I'm sorry, we broke down and then—' He couldn't meet her gaze and he turned to Ste instead, who slowly nodded his head.

'And then *what*?' Ella was all too aware of the crowd watching them and she could almost feel Jed's breath on the back of her neck. So much for not wanting to be the centre of attention.

'You've got to tell her, mate.' It was Ste's voice, urging Weller to spit it out, but he was still looking at the floor. 'Go on, we talked about this.'

'I'm sorry, Ella. When the Lambretta broke down, my first thought was to hail a cab and get here as quickly as I could. I wanted to marry you, so we could move into the flat and start a family, just like we talked about. I really did. At least I thought so.'

'You thought so?' Ella repeated the words, wondering if she was going to wake up in a minute and find herself still lying in bed at the Dorset Square Hotel. But she couldn't be imagining how tight her dress felt, as she struggled to steady her breathing, while the crowd watched on. If Weller had noticed them he didn't seem to care, and he carried on regardless.

'We got a cab straight away, but the closer it got to you, the more I got the urge to ask the cabbie to just keep going. So we did. We've been past here six times already.'

'Did you see me standing here waiting?' Her voice sounded quiet, even to her own ears, and she was barely able to believe she was asking the question.

'I did and I'm sorry. But it felt like a sign: the Lambretta breaking down. The last chance to stop things before we both did something we'd end up regretting.' He tried to reach out and touch her, but she pulled away as if she'd been burnt. 'We're just too different you and me. We don't want the same things, I don't think we ever have, but I knew it for certain when I was in the back of the cab. I had that song by The Jam playing on a loop in my head.'

'What the hell are you talking about? What song?' This couldn't be real. The noise of the busy London street seemed to have faded away and the crowd didn't even murmur, all of them waiting to hear what Weller said next.

'You know that song I'm always playing, "I've Changed My Address", when Paul Weller sings about not seeing the point of marriage and being tied down to a mortgage and kids? It was like he was talking about me and I realised I was doing all of this, settling down and getting married, because I'm thirty-five and that's what the world expects, not because I want to.'

'And it took seeing me standing on the steps outside our wedding venue for you to realise that?' Ella shoved the bouquet she was holding against his chest and he tried to grab her hand again, but she was too quick for him. He didn't get to patronise her with words of comfort, he'd already done enough by humiliating her and her parents in front of a crowd of strangers. 'For your information I had my doubts too, but I would *never, ever* have treated you the way you've treated me. You don't do that to someone you love.'

'No, you don't.' Weller shook his head. 'I don't love you, Ella, I'm so sorry. I think if I could ever have loved someone enough to make them my wife, it would have been you, but I can't keep lying to either of us.'

'You absolute—' Ruth launched herself at him and it took Jed and his videographer, Jimmy, to hold her back, her arms and legs flailing in all directions. 'This lot might be able to stop me now, but when Jago finds out about this, you'll wish you'd never been born!'

'He's not worth it, Mum.' Ripping off her engagement ring, Ella threw it into the crowd, scattering them apart as they fought to retrieve it. She was beyond caring whose social media page she, or her ring, turned up on.

'I'm sorry, Ella, please—' She turned away from Weller as he called out. Easing his guilt was his problem, not hers. Ignoring the commotion still going on behind her, she headed back up the steps to break the news to her father and she felt an arm go around her shoulders. It was Petra, of all people, and she had a look of genuine sympathy on her face.

'You'll be glad he did this one day, I promise you.'

'You think?' Tears choked at the back of Ella's throat, but she couldn't seem to cry.

'I'm certain of it.'

'She's right you know, you can do better.' Her mother was suddenly at her other side, her rage seeming to subside and her voice taking on a far gentler tone. 'It's going to be hard telling everyone. But like you said, at least there aren't loads of guests here, and this will all soon be yesterday's news.'

'Hmm, except that what goes on the internet is out there

forever.' Jed shrugged as he came towards them. 'And there was a fair portion of the crowd taking photos, some of them were even filming it.'

'This day just keeps getting better.' The first tears plopped onto Ella's cheek and once they'd started, she wasn't sure she'd ever be able to stop them. She'd always thought her wedding day would change her life, but she was pretty sure no one could have predicted it would turn out quite like this.

2

Ella breathed in for the count of three, held her breath for four seconds and then released it to a silent count of five. As a midwife, she'd been ahead of the curve about the so-called power of breathing. It had always been essential to life, but now the self-help gurus were keen to say they'd created something new. The three, four, five breathing technique was supposed to be the equivalent of a double gin and tonic, and since she couldn't turn up to her first day at the Port Agnes midwifery unit the worse for wear, she just had to hope it was going to work. It might only be a six-month contract to cover the secondment of another midwife, but that was all she needed. Six months should be more than enough time to get her life back on track and forget that Weller had even been a part of it.

Parking her Fiat 500 in the last available space in the staff car park, she repeated the breathing exercise a few more times. She could do this, as long as no one mentioned her fifteen minutes of fame. Her hair was a different colour, back to its original dark brown, and much wavier than it had been when she'd been videoed on the steps of The Old Marylebone Town Hall. It was a classic *get-that-man-out-of-your-hair* move, but the hairdresser had been a bit overly enthusiastic, cutting in shorter and shorter layers to make the most of her hair's natural curl. So the last month had been one long bad hair day. It had taken some moulding clay and half a can of hairspray to get it all to lay flat for the job interview. But six weeks later, on day one of her new job, she finally had the soft curls she'd been going for, instead of looking like Brian May in his seventies heyday.

Getting out of the car, she headed across the car park and through the entrance to the midwifery unit. It was a sunny day, but it would probably have been just as bright inside the building, even if the skies outside had been grey. The walls were painted sky blue, except for the one that wrapped around the waiting area in reception, which was a brightly coloured mural of families playing on the beach in Port Agnes. When she'd come for her interview, the head of the unit, Anna Jones, had told her the mural had been created by a local artist, who'd donated his time for free as a thank you to the team for helping a family member through a difficult delivery. Whatever the reasons behind the mural, it was hard to look at it and not feel happy.

'Good morning.' Ella stopped at the reception desk and smiled when the young woman behind the counter looked up at her. 'I'm Ella Mehenick, the new midwife, covering Sadie Turner's secondment.'

'Ah yes, Anna told me you were starting today.' The receptionist stood up and took a package out of the drawer. 'I've pulled together all the things you need to get started. Here's your ID badge and a fob for the door, as well as a permit for the car park, which you'll need to put in the window any time you're here for more than two hours. I think Anna is going to have you shadow her today, so you can pop it in your car when you go out later. She'll give you all of the kit you need for when you go out and do your rounds, too. I'm Penny by the way.'

'Pleased to meet you, Penny.'

'You too. I've only recently moved to Port Agnes, so I'm just getting to know people. But Anna said you grew up here?'

'That's right, but I haven't lived here in over ten years, so I hardly know anyone any more either. All my old friends left for uni and never came back. I think it's because the choice of jobs on offer are brilliant... as long as you want to be in the hospitality industry or buy yourself a fishing boat! That's started to change since they built the unit, though, and it was part of the draw of deciding to come home for a few months.' She wasn't about to offer the other reasons up if she didn't have to. It was just good to get through an introduction, back in Port Agnes, without being outed as the jilted bride who'd become the sort of viral internet sensation no one wanted to be. Even two months on, she was still getting emails asking if she was willing to be interviewed on some daytime TV show or other about what it felt like to be jilted. She could probably have summed it up in one word, but it wasn't the sort of thing you could say on daytime TV, or to her new colleagues. Even if they were only going to be temporary.

According to her parents, the local press in Port Agnes had run stories on her for the best part of a month after fans of Jed Harris and Petra Alexia had posted the video of Weller telling her, in no uncertain terms, that she was dumped. The online video had circulated worldwide and someone had even made a meme featuring Ella in her wedding dress, with text saying, '*this is what a bad day really looks like*'. She doubted if anyone was hounding Weller. He seemed to have gone to ground and even Ste claimed not to know where he was. Not that she wanted to speak to him, she just wanted to know where to dump his stuff. In the end, after giving him a whole forty-eight hours to respond to her messages, the local Oxfam shop had been gifted everything he'd left behind in their rented flat. It was a compromise, seeing as her father had wanted to burn it all and then post the contents of the dog poo bin at the end of their road on to his forwarding address. Lucky for him, Jago Mehenick didn't know where Weller was. Thank God they'd never actually got as far as putting down the deposit on the place they'd been planning to buy, that would have made things even messier. Some people might say Weller had ended things just in time, but none of them were standing jilted on the steps of their wedding venue.

'I'll just give Anna a call and see if she's free to come and collect you.' Penny smiled, bringing Ella back to the present.

'Thanks, that's great.' Ella's eyes were drawn to the mural again while she waited. One end started with a scene on a hillside and then the rolling fields led to a row of houses. At the far end of the mural was the artist's interpretation of the harbour. It was a jolly scene filled with children running after kites, and dogs chasing across the grass towards the beach. The row of houses that flanked one side of the harbour was painted in the same bright colours as its real-life equivalent. There was Mercer's Row, the terrace of old fisherman's cottages, that had been owned by a holiday rental company for as long as Ella could remember and where she'd had her first official part-time job as a cleaner when she'd still been in sixth form. Her cheeks went hot as another memory of Mercer's Row came to mind and she tried to shake it off. But there were just some things she couldn't forget, no matter how much she might want to.

The house with the bright red door and the big bay window, in the middle of the harbour scene, was Mehenicks' Bakery, where her parents had lived and worked for their whole married life and where she'd called home until she'd left for university. Peering at the mural, she half expected to see an image of herself staring out from the upstairs window across the harbour, like she'd done so often growing up. Back then she'd longed for the adventure of London and leaving behind the confines of the pretty Cornish fishing village. She didn't want to spend her life telling anyone who'd listen that she was Port Agnes born and bred, like her parents and grandparents; she'd so desperately wanted to make them proud of her for doing something different. Her mother had been denied that opportunity and had given up her dreams of singing to run the bakery, but Ella had been given every chance and she'd had no intention of wasting them. Yet here she was, back living in her old bedroom above Mehenicks' Bakery and not sure if she'd made the best decision of her life, or taken a backward step she'd never recover from, in committing to come home for the next few months.

'Oh, Ella, brilliant, you're here!' Anna emerged from behind the door to the birthing suite and hugged her, rather than offering the expected handshake. 'Sorry if that's a bit full on, but I couldn't let myself believe you were actually going to show up until I saw you here in the flesh. I still keep pinching myself that we're getting someone with your experience for a post at this level and for a temporary contract at that.'

'I just hope I don't disappoint!'

'Of course you won't. Come on in and I'll introduce you to the rest of the team. I thought Jess could take you out on her rounds this morning and you could shadow me this afternoon. Then tomorrow you can hit the ground running! We all pretty much muck in here with everything, though, so just because I'm head of the unit, it doesn't mean I don't still get stuck in. In a rural midwifery unit, with our patients spread across such a wide geographical area, there's never a dull moment.'

'I'm counting on it.' Ella smiled and a frisson of nerves twisted in her stomach. She'd been a hospital midwife for so long and had specialised in high-risk pregnancies and deliveries over the last few years. It was going to be really different working at a midwifery unit where they automatically transferred any kind of high-risk mum-to-be to the nearest hospital maternity unit in Truro.

'Well, you picked a good morning to meet the team.' Anna held the door open for her and they headed down the corridor. 'We've only got one lady in labour this morning and none of our clinics start for another half an hour, so most of the team who are on duty are in the staffroom.'

'Great, it'll be good to meet everyone.' Ella just hoped none of them were devotees of YouTube and Instagram. It had been less than two months since the wedding-that-never-was, but she'd already come to hate hearing those dreaded words: *I'm sure I recognise you from somewhere...*

'Everybody, this is Ella Mehenick, the latest addition to our team.' Anna who was tall and slim, with long red hair which was doing its best to escape from a plait, stepped to one side.

'Nice to meet you, Ella, I'm Frankie, one of the maternity care assistants. There are four of us all together, working on rotation. There's usually two of us here, but Bobby's assisting with the delivery. He's the only man on the team, so you can't miss him!' Frankie gave Ella a wink. She appeared to be in her late forties and she was very pretty. It looked as if she'd gone up a couple of dress sizes since she'd been issued with her uniform, but she clearly wasn't giving in until the fabric did.

'Great to meet you, Frankie. I always relied on the MCAs for everything in my last job, so I'll probably drive you mad asking questions.'

'Ask me anything you like. The only thing I won't reveal is my weight! That's between me, the scales and my fat club leader. Although she threatened to chuck me out if I don't start losing... or at least stop gaining!' Frankie had the most infectious laugh and Ella already felt better about taking the job. What she needed, more than anything, was to be surrounded by people who could make her smile.

'I'm not sure if I can follow that, but I'm Jess.' The blonde woman sitting opposite where Anna was standing stood up and shook Ella's hand. 'Thanks to your arrival, I'm no longer the newbie here. Although it hardly feels like that after the best part of a year anyway! But it's the sort of place that people don't want to leave, which means everyone's been here for ages. So watch out, just because you think you're only going to be here for six months, it doesn't mean it's true!'

'That's because you've got such an understanding boss, right?' Anna grinned.

'Of course, although the fact that one of the other midwives, Gwen, brings in cakes and biscuits she's baked for us almost every time she's on shift, might have something to do with it.' Jess had barely got the words out before Frankie cut in.

'I made the mistake of mentioning that to my fat club leader and she threatened to come in here and tell Gwen not to let me have any more of her baking.' Frankie wrinkled her nose. 'She'll be putting posters of me up in the chip shop and Mehenicks' Bakery at this rate, with a note saying: *if you see this woman, don't serve her!*'

'My parents own Mehenicks' Bakery.'

'Ooh, Ella, you lucky thing! Although God knows how you stay so slim.' Frankie pulled another face. 'If I had unlimited access to your dad's pasties and those split cream buns, I'd be the size of a house. Now you come to mention it, though, I can see the resemblance between you and your mum, you've got the same blue eyes. She came to fat club for a bit, not that she needed it, but there was a big family wedding or something and she said she wanted to look good in the photos.'

'Ah, talk of the cake-making guru, Ella, this is Gwen.' Anna swiftly changed the subject as a woman with grey hair pulled up into a neat bun came into the room. Anna was probably almost as grateful as Ella for the timely interruption. She was fully aware why Ella had been so willing to accept a demotion to return to Port Agnes for a temporary role, but she clearly hadn't shared it with the others and Ella liked her new boss all the more for it. No doubt it wouldn't be long before Frankie put two and two together and worked out it was Ella's wedding her mother had being dieting for. Hopefully she'd be able to get through the first morning without having to talk about it, though.

'Nice to meet you, Ella. Welcome to the team!'

As well as Gwen, the oldest of the midwives at the unit, Ella was introduced to Toni, another community midwife. There were two other MCAs, who worked opposite shifts to Frankie and Bobby, who she didn't get to meet, three more midwives, currently on nights, and one who was on annual leave. It was quite a big team, but they covered the stretch of Cornwall from Port Agnes up as far as Port Kara which was twenty miles north. The boundaries of the region they covered went about five miles inland too, all along that stretch of coast. Any patients unable to give birth in the unit could still have their antenatal care in the community, or at the unit, but they had to travel to the hospital in Truro for the delivery.

'Right, I'll just get the morning briefing out of the way.' Anna smiled at Ella. 'Then Jess can take you out on the road. You probably know Port Agnes better than most of us, but there might be parts of the area we cover that you don't know so well, and Jess has got at least one appointment up at Port Kara and you'll be taking over the care of a couple of the ladies you'll meet today.'

'I'm looking forward to working in the community.' Ella felt her shoulders relax a bit. At least outside of Port Agnes, she might not have to worry every five minutes that *the-wedding-that-never-was* would get a mention at any moment. To anyone outside her home town, her fifteen minutes of fame were already very old news and, at worst, a discarded newspaper lining the bottom of a bird's cage. But in the town where she'd grown up, there were people who'd never forget what they'd read about her in the papers and, worse still, those who wouldn't let her forget either. Whatever Jess might think, six months back in Port Agnes would be more than enough for Ella.

* * *

Jess was one of those people who had no inhibitions about singing along at the top of her voice to whatever song the local radio DJ was playing. So what if she made her own words up to half of the lyrics? It clearly didn't bother her, and neither did the fact that she couldn't hold a note. Ella would have loved to have had that sort of confidence but hiding in plain sight had always been more her style. Three Ports Radio, the station serving the coast from Port Agnes to Port Kara, seemed to be stuck in the seventies and eighties, if its preferred playlist was anything to go by. Although, according to Jess, there was a good reason for not changing stations.

'I know he's got a bit of the Alan Partridge about him.' Jess turned her head for a second and grinned at Ella, before fixing her gaze firmly back on the road ahead. 'But it's the only radio station where you're guaranteed to hear if Johnny Tingal's sheep have escaped onto Holly Bay Road before it's too late and you find yourself in a traffic jam that can only be shifted if you've got the stamina to herd thirty clinically stupid ewes back into the safety of their field. Trust me, I've done it, and it's even harder than it sounds!'

'That was Donny Osmond with "Puppy Love"!' The DJ shouted the announcement, so that it came out of the speakers about three times louder than the song that had just finished playing. 'Talking of puppy love, did anyone read the article in this week's *Three Ports News* about local woman, Kayleigh Mackenzie from Port Kara, who's fallen in love with her goldfish? I don't know about puppy love, that sounds more like guppy love to me!

What better song could I play next than "Kayleigh" by Marillion, whose lead singer is... you've guessed it, Fish!'

'I think I might prefer to herd sheep than listen to this.' Ella couldn't help smiling, though. At least she hadn't been in love with a goldfish, just a bloke who'd turned out to have the memory of one when it came to remembering why he'd wanted to marry her. Poor old Kayleigh Mackenzie was having her fifteen minutes of notoriety on Three Ports Radio now, and making headlines in its sister paper. Although, maybe Kayleigh was one of those people who wanted fame at any cost; even if it meant getting engaged to a fish.

'You'll get used to it. I expect this is all a bit of a culture shock, coming back here, after spending so long in London? Did you never think about coming back before now?' Jess navigated a bend in the road as they began to climb upwards and inland towards their first home visit – a second time mum-to-be called Lissy Holmes, whose care Ella would be taking on. The steep banks and stone walls cut off the view of the sea back in Port Agnes, and Ella shifted in her seat.

'I stayed in London after I finished my degree, mainly because Mum and Dad had insisted on using up their savings to pay for my course, instead of just letting me take out a loan. I felt like I owed it to them to stay up there and make the sort of career for myself that would repay their investment.' Ella still wished she'd been able to persuade her parents not to spend all their money on her, but the impasse they'd found themselves at had led to one of the biggest rows they'd ever had. All her father had needed to mention was his blood pressure and she'd had to agree to their plans.

'And what about now?'

'I met someone, but things didn't work out and I realised there was some truth in what my dad had been saying for years. *You can take the girl out of Cornwall, but you can't take Cornwall out of the girl.* I just had this longing to come home and do some work in the community where I grew up, at least for a while. I was delivered by a local midwife in my parents' bedroom, so community midwifery was always close to my heart, even though I took a different route. Mum and Dad tried for a baby for a long time before me and I was in a bit of distress after I was delivered. It's why my middle name is Abigail, after the midwife who delivered me, because Mum and Dad were so grateful to her and they were convinced she was the only reason I survived. I grew up being told that midwives had the most important job in the world and so it was all I ever wanted to be. But the midwifery unit wasn't even built when I first completed my training.'

'I'm so sorry about what your parents went through.' The look on Jess's face suggested she meant what she'd said. 'But I can't help agreeing with them that we really have got the most important job in the world, and the best one too.'

'Me too, but I just hope I've got what it takes to be a good community midwife, while I'm here. I might be a Cornish girl at heart, but, as my dad is so fond of saying, it's not the place it was twelve years ago, when I last time spent any length of time here.'

'Deep down, I think you'll find that things haven't changed that much at all. Especially in the community.' Jess smiled. 'We can support our mums to give birth at home much more readily than a generation ago. Now it's not just tree-hugger types, who want to throw a dinner party with their placenta as the main course, who choose to give birth at home. If a mum is low risk and thinks she can handle the pain with no support from an anaesthetist, then there's no better place to deliver in my opinion. For anyone a bit more cautious, but still low risk, there's the birthing suite at the unit. In some ways we're going back to how my nan did things when she was a midwife in the fifties. Only with better hygiene!'

'Even in a place like this?' Ella tried not to wrinkle her nose as they turned up a farm track, but the distinctive smell of slurry hit her nostrils before she even caught sight of the steaming piles of manure banked up against the side of a barn.

'The place is spotless inside.' Jess laughed at the look that must have crossed her face. 'Although it's always worth having a pair of wellies in the back of your car as a community midwife around here.'

Ella looked down at the suede shoes that probably weren't going to survive this trip. Although seeing as they'd been a gift from Weller the previous Christmas, it was hardly the end of the world.

'So this lady's low risk?' Ella asked, as they pulled to a halt outside the chalet-bungalow style farmhouse. It definitely wasn't chocolate box pretty. In fact, it looked like it had been built in the sixties, when putting character into a house didn't seem to be a top priority. Still, Ella knew better than anyone that not every house in Cornwall was thatched, or a stone-built fisherman's cottage with views straight out to sea. This was a working farm, and as much a part of the real Cornwall as her parents' harbourside cottage.

'On paper Lissy should be low risk. Her blood pressure is great and there are no other concerns for mum or baby. But this is baby number two and, when she had the first one eighteen months ago, he turned breech at the last minute. She'd chosen to give birth at the unit and there wasn't time to get her to the hospital, so Anna had to help her through it. The baby got distressed and it was touch and go for a while, but thankfully he picked up. She wants to try and give birth at home this time, but she's quite nervous in general about the pregnancy, and her husband works away, so we're checking on her once a fortnight, just to make sure she doesn't get too anxious about things. It's a lot more often than normal, but being able to support women like this is one of the benefits of community midwifery.'

'I think I'd err on the side of caution about home delivery if I was her,' Ella said, making Jess raise her eyebrows as they got out of the car. 'Sorry, I probably shouldn't say that.'

'Maybe not quite like that, but it's important that we're clear about the risks and share as many of the *what ifs* as possible, so our mums-to-be can make an informed choice. Lissy seems to know her own mind, though. I think the only way she's been able to deal with her anxiety about going through another labour, is to plan a very different delivery from last time. Unfortunately, I don't think her husband's as supportive as he could be, mainly because he has to go away so much.'

'Who's helping her run this place, then? Oh God!' Ella nearly jumped onto the bonnet of the car, as four cows galloped past and charged through the open gate just beyond the house.

'Ah, I forgot to mention that. Lissy runs a free-range farm in the truest sense of the word! And pretty much on her own from what I can gather.'

'How's she going to manage this place, with a baby and a toddler?'

'I'm hoping her husband might rethink his other commitments and be around a bit more, at least at first.' Jess smoothed her hair as they reached the front door. 'But we're not social workers, or even agony aunts, so if we've got any concerns after the baby arrives, we'll have to refer her on. That's the one downside to getting to know the mums as well as we do in community midwifery; it can be really easy to cross the line into something else.'

'I'll bear that in mind.' As Ella spoke, Jess rapped her knuckles against the door of the farmhouse and a voice called out in response.

'Just a minute.' Seconds later the door was pulled back and a visibly pregnant woman, with hair piled high onto her head, smiled at Jess. A jolt of recognition made Ella catch her breath. 'Sorry, I was just locking up the dog.'

'No problem, I thought you might be making sure Noah couldn't escape!' Jess laughed and turned to Ella. 'Lissy's little boy has just gone from walking to running and, last time I popped up to see her, he tried to make a break for it. If I hadn't grabbed him on the way past, I reckon he'd have made it halfway to the cow shed before I caught up to him.'

'He's getting faster every day. There's certainly no sitting about taking it easy with this pregnancy; not with Noah around. Thankfully he's worn himself out this morning and he's having a bit of a nap.' Lissy gave a little sigh and then she looked straight at Ella for the first time.

'On my God! Is that really you?'

'Fizzy?' Ella looked at the woman standing in front of her. It had been ten years since she'd done more than catch a glimpse of her around town, when she'd been back for a visit, but she'd still have recognised Dan's sister anywhere. 'I thought Jess said your name was Lissy?'

'It is, no one's called me Fizzy for years, I think Dan found it too embarrassing that his inability to pronounce Felicity when we were kids had stuck for so long and he refused to call me it any more when he hit twenty!' Lissy laughed. 'But being called Felicity always made me feel like I was back at school, getting told off for something, so Lissy seemed like a good compromise.'

'You'll have to forgive me, if I forget. You'll always be Fizzy to me.' Ella was surprised she was managing to string a sentence together at all. If there wasn't already enough to worry about being back in Port Agnes, then constant reminders of Dan Ferguson added another layer of discomfort. She'd caught sight of both Dan and Lissy a few times on her trips home after they'd split up, but flying visits made it easy to avoid anyone she didn't want to spend too much time with. Being back for the next six months would make avoiding Dan much more difficult. Especially now his sister was one of her patients.

'I'll happily answer to Fizzy, it makes me instantly feel ten years younger!' Lissy grinned. 'It's so lovely to see you after all this time, Ella. Dan won't be able to believe you're home.'

'I take it you two know each other then?' Jess looked from Lissy to Ella and back again, as they all stood around the front door of the farmhouse.

'Yes, sorry, Jess, come in, both of you. I'm just so shocked to see Ella after all this time. She was the love of my younger brother's life.' Lissy grinned again, as the breath caught in the back of Ella's throat for a second time. 'At least when they were eighteen and thought the world started and ended at the boundaries of Port Agnes.'

'A lot has changed since then.' Ella had half expected uncomfortable conversations in her first day on the job, but she'd never dreamt this would be one of them.

'I'm only teasing you.' Lissy ushered them into the house. 'Don't worry, Dan's not about to jump out from behind the sofa and ask where you've been all this time.'

'That's good.' Jess raised an eyebrow, as she turned towards Lissy when they went through to the lounge. 'Because you're not allowed to scare Ella off on her first day on the job. Getting a midwife with her experience to come and cover a six-month contract had our boss dancing down the corridors for the best part of a week!'

'I promise I won't, that would be a disaster! We're so lucky to have community midwives close by. What with Noah and the farm, it's a military operation for me to even get into Port Agnes these days, let alone make an appointment I've got to keep to. We'd starve to death it wasn't for the fact the supermarket delivery finally makes it out this far.' Lissy ushered them in. 'But your luck's in today, the delivery only came yesterday, so we've still got at least one packet of chocolate biscuits left!'

Dan clearly had other priorities, if he'd let his sister get so overwhelmed that she was in danger of running out of food, and he didn't offer to help. Ella had heard plenty from her father over the last ten years or so about Dan's empire building, and his sister obviously came way down the list. But despite Lissy saying how frazzled she was, much to Ella's surprise the inside of the bungalow lived up to Jess's description. It smelt of vanilla and there wasn't a single scuff mark on the light grey walls. She had no idea how Lissy kept the place so tidy, while running a farm – not to mention sharing her home with a toddler and at least one dog, which had come bounding down the hallway to greet them as soon as she'd opened the kitchen door. Ella was desperate to ask why Lissy had left the beautiful old Georgian farmhouse that she and Dan had lived in when they were growing up, but her father had told her years before that it had been sold and set up as a boutique hotel. Dan's decision, apparently, and the last thing Ella wanted to do was rake up any old hurt.

'I've got the kettle on for tea if you want some, or there's the coffee machine?' Lissy shrugged. 'Although I might need some help with that. My husband bought it, but you have to grind the beans and everything and I think you need three months training at Costa before you can work it out!'

'Tea's fine, but I can make it if you like, and Ella can get up to speed on how you're feeling and any questions you've got about your planned delivery?' Jess looked at Ella, who nodded in response.

'That's a great idea, if you don't mind, Lissy? And then I can examine you, if you're okay with that?' The sooner Ella got started with helping patients again the better, even if it did feel a bit strange when the first patient turned out to be an old friend. Lissy was five years older than Dan and, at just twenty, she'd taken on his legal guardianship, when both their parents had been killed in a plane crash. The two of them had been incredibly close as a result and Ella had inevitably become quite close to Lissy too, when she'd been dating Dan. But all of that was so far in the past and she desperately needed to get back to being a midwife. Work had always been the best distraction when she didn't want to think too much about the rest of her life. The fortnight between finishing up her job in London after working her notice, and starting at the midwifery unit, had seemed interminable.

'Of course I don't mind. Like I said, I'm just so grateful for the home visits and I know I'm in good hands. You were always brilliant at everything you did.' Lissy smiled. 'I'll have a cup of tea too please, Jess. What about you, Ella?'

'Tea would be great, thank you.' Ella nodded, as Jess headed out to the kitchen.

'Shall I lie on the settee?' Lissy indicated towards the long red sofa, which was covered in a sort of tapestry design. 'Jess usually examines me there. I'm a bit obsessed with whether the baby is head down. I was thrilled when the sonographer said the baby was already in that position at my twenty week scan, but every time I feel a vigorous movement or kick, I can't help worrying the baby's flipped and I'll have another breech birth! I'm terrified of it happening again and I'm just so grateful that I get seen so often.'

'Try not to worry, babies can go head down any time between twenty and thirty-nine weeks. So, even if baby is bottom down at this stage, there'll still be time for it to turn, but let's have a look, shall we?' Ella rubbed her hands together to warm them up and placed them on Lissy's stomach. At this stage, it was much too early to hazard a guess just from looking whether the baby was still head down. After she'd palpated Lissy's stomach, and felt what she was certain was the baby's bottom higher up in the abdomen, she was more confident. What she wasn't going to tell Lissy was that the baby could turn bottom down, just as easily as it could turn head down, until she was much further along. 'It looks like baby's still the right way up, or should that be the right way down.'

'Thank goodness for that.'

'I'm just going to measure you, to check the baby's on track for your dates.' Ella took out her tape to measure the height of the fundus and it was bang on expectations; another good sign that this pregnancy was going to plan so far. 'That all looks good. Do you know what you're having?'

'No, my husband didn't want to find out. It might have made planning a bit easier and I'd know whether I could get away with handing down all of Noah's stuff to the baby or not. I know a lot of things are supposed to be gender neutral now, but whenever I'm out shopping for Noah's clothes, there are always so many pretty outfits for girls. Little dresses and matching tights. The sort of things that would be completely impractical for life on the farm!' Lissy laughed.

'I have to say I can see both sides of the argument about finding out the gender. There's always an air of excitement in the delivery room when no one knows what we're expecting. Shall we have a listen to baby's heartbeat?' Ella placed a Doppler on Lissy's stomach, moving it around until they could both hear the rapid beat of the baby's heart. It didn't matter how many times Ella did it – even when there were no indications that anything was wrong – the reassuring rhythm of the baby's heartbeat was always the best sound there was. Between the shape of Lissy's bump and the pace of the baby's heart, which hit the higher end of the normal range, Ella's guess was she'd be getting her wish for a little girl. It was still just a guess, albeit one with odds ever-so-slightly better than fifty-fifty. 'That all sounds perfect too. Baby seems to be fighting fit. How are you feeling?'

'Exhausted if I'm honest!' Lissy smoothed down her top as she pulled herself upright. 'When we sold Six Acre Farm, Dan and I split the proceeds. He kept the old stables and a bit of cash to start his business. I had enough to buy this place, with what my husband, Niall, put in. He was really keen to get the farm up and running, but we struggled just to break even at first and he took a job, just before Noah was born, which means being away a lot, even though we could probably get by without his salary now.'

'Could you get some outside help?' Ella had to dig her fingernails into her palms, to stop herself from telling Lissy that Dan should be the one making that offer. After all, his sister had barely been more than a child herself when she'd stepped in to take care of her little brother. The least he could do was help her out when she needed it. Jess had only just warned her how easy it could be to overstep the mark as a community midwife, let alone when she had a history with the family. Ella couldn't let the fact that her feelings about men in general had taken a severe nose-dive, since being publicly dumped by Weller, influence her either. She didn't want to become one of '*those women*': the bitter men-hating sort who tarred the whole gender with the same brush and had to be sent on diversity training every year, just to learn how to rein their animosity in to an acceptable level.

'I've got a bit of extra help at the moment luckily, so it's okay, really. I'm just having a moan, like we all do when we're a bit tired.' Lissy paused, as Jess came in with the drinks. 'Oh lovely, thanks, tea is always so much nicer when someone else makes it for you!'

'How are you getting on in here?' Jess turned towards Ella and smiled.

'Everything looks great with the baby. I was just about to check Lissy's blood pressure and we were catching up with how she's feeling and what a challenge it is running a farm.'

'I've got to say, I don't know how you do it.' Jess sat down in the armchair opposite, but she was straight back to business before Lissy had a chance to respond. 'We did a urine test last time I was here, didn't we? It all came back clear, so I think we're okay to leave it today, unless you've had any symptoms?'

'I'm fine, apart from feeling like I haven't had enough sleep for about two years! But like I said to Ella, that's all completely normal for someone with a job and a toddler, even if they aren't pregnant.' Lissy shrugged and Ella could see Jess was right. Unless they had reason to believe Lissy wasn't coping, it wasn't their place to step in. Just the fact that her brother could be a bit more helpful, if he felt like it, didn't give them grounds.

'Someone wants his mum.' A tall man walked through the door to the living room, holding a blond toddler in his arms. Thank God he hadn't even glanced in Ella's direction, or he'd have seen her staring at him, open-mouthed. 'He's been chatting to himself for about ten minutes, but then he started moaning and I thought I'd better get him up before it turned into full-scale wailing.'

'Oh God, I'm sorry. I must have had the monitor turned off. And you were up there trying to work!' Lissy almost yanked the blood pressure monitor out of Ella's hand as she stood up. 'But look who's turned up out of the blue!'

'Hello, Dan.' Somehow Ella kept her tone steady, as he finally turned to face her.

'Don't worry, I've always got time for my favourite boy. I said I'd be here to watch him while you had your check-up and the work calls can wait.' Handing Noah to Lissy, he smiled at his sister, not missing a beat. Clearly unexpectedly bumping into an ex he hadn't spoken to for years was no big deal for Dan. 'Ella Mehenick, it's been a long time.'

'Can you believe she's back?' Lissy nudged him in the side, as if Ella couldn't overhear everything they were saying.

'I'd heard that you might be coming back.' There was a hint of a smile playing around the corners of Dan's mouth as he looked at her again. If he found the fact she was back in Port Agnes amusing, then she wasn't going to let it bother her. What did bother her was the fact that somehow he'd got even better looking over the last ten years. He was over six feet tall and the boy had definitely become a man, somewhere along the line. He'd broadened out and looked like he could scoop her into his arms without any difficulty if the mood took him. Why the hell was she even thinking like that? Being suddenly confronted by her first love seemed to have scrambled her brains and she was back to being that lovesick teenager, scrawling Dan's name on her exercise book and daydreaming about him – the dark hair and sky blue eyes that had half the girls in the Three Ports area wishing they were Ella back then. But she wasn't a lovesick teenager any more, she'd grown up too and there were bits of her heart that were still patched up because of him. The last thing she wanted was to be confronted by that, not now, when she had a whole new set of scars on her heart to deal with.

'I'm only here for six months and then it's back on with the game plan.' If she could have got away from Dan in the next six seconds it would have suited Ella.

'You're still going from five-year plan to five-year plan, then?' Dan wasn't even trying to hide his amusement any more.

'I thought you'd be a fan of plans too nowadays?' Ella wrinkled her nose. It would be so easy to let him get under her skin and every time he smiled she had to drag her eyes away from his lips. She might be the biggest laughing stock in Port Agnes, but however amusing he was finding all of this he couldn't hurt her any more. Not like he'd done before. After Weller, she had no intention of letting anyone get close enough to do that again. Least of all Dan Ferguson. And he wasn't exactly flavour of the month in town either. 'From what I hear you've got a pretty grand plan to turn Port Agnes into a second-home owners' paradise?'

'I'm obviously still one of your dad's least favourite people.'

Dan's smile didn't slip. 'But never mind all of that, how's Lissy doing?'

'Everything's spot on, she could just do with taking it a bit easier.' Ella gave him a pointed look and he nodded. Sticking to the job she'd come to do made things easier, bickering with Dan was pointless anyway. She had enough on her plate dealing with the fallout of her most recent break-up, without wasting energy on something that had been over for a decade.

'If you can persuade Lissy to take it easier, then you've got my vote.'

'Dan-dan, Dan-dan!' The little boy reached out his chubby arms towards his uncle.

'Sorry, buddy, I've got to get to Padstow for a meeting.' He planted a kiss on the top of Noah's head and Ella bristled again. So much for saying he wanted his sister to take it a bit easier, he couldn't even wait until Lissy's check-up was finished. 'Nice to see you again. It's great to know you're looking after Lissy so well, especially after last time. Are you okay if I head off now?'

'Like Ella said, everything's fine. Don't let us hold you up.' Lissy smiled as Dan planted an absent-minded kiss on her head, in much the same way he had with Noah, and Ella had a flash-back to the last few weeks with Weller. He'd stopped kissing her, at least on the mouth, and she should have seen it coming: that slow drawing away that had led to those final moments, standing on the steps, watching him walk away. She'd put the lack of sex down to how busy they'd been in the run up to the wedding, but, looking back, there'd been none of the usual intimacy in those last few weeks. It was easy to see the signs, watching the way Dan kissed Lissy; if Weller had felt any kind of love for her at the end it had been the platonic sort. Another image flashed into her mind of what it had been like to kiss Dan. The first time was imprinted on her memory, however much she might wish it wasn't. All that pent-up passion only teenagers could muster and, when he'd finally kissed her, her whole body had tingled, crying out for his touch. She'd had no idea that a kiss could do that and no one but Dan had provoked that reaction before or since. But Lissy had summed all that up – they'd been eighteen and stupid. Thank God a relationship was so much more than physical, otherwise she'd never have moved on from Dan.

'See you later.' With another casual smile, Dan disappeared back through the door to the hallway and Noah started his chant all over again.

'Dan-dan, Dan-dan!'

'It's not fair, is it?' Jess grinned. 'You do all the work with the little ones and yet they never seem to learn to say "mum" first to show their appreciation!'

'You're right, it's not fair.' Lissy gave another shrug. 'But then when you're competing with someone like Dan, it's never really a level playing field, is it?'

'Shall we try again with your blood pressure?' Ella wasn't sure what else to say and, if she was going to have a good relationship with Lissy as her midwife, the less said about Dan Ferguson the better.

3

Reaching over to the bedside table, Ella scrabbled around in the darkness of the room trying to find her iPad and shut off the alarm that sounded like a heavy goods vehicle going into reverse mode. She could have sworn she'd turned it off the night before, because for once she didn't have to be up at a specific time. It was her first weekend off since starting at the unit and she'd been intending to sleep in until she woke up of her own accord. The smell of freshly baked bread filled the air, just as it did six days a week in the Mehenick household. Living above a bakery had definite advantages, but trying to diet when you were constantly confronted with that smell wasn't one of them. Thankfully her appetite seemed to have disappeared at the same time as Weller, so for once in her adult life she wasn't thinking about her weight. The irony was that she'd have room to spare in that too-tight wedding dress now, if her father hadn't set light to it in the small courtyard garden behind the bakery, while ranting about Weller burning in hell.

By the time Ella had showered and dressed, after scrolling through her social media feed on her phone for a good hour, it was past nine a.m. She'd done the usual Google check of her name, to see how easy it was to find the viral video that had received over four million views the last time she'd looked. As luck would have it, there was an Ella Mehenick out in Canada, who'd shaved her head for a children's charity and was now walking the circumference of all five of Canada's Great Lakes to boost donations to the fund. Ella's video had almost slipped off the first page of entries as a result and, thank God, or more accurately thanks to her Canadian alter ego, it looked like her unwanted brush with fame was finally over.

There was already a queue of people in the bakery when Ella went down to find her parents and offer her help in the shop; they took a day off even less often than she did. They'd spent a fortune on fertility treatment to finally get their much longed-for baby and any savings they'd built up since then had all but disappeared putting Ella through university. God knows when they'd ever be able to retire, so it was the least she could do. Watching them had instilled a really strong work ethic in her too and she'd spent every Saturday from the age of about thirteen, until she left for university, working in the bakery, and up to six days a week when she'd been on holiday from uni too. Some of her happiest memories were of working alongside her parents and exchanging banter with the regulars. Her father had warned her that things had changed in Port Agnes; things she wouldn't have noticed on her relatively infrequent visits home. There were less of the regular customers and more holidaymakers and weekend home-owners, because of people like Dan, according to Jago. Although this came from a man who had the Cornish flag tattooed in three different places on his body, one of which Ella would have to take her mother's word for. It made her cringe just thinking about it.

God help anyone who suggested Jago should take down the flagpole outside the shop, which flew the Cornish flag three hundred and sixty-five days of the year. Someone had complained to the council that it was a hazard, about three years after Ella had finally left home for good. Her mother had sent her the newspaper coverage of Jago chained to the flagpole after the council threatened to remove it and she'd been terrified that he'd have a heart attack over something that must have seemed ridiculous to most people. Eventually her father had won the case on appeal. Heaven knows how much it had cost him in legal fees, but for Jago it would have been worth it, and it was one of the many things she loved about her dad. Not many people stuck up for what they believed in to the extent that he did, even if it was a bit hard to live with at times. For the bakery to survive all the financial knocks they'd taken over the years, he had to smile and serve people who had holiday homes and weekend retreats, even though he wouldn't have given them the time of day otherwise. But it was the locals who'd get an extra fresh baked roll with their order, or a complimentary cream slice.

'Morning, Dad. Shall I get my apron on and give you a hand?' Ella caught hold of her father's elbow as she spoke, making sure he heard her over the chatter of the queue, which was already snaking out of the door.

'That would be great, Ysella. But only until ten when Maddie gets here. There won't be room for four of us behind the counter. Even if you are disappearing before my eyes.' He looked her up and down, but she wasn't going to get into that conversation again. Anyone would think she'd halved her weight the way he went on, instead of losing just shy of a stone and finally fitting into a size twelve. Jago was the sort of man who thought anyone without enough meat on their bones to survive a month stranded alone on Enys Samson – an uninhabited island off the Cornish coast – was about to waste away.

Maddie had started off as just the Saturday girl a few years back, but she was now at college training as a patissier and working three days a week in the shop. Jago had admitted it was a godsend to have her skills now that he had customers demanding what he called 'mucked about London pastries', but Maddie had her sights set on a career in Paris when she finished her course. It was another subject Ella avoided raising with her dad, after she'd spent half an hour listening to him ranting about how a croissant could never hold a candle to his own breakfast of choice: a bacon, leek and cheese pasty.

'You don't want to give up your precious day off working here, my love.' Ella's mum, Ruth, squeezed her waist as she was tying the apron strings around at the front.

'I do, Mum, honestly. It'll be like the old days, the three of us working behind the counter together on a Saturday morning, like we always used to.' For some inexplicable reason Ella's eyes suddenly filled with tears. It was good to be home. Not just because she'd needed somewhere to run – to escape London – but because there was a sense of belonging here that she'd spent so long trying to fight, to achieve all the things she thought she should. Deep down she was as Cornish as the solid slate floor beneath her feet. At this rate, she'd be getting the Cornish flag tattooed on her left bum cheek before the summer was out.

There was little chance to do anything other than serve customers for the first forty-five minutes. Everyone seemed determined to make sure they didn't miss out on the Mehenick specialities and, whatever her dad might think about how things were changing, there was far more call for the traditional baking he'd always done than any of those *'fancy London pastries'*, which he'd stare squint-eyed at whenever someone ordered one.

There was a brief lull of customers about ten minutes before Maddie was due to start her shift, when a tall man with vibrant ginger hair walked past the shop window. As he passed through the doorway, Ella couldn't help noticing how he filled the space, his shoulders seeming to skim the door frame on either side and she recognised him instantly, before her father even greeted him.

'Ah morning, Brae, I've got your order put by, my boy.' Jago shook his hand enthusiastically, like friends being reunited after a long time apart.

'Thanks, Jago, my customers would go mad if they couldn't have some of your rolls with their orders. Even them emmets have to admit they can't be beaten, especially not when they're stuffed with juicy chips made from Cornwall's finest taties. When they ask me why the taties taste so much better here, I tell them it's because even our earth is superior!'

'Are you just going to pretend you don't know me now then? Or am I an emmet to you too after all these years?' Ella came out from behind the counter and seconds later Brae had literally swept her off her feet.

'You could never be an emmet, Ella, you're Port Agnes born and bred, and Jago and Ruth Mehenick's daughter which makes you royalty around these parts!' Brae laughed, just like he had so many times before, when they'd sat next to each other in maths classes at Three Ports High School. The one and only time she'd ever got detention had been because they hadn't been able to stop laughing when the teacher had been explaining the purpose of a Cox-Zucker machine, which was apparently an algorithm used in the study of curves. It had been pure comedy gold to a classroom full of teenagers, though.

Back then, Brae was the last person Ella would have expected to use a derogatory term like emmet to describe the tourists and incomers to Cornwall. Tourism had been the lifeblood of coastal towns like Port Agnes for the whole of Ella's life, especially since some of the traditional industries had been squeezed out, and Brae's family had run a fish and chip restaurant for generations that relied on those very tourists. Jago's main issue was with the holiday homeowners who had pushed the price of property up so high that some locals, especially those with young families, could no longer afford to buy a house in the area. Ella had heard him use far harsher terms than emmet to describe them and it sounded as if there was a good chance that Brae felt the same.

'It's so nice see the two of you together like you always used to be. I always hoped...' Jago just about stopped himself before he said something really embarrassing. 'Well, never mind that, it's just lovely that you remember Ysella so well, when she's stayed away for as long as she has.'

'Of course I do, Jago. But I thought we'd lost her to London!' Brae laughed and Ella suddenly felt like the butt of some private joke that only someone who'd never left Port Agnes would understand.

'I thought you wanted to get out and see the world beyond Port Agnes too?' The last time Ella had seen Brae had been just after their A-levels and he'd been determined not to just join the family business.

'I did. I joined the Navy straight from school and did my ten years, then last year I came back and took over the fish and chip shop.' Brae shrugged. 'Dad was ready to retire and I'd finally seen enough of the world to realise none of it compares with Port Agnes.'

'See, here's a fella who knows what's what. The two of you must have a lot to catch up on.' Jago looked from Brae to Ella. 'You should go out for a drink some time.'

'Oh, I don't think—'

'I'd like that. When are you free?' Brae had spoken over Ella's protests, before she'd even had a chance to come up with an excuse. It wasn't that she didn't want to catch up with him – he'd always been great fun at school – but she definitely didn't want to give her father ideas about fixing her up with any of the locals. If she ever went out on another date again, it definitely wouldn't be in Port Agnes, where everyone but everyone knew who she was and what she'd been through with Weller. Not to mention the fact that Brae seemed to think exactly the same way as her father did; one Jago in the family was more than enough to contend with.

'She's free every night of the week when she's not working a late shift!' Ella's dad was clearly a man on a mission, and, if he'd picked up on her reluctance, he was thick-skinned enough to ignore it. Even when she turned to her mum for support, all she got was a sympathetic smile. Ruth knew better than to try and deter Jago when he got an idea into his head. Still, the path of least resistance was one Ella could take too and going out for a drink with Brae couldn't do any harm, as long he knew exactly where they stood – even if Jago didn't. Aside from Dan and Brae, her old friends from school had all long since moved away and it would be nice to have a friend in Port Agnes while she was here. It would make her dad happy too, and anything that helped keep his blood pressure down had to be a good thing.

'I'm off for the whole weekend, but I'm guessing Saturday night in the shop is a busy one for you?' Ella turned to Brae as he nodded.

'It is, but I'm free tomorrow. We haven't bowed to the pressure from the emmets to open on a Sunday yet, just because they want the same twenty-four-seven lifestyle they've got in the cities. Like I tell them, this is Port Agnes, not Las-bloody-Vegas.'

'How about we meet at eight o'clock in The Jolly Sailor tomorrow night then?' It was late enough that she could say she'd already eaten if Brae suggested dinner. And she could cite work early on Monday, if she wanted to get away after one drink and he wasn't nearly as much fun as he'd been when they were at school. Although if her recent track record was anything to go by, he might be the one who wanted to duck out early, and giving them the option of a get-out would save both their blushes.

'Nonsense, I'll come by and pick you up at seven-thirty and we can go over together.' Brae nodded as if it was already agreed.

Even if she'd wanted to protest, her dad wasn't giving her the chance.

'That's set then.' Jago gave Brae an enthusiastic thumbs-up, as Ruth handed over his order of rolls for the Saturday rush in the fish and chip shop. 'And the two of you have got my blessing for whatever the drink turns into.'

'Dad!' Ella flushed right to the roots of her hair this time. Even for Jago that was a new low.

'I just meant if you wanted to start dating, nobody needs to ask my permission.'

'You're unbelievable.' Ella shook her head. But when Brae winked, she instantly felt better. Okay, so he might be a dyed-in-the-wool Cornishman like her dad, but he had a twinkle in his eye that proved he not only understood, but he was still the same old Brae she'd known at school. It was just a drink in The Jolly Sailor and there was absolutely no chance of anything more, no matter how much fun she had. Weller had seen to that.

* * *

Daisy, the Mehenick family dog, was of indeterminate age and breed. She could have been a West Highland terrier, except for the fact that her fur was covered in dark brown splodges. Ella's dad always insisted that the rescue centre called her a Yestie – a mix of Westie and Yorkshire terrier – but no one knew for sure. The staff at the centre had guessed she was about four when she was rehomed, which made her pretty ancient now. She'd been Ruth's reaction to Ella leaving for university – a four-legged, fluffy, fur baby to help fill the space she'd left behind.

They'd never talked in detail about the reason why there'd been no more children, but Ella had a memory of hiding behind the counter, sneakily eating an iced finger bun, and hearing her mother discussing with her best friend – in the otherwise empty shop – that Jago's tadpoles swam in circles. Ella had been so excited she'd jumped up and asked her mother when the tadpoles would turn into frogs and if she could keep one as a pet. Ruth had been cross, something she rarely was, and she'd shouted at Ella and sent her to bed. Neither of them had ever mentioned the tadpoles again and maybe Ruth thought she'd forgotten about it over the years. Her father was such a proud man and so traditional, he'd have been mortified if people thought he was less of a man in any way because of it, however ignorant that might be.

She'd found out years later that her parents had gone through the IVF process seven times in their attempt to have a child and they'd suffered a miscarriage after their sixth round of treatment. When Ruth had eventually fallen pregnant with Ella, she'd been terrified that things might still go wrong. When Ella had finally arrived, Ruth credited her wonderful midwife, Abigail, who was the reason for Ella's middle name, with saving her daughter's life by acting so quickly to clear the fluid that had filled the baby's throat during delivery. As far as the Mehenicks were concerned, midwives were miracle workers and because of Abigail they'd got their longed-for baby at last. So they couldn't have been more pleased when Ella announced, at the age of ten, that she wanted to be a midwife when she grew up.

Even now her mum took every chance to cuddle a baby when she got one. It didn't matter if there was a queue out to the pavement, she couldn't be hurried when there was a baby in her arms. It was why Ella could forgive her mum so easily for colluding with Jago and engineering the date with Brae. Neither of her parents had particularly warmed to Weller. But in Ruth's case, it had nothing to do with the fact that he wasn't a Cornishman. Her mother had confided on Ella's hen night, after her first experience of a gin festival, that she'd never felt able to get below the surface with her soon-to-be son-in-law. Ruth had described him as hard to get to know and Ella hadn't been able to argue with that. Sometimes it had felt as if their relationship was a rehearsal before the real business of life began. At the time she'd told herself she was overthinking things, but now she hoped it was true. His only saving grace, as far as Ruth was concerned, was the fact that he'd been keen to start a family and she might finally get those longed-for other babies in her life. Ruth had promised she wouldn't be one of '*those mothers*', who was always asking when she could expect to become a grandma. But they'd both known she would be thinking it and praying for the day when she'd finally have another baby in her arms, when the prospect had seemed so much closer. Only it had turned out Weller wasn't keen to start a family after all. At least not with Ella.

All of that meant Ella could understand Ruth wanting her to start dating again so desperately and nodding along when Jago was giving his permission for Brae and Ella to take things as far as they liked. She was going to disappoint her mum, though. She'd have a very long wait before she got a grandchild now, but there'd be one, one day. Even if it meant Ella being a single parent, through adoption or fostering, she had the same drive to be a mother as Ruth had always had. Going into midwifery, she'd naively believed it was at least as much about the babies as the mothers. In truth it was the women – and more often than not the baggage they brought into their pregnancies with them – who were the main focus of her work, but she'd grown to love it all the same and she really hoped she was living up to Abigail's legacy.

Heading out to the patch of grassland behind the cottages that flanked the harbour, Daisy tugged hard on her lead. Given that the dog must have been at least sixteen, she could still ramp up the pace when her terrier instinct kicked in and she picked up the scent of some long-gone prey. Ella didn't dare let her off her lead, not after the last time. There'd been a young seagull, too busy making the most of a pile of discarded chips to notice Daisy approaching. When the bird finally noticed her and bounced, rather than flew, down towards the harbour, the dog had given chase. Despite screaming Daisy's name until it felt like Ella's lungs were about to burst, the dog took no notice whatsoever. When the seagull finally reached the edge of the harbour, and found itself cornered, it had launched towards Daisy, pecking at her back, and the dog had turned and run, not stopping even as Ella sprinted after her, still shouting her name. Daisy had been gone for almost twenty-four hours before she finally skulked into the garden behind the bakery. Ella had spent every spare moment during the dog's disappearance searching for her and printing out enough flyers for every lamp post in Port Agnes. If it was possible for a dog to look embarrassed, then Daisy had mastered the expression when she'd finally returned. The incident hadn't stopped her barking at seagulls when she saw them, but there was no knowing how she'd react if she came into close contact with one again. Ruth had cried when she'd heard about Daisy's disappearance, so Ella definitely wasn't going to risk it this time.

Letting the dog dictate the pace of their walk, which veered from speed walking to a slow crawl each time Daisy encountered a bush or post she just had to sniff, Ella let her mind drift. If she was going to get her career back on track, it wouldn't be long before she needed to start looking for another job again. Setting her up on a date with Brae would probably be just the start for her parents and, before she knew it, she could find herself sucked back into life in Port Agnes and the sacrifices her parents had made for her would come to nothing. Even if they didn't manage to marry her off to a local, she didn't want to be in her thirties and still living above the bakery. She'd even been thinking about the possibility of qualifying as a lecturer, so that she could teach midwifery at Plymouth University. It might be Devon, rather than Cornwall, but at least that way she'd be able to see her parents more often, but still be doing something that made them proud.

She might even be able to buy a house somewhere like Saltash or St Germans, on the eastern edge of Cornwall, which would make a commute to Plymouth doable. Maybe then her father wouldn't mind so much when she told him she wasn't going to start dating Brae, let alone marry him – permanently uniting Port Agnes' fish and chip dynasty with its bakery one.

'Come on, girl, let's walk back via the high street.' For once Ella pulled Daisy in the direction she wanted to go. There was only one estate agent in Port Agnes' winding street of shops, and now was as good a time as any to check the sort of price she might have to pay for a house in her home county, which could vary greatly if she went inland, away from the popular seaside resorts. It wouldn't be open, being a Sunday, but it meant she could browse the details in the shop window without the risk of being dragged in and signing up to a mailing list before she'd even broken the news to her parents that she was thinking about it. She'd probably be able to get a senior midwifery job at the hospital in Plymouth too, while she was completing her training. For the first time since Weller had dumped her, it started to feel like she had a plan for after her temporary contract in Port Agnes came to an end.

As it turned out, there was only one property in the window that was the sort of thing she was after, if it had been located on the east of the county. Instead the conversion of the old telephone exchange was slap bang in the middle of the countryside between Port Agnes and Port Kara. It was a cute, brick-built, whitewashed building, into which they'd somehow squeezed two bedrooms, a bathroom and an open-plan kitchen, dining and living room, with beautiful parquet floors throughout. The details described it as the 'perfect lock up and leave' holiday property. Ella just hoped Jago wouldn't spot the advert and graffiti the estate agent's window for encouraging more incomers into the town. At least it gave Ella some hope that the perfect place might exist on the east side of the county too, if her plans worked out. Getting one over on the emmets would give her father another reason to love the idea of her buying up a similar property, even if it wasn't in their home town.

Two doors down from the estate agent there was an art gallery, Pottery and Paper, which these days was open on Sundays, at least in the summer months. It was the perfect place for visitors to buy a reminder of their time in Port Agnes, or for day trippers to purchase a souvenir of a holiday spent elsewhere on the Atlantic coast. There were paintings, of course, originals and prints, but also pottery pieces and a whole range of items crafted from driftwood and other reclaimed material. Ella had bought a few things from there over the years to decorate the flat in London and remind herself of home. Those things were packed up in a box now, in the attic above Mehenicks' Bakery, after narrowly escaping the bonfire Jago had made to wipe out Ella's life in London, as though it had never existed.

In her head, Ella was already decorating a property just like the old telephone exchange with pieces from Pottery and Paper. Just enough little touches to be tasteful and tell the story of her home county, without tipping into looking like a seaside-themed café. It would be so different to the flat she and Weller had shared in London too, which made it all the more appealing. There was one painting in the window that caught her eye and, without even checking, she knew it would have the same signature in the corner as the mural at the midwifery unit. It was the same style, the town represented exactly as it was, quirky and distinctive, but with a warmth it would be difficult to put into words as effectively as the painting somehow did. The picture in the gallery was the view from the lighthouse down towards the town, and the people in the harbour were celebrating the annual Silver of the Sea fishing festival, which took place every August. The painting was big, about four feet high by two feet wide in Ella's estimation, but she could have been shown any four-inch-square portion of the painting in isolation and known it was Port Agnes. That was the level of detail the artist had captured, and she'd fallen in love with it instantly. The price tag of almost two thousand pounds brought her back down to earth with a thud. Still, if she knew Verity Grainger, who ran Pottery and Paper, and who had a reputation for valuing cash over creativity, there'd soon be a 'limited edition' of the original available for sale, negotiated with the artist, both online and in the shop. Ella would just have to bide her time. Buying a place to live that fitted her five-year plan was the priority and spending a chunk of the deposit on a piece of artwork wasn't going to get her there.

They were almost home again when Ella had to drag Daisy away from the stack of lobster baskets on one side of the harbour wall and pull her towards the narrow part of the harbourside road that led back towards Mehenicks' Bakery. For a good ten seconds she'd thought about pretending she hadn't seen Dan. He was taking photographs of the row of old fisherman's cottages in Mercer's Row, which had recently been sold at auction, after the holiday firm that owned them went into liquidation. Her father had been trying to find out who'd bought them ever since, but no one seemed to know. Having spotted Dan, it didn't exactly take a genius to work out who the new owner was, but the last thing she was in the mood for was another awkward conversation with her childhood boyfriend. She'd been just about to slip off unseen when he glanced up and smiled.

'Afternoon! Ella, can you hear me?' Dan called out, even as she kept up the attempt to put her head down to avoid him, but then the shouting started. 'TAKE YOUR AIRPODS OUT!'

'I haven't got any AirPods in. Sorry, I didn't see you, I was miles away.' It was a lie, but suddenly she wished she really was on the other side of town from Dan, at the very least. 'They're not the best-looking buildings in Port Agnes to photograph, they look like they could fall down in the next big storm.'

'I know, but you must remember what they used to be like?' He caught her eye and she did her best to adopt what she hoped was a neutral expression.

'What they *used* to be like?'

'When you were working there as a cleaner in the summer holidays? You were on the go all weekend, working in the bakery on a Saturday and cleaning here on Sundays, ready for the changeovers.' Dan gave her one of his easy smiles. 'As I recall, if I wanted to see you at the weekends, I had to come down here and muck in with the cleaning. And there's one particular Sunday I'll never forget.'

'So you've bought the houses?' She'd cut him off before he could go into more detail. She'd never forget that day either, but it didn't mean she wanted to talk about it. She'd rather die than tell him that she still thought about it every time she looked out of her bedroom window and caught a glimpse of the last cottage on the row. How gently he'd kissed her, slipping the strap of the top she was wearing off her shoulder, but her body had been impatient, her reactions racing ahead of him trying desperately to take it slowly, to make sure she was certain it was what she wanted. In the end it was her who had left him in no doubt, who had unbuttoned his shirt and pulled her top over her head as quickly as she could manage without ripping it. If it had been brazen, Dan certainly hadn't seemed to mind and she'd wanted him far too much to care. Shaking off the thought, she looked at him levelly, hoping she didn't look as hot as she felt.

'I have. Like I said, I thought it was time they had a makeover, but judging by the look on your face you don't agree?'

'They're part of the character of the place, and anyone who comes to Port Agnes thinking they can change things for the better should just turn around and head back out the way they came in.' Ella wasn't sure how it had happened: it was like she was speaking, but Jago's words were coming out. Infuriatingly, Dan just laughed.

'How long does a person have to live in Port Agnes before they become a local? It's been nearly twenty years for me now, two-thirds of my life, but I'm still an emmet, so it seems.'

'It's not about how long you've lived here, it's what the place means to you.' Ella's hand involuntarily moved to cover her heart, as if she was about to take a pledge of allegiance to Port Agnes. Dan might have moved to Six Acre Farm with his parents when he was ten, but he'd spent most of the time at boarding school until their death when he was fifteen. After that he'd come home to live with Lissy and he'd started at Three Ports High School just after he'd turned sixteen. Everyone had thought he was just moody, mysterious and incredibly good-looking, until someone had found out about his parents dying. That had made the girls all the more interested in him, but it was Ella he'd formed a bond with, when she hadn't even been trying. A boyfriend was never part of her plan while she was still at school. What with working so hard in two part-time jobs, she didn't have the time if she wanted to get the grades she needed. But Dan had wormed his way into her affections and there had been a time – almost two years – when she'd found it hard to focus on anything but him. Everything about him had seemed perfect back then. It hadn't just been about the way he looked; there was something about him that drew her in and made her forget whatever else was on her mind, especially when he smiled; it was like the sun coming out, because he'd seemed to reserve it just for her. After losing his parents, smiling hadn't come as naturally to Dan as it might have done otherwise and it had felt so good to have the power to change that – oh the folly of youth. Somehow she'd still got the grades she'd needed, but her rude awakening had come eventually all the same.

'This place means a lot to me too, Ella. I wasn't the one who chose to leave it, remember?' Ella bit back the retort that flashed through her head, her scalp tingling. He was the one who'd changed his mind and broken all the promises they'd made to each other. Now he was trying to make it sound like it had all been down to her. What annoyed her most was that it still bothered her whose fault it had been, when it was ancient history.

'You might still live here, but you're probably also the sort of person who thinks a drastic overhaul could improve the appearance and make the harbour look less like a working fishing port and more like the Disney-themed version so many incomers expect? God forbid that the clients who buy your so-called makeover properties might actually encounter the smell of fish.' Ella couldn't seem to stop herself. Something about Dan had rubbed her up the wrong way from the moment she'd seen him again. Maybe it was just the reminder that Weller hadn't been the only man to let her down.

'Actually no, I love the harbour exactly the way it is and I think Mercer's Row was perfect the way it used to be too, before it fell into disrepair when Trethowan Holidays went bust. That's why I was photographing the terrace, I wanted to make sure all of its charm is retained after the renovation.'

'You can't just have a façade of history like that, it's generations in the making and from what I've heard about your business, they'll be sold to second-home owners and they'll be empty ninety percent of the time. If anything can rob a place of character, that's it.'

'Fair point.' He looked at her levelly for a moment, before deciding a change of subject was called for. 'So, how's Lissy doing? Anything I should know?'

'She could do with more help with Noah and the farm.'

'I know, I wish I could do more.'

'Why can't you then?' It was no good. Jess might have warned

Ella not to overstep the mark, but sometimes things just had to be said.

'The farm is Lissy's thing and she's already told me to butt out more than once and get on with my own job.'

'Do you ever think she might be doing that to make life easier for you? Sometimes people don't always come out and say what they want, because it's hard to admit that you need someone's help. But you don't have to look all that hard to read between the lines.' Ella could still picture the look on Dan's face when they'd walked along the coastal path which led in the direction of Padstow, an hour before she was due to leave for uni. Her parents' car had already been packed up with everything she thought she was going to need in the halls of residence, and Dan had wiped away the tears that had filled her eyes, which had nothing to do with the fresh sea breeze blowing across the clifftop.

'It's only for a year, El, and that'll give me time to get everything on the farm sorted out with Lissy. Then I can come to London too.'

'A year just seems so long.' Even as she'd wanted to plead with him to come with her straight away, Ella had known that Dan was doing the right thing. He could hardly just up and leave Lissy to run the farm by herself without making sure she had all the help she needed first, and it took time to find the right person for the job. Dan had already made the commitment to come by applying for a place at an art college to study graphic design a few miles from Ella's university, and deferring it for a year. But when the year had turned into a year and a half, and then into two and Dan was still in Port Agnes, she'd finally realised he wasn't coming at all. When she'd seen him on her visits home during that second year, she'd never once confessed to just how much she'd needed him; to how much she missed everything about Port Agnes, but especially him. He wouldn't have needed to look very hard to see it, though, and after everything he'd promised her she shouldn't have had to say it out loud. Instead, he'd asked for just one more year, but he'd gone more and more silent about his plans to move to London, until he'd almost stopped saying anything at all. Nowadays they'd probably call it ghosting, but back then she hadn't understood how he could be so cold. In the end, she'd finally found the strength to walk away and let herself make the new start in London she'd put on hold waiting for Dan, while he'd begun the process of building the property development business that had turned out to mean far more to him than her. Now it was Lissy coming second to his business. Not that much had changed after all.

'You're right. I've got to stop taking Lissy's word for it when she tells me she's managing okay. I need to be there for her, especially while Niall is away. God knows she's made enough sacrifices for me over the years.'

'Exactly.' The fact it might mean there was an increased chance of Ella running into Dan more often too made her wonder if she really should learn to butt out sometimes. Being around him raked up a strange mix of feelings. Remembering quite how badly he'd broken her heart was weirdly comforting. She'd got over what had felt like the end of the world back then and moved on, so she could definitely get over what had happened with Weller. But she couldn't relax around Dan, there were too many memories that just a familiar look could bring crashing back to the forefront. All of that meant the thought of seeing him every time she went to the farm to see Lissy was uncomfortable, but she couldn't just keep her mouth shut, not when the health of Lissy and her unborn baby might be at stake.

'I'll swing by the farm now and talk to her.' Dan put the camera back in its bag. 'This time I'm not going to take no for an answer!'

'You could always be persuasive when you needed to be, but just don't make any promises you can't keep.' Ella frowned. She wasn't being fair and Dan was definitely suffering for Weller's actions because he was the one standing in front of her. It would be him desperately trying to avoid her next time around, but she couldn't afford to let it affect the support she offered his sister. Maybe it wasn't as easy for him as it seemed to be either. When he'd said she was the one who'd decided to leave, there was just a hint that it might have hurt him as much as it hurt her when they split. But his sister was all that mattered now and they both wanted the best for her. They might never get back to being friends again, Ella wouldn't be around long enough for a start, but at least looking out for Lissy was one thing they'd have in common. 'I'm sure she'll be grateful for whatever help you can offer and please tell her from me, if she's worried about anything to do with the pregnancy, all she needs to do is call.'

'Thank you, I will.' Raising a hand, Dan walked quickly in the opposite direction to the bakery, as if he couldn't get away from her, or Mercer's Row, soon enough. At least he wouldn't be tempted to talk about that Sunday afternoon again, when they'd lain on the freshly remade bed she'd prepared for the next changeover. Dan hadn't needed to do anything to persuade her to take the next step in their relationship, and it had been Ella who'd made the first move. She'd never regretted it, not even when he'd ended up breaking his promises. It was all so long ago now, though, and some things, like the charm of Mercer's Row, were definitely best left in the past.

4

By the time Ella got to work the morning after going for a drink with Brae, there were already six text messages on her phone: four of them from him. She had no idea until she read the last message how he'd even got her number.

Really enjoyed last night. When can we do it again? Brae x

How about tonight? Or tomorrow. I can do any day this week, I just need to get cover for the shop. Xx

Maybe we could have dinner this time. Or I could make us something if you like? I didn't ask if you like fish? Hope you do! Xxx

Sorry if I've come on too strong. My cousin reckons texting you three times before you answer might come over a bit stalkerish. I'm really not, I just really enjoyed reliving our old school days and I lost touch with most people from Three Ports High when I was in the Navy. Can you just let me know if you're getting these messages okay? Xx

You snuck out early this morning, I was dying to hear how the date with Brae went! Give me a call later if you can. I'll take it even if I'm in the shop, Mum xxxx

I gave Brae your mobile number when I rang him last night to see how the two of you got on. He's smitten! I knew you'd be made for each other. Love, Dad.

It was no surprise to discover her father was the guilty party and both her parents still insisted on putting their names at the end of every message they sent, as if she might not know who it was. She typed out a reply to Brae before she got out of the car.

Thanks for all the messages. Don't worry, I don't think you're a stalker! But your cousin might be right about waiting for a reply 😊 Maybe we could arrange another drink on Sunday, that way you won't have to take time off work? I enjoyed talking about school too, I'd forgotten all about Mr Stark and his skintight corduroys and now I can't get them out of my head! Have a good week x

Ella had agonised about whether or not to add the kiss. She didn't want to give Brae the wrong impression, but she didn't want to upset him either. He was a nice guy and he'd confided in her about his lack of luck with women and how he seemed destined for a life in the friend zone. By that point, Ella had already decided they'd never be more than friends, even if she'd wanted a relationship – which she definitely didn't. It had been her get-out-of-jail-free card, too, the plan to tell him that she'd been badly hurt by Weller and wasn't in a position to start anything new. Then he'd reeled off a list of excuses his past dates had used to friend-zone him and, right at the top of the list, was being hurt by a past relationship, so she'd kept her mouth shut and sympathised with him instead. Now it looked like they were going on a second 'date'. At this rate, she'd probably end up marrying him just to avoid hurting his feelings. At least she still had her plan to leave Port Agnes when her contract was up and she'd emailed the admissions team at Plymouth University about potential start dates for her teaching qualification, so she could make a decision about when to apply. Heading off to university had done a stellar job of ending her relationship the first time she'd gone, so if all else failed that should do the trick.

Her phone pinged again as she crossed the car park, and she steeled herself for a fifth message from Brae. But it was worse than that. She'd forgotten to unsubscribe from the newsletter that Weller's record label sent out when there was big news to share and an email had come through on her phone delivering the latest edition. She couldn't stop herself opening it and the headline said it all:

Modska Records are delighted to announce the signing of The Undermods, straight from their sell-out tour of Japan.

Ella might not have loved Weller's choice of music when they were together, but even she knew who The Undermods were and he'd been hoping to sign them ever since he'd started the label. He'd told her more than once that it would be a game changer and he was clearly making all of his dreams come true, but she couldn't hit the unsubscribe button quickly enough. Weller could stick his breakthrough news where the sun didn't shine.

'Morning.' Ella directed the greeting at Toni, one of the other midwives, and Bobby, the maternity care assistant on duty, as she walked into the staffroom. Anna had told her that Bobby was studying for a degree apprenticeship in midwifery, and he and Toni had been sitting together when Ella came in, looking at something on the desk, so close their heads were almost touching. When Ella spoke, Toni had sprung away from Bobby and got to her feet in a single movement a gymnast would have been proud of. She deserved ten out of ten for artistic impression alone.

'Sorry, did I make you jump?'

'I was just helping Bobby run through some questions for an assignment he's got coming up.' Toni turned back towards the desk as she spoke and slid what looked like a glossy brochure under a pile of paperwork.

'I'm at university part-time, but most of the learning is on the job. Like midwifery used to be when no one would ever have dreamt of a man studying it!' Bobby grinned. He was probably ten years younger than Toni, but it was hard to tell because he had the sort of boyish complexion that made it look as if he still didn't need to shave more than once a week. If there was something going on between them and they wanted to keep it secret, Ella wasn't going to blow their cover.

'I think it's brilliant, but I'm guessing you might still get a bit of stick about that from some people?' Ella put her bag down as she spoke.

'Definitely!' Bobby grinned again. 'I mucked around a lot at school and left with only two GCSEs. If you'd told me back then that I'd get into any kind of nursing, let alone midwifery, I'd have laughed in your face!'

'So how did you end up here?' It was difficult to imagine anyone falling into midwifery by accident; it was hardly the easiest of jobs but it was the only thing Ella had ever wanted to do, and that path had been set for her almost before she was born.

'When I left school, there were two choices around here for someone like me. Get a job in the hospitality trade, or work in a care home. Believe me, when I first left school, I'd have done anything to avoid working in care. But I got disillusioned with working in hotels and restaurants pretty quickly. If the other staff weren't moaning, the customers were. And most days it was both. I walked out of one job with nothing else to go to and I needed money to pay my rent. I figured I'd work in the care home for as short a time as possible and then I'd get something else. Except I discovered I loved it. I liked looking after people and the residents were always so appreciative of what I did for them. Well, most of the time! Some of them were really suffering, but they were tough. Most of them had been through a lot in life and they didn't moan because someone on a neighbouring table had apparently got more chips than them.'

'I can imagine care work was a lot more rewarding.' Ella glanced at Toni, who was watching Bobby with an intense look on her face, like she was trying to commit every word to memory. Whatever was going on between them, it was obviously more than friendship on Toni's part.

'It really was, and then the opportunity came up as a health care assistant and eventually I got placed here as a midwifery assistant. My mates from school still think it's hilarious that I'm pursuing a career with the word *wife* in the title, and they make jokes I couldn't repeat about what I do all day. But you know when you find something you love and no matter what anyone else says, you can't let it go?'

Ella was certain she saw Toni blush as she nodded. 'Good for you. From what I've heard, you'll make a great midwife. Hopefully we'll get the chance to work together on a delivery before long, although I mainly seem to be rostered on clinics and home visits at the moment. Not that I'm complaining, it means less night shifts!'

'We're lucky here.' Toni moved to the far corner of the staffroom to flick the kettle on. 'There are three of the midwives who prefer the night shift for various reasons, so it means the rest of us don't have to do nights quite as often as we would otherwise.

I mainly do them when I've been looking after a mum-to-be and I've promised to be at the birth if I can. Babies have a habit of coming at the most inconvenient times! Do you want some tea, or coffee?'

'Tea, please. And, yes, babies certainly pick their moments! Anna has rostered me on clinics and home visits, so I can get to know some of the mums and get a real feel for the differences between community midwifery and what I did at the hospital.'

'How are you liking it so far?' Toni dropped teabags into the cups.

'I'm really enjoying it, but Jess warned me it can be hard not to cross the line when you're working in the community. I find myself wanting to offer the women advice that has nothing to do with antenatal care!' Ella's thoughts drifted to Lissy and Dan. She'd mentioned to Brae that she'd bumped into Dan a couple of times, and Brae had soon been reminiscing about the old days, saying how sad it was that Dan had lost his parents just before joining their school. He'd been through more than his fair share of hard times over the years and Ella had jumped on the opportunity to give him a hard time again for something that was ancient history. Next time she saw him, she was definitely going to make the effort to be more civil. There were only so many grudges one person could hold and Weller definitely had the number one spot right now.

'Finding the right balance between caring and interfering is tough and sometimes I can't help myself.' Toni shrugged. 'I think that's why labour and delivery is easier than antenatal and post-natal check-ups. There's such a focus on just getting mum and baby through the process safely, in those hours nothing else really matters.'

'That's so true.' Ella smiled. 'I take it you're covering the delivery suite this morning?'

'Yes, Gwen and Jess are here too. They're both in delivery

rooms already. I'm expecting one of my ladies in soon. She phoned earlier to say her contractions were around fifteen minutes apart, so when they start getting closer she'll be coming in too.'

'We'd better make the most of this cup of tea then.' Ella took the mug Toni passed her. 'I'm running antenatal clinics all morning and then out on rounds this afternoon.'

'You might even get some biscuits when you're out and about.' Toni passed Bobby a cup and gestured towards the tins of biscuits and boxes of chocolates in the corner. 'Although we don't do too badly here with thank you gifts.'

'I've been here less than two weeks and I've already been offered everything on my rounds from cider to red diesel!'

'I can beat that.' Toni laughed. 'I was offered a ton of manure for my garden once.'

'Did you take them up on the offer?' Ella looked over at Toni as she shook her head.

'I might have done, had it not been for the fact that I live in a top-floor flat and I'm not sure I could fit a ton of manure into the window box!'

Anna had been right about the antenatal clinics being a good way to get to know the mums-to-be. By eleven thirty, Ella had seen a woman who had no idea who the father of her baby was, though at least three members of the local darts league were in the frame. Then there was the woman who brought in not just her mother, but her grandmother and great-grandmother to her check-up, so they could all hear the baby's heartbeat. Ella had nearly been in tears herself at the look on the eldest lady's face. She kept announcing that she was ninety-two and she couldn't believe she'd lived long enough to hear her great-great-grandchild's heartbeat, especially since she'd suffered from TB as a child, losing most of the function of her right lung, and had been warned she might not make it to thirty.

Ella's last appointment for the morning was with a young woman called Sophie Brighouse. She was coming up to twenty weeks pregnant and the notes said she'd been suffering from anaemia.

'Hi Sophie, come on in and sit down.' Ella held out her hand as the woman took a seat opposite her. 'I'm Ella Mehenick. We haven't met before, but I joined the team a few weeks ago, taking over from Sadie Turner, while she's on secondment for six months.'

'I heard Sadie had gone and they said I might be seeing Gwen today, but I was hoping to get someone a bit younger like you. Someone who might understand.' Sophie bit her lip and Ella forced herself to wait. If she interrupted, Sophie might never say what she clearly wanted to. 'No one knows about this baby, except the midwives and Dr Taylor.'

'Do you want to tell me why you haven't told anyone?' It was obvious Sophie was struggling to keep her emotions under control and Ella was glad she didn't have to rush the appointment. She had a break for lunch afterwards and she didn't care how much of her own time this ate into; she wanted Sophie to go away from the appointment less troubled than when she'd arrived.

'My parents will be so disappointed. This is supposed to be a gap year before I go to uni and train to be a teacher.' Sophie's eyes filled with tears. 'All my mum says whenever we go to a family event, or bump into one of her friends, is how I'm the first one from my generation in the family who'll be going to university. None of my cousins have done it, but she won't want to boast about me being a single mother, will she?'

'She might be shocked at first, but in my experience, most

parents rally round to support their daughters in the end.' It was tempting to promise Sophie it would all be okay, but she couldn't do that. She'd known one couple turf their fifteen-year-old daughter out onto the street when she'd announced she was pregnant, for 'bringing shame on the family'. The poor girl had turned up at the hospital where she'd been due for a scan, with all her belongings in three black bin liners. The sonographer had phoned the midwifery team and Ella had been the one to call a social worker and get the ball rolling so the girl would have somewhere to sleep that night. She'd eventually been taken into a foster placement in another part of London. Ella had often wondered how things had panned out for the girl, but she hadn't been able to support her once she'd moved on to the care of another team. She wanted to help Sophie, though.

'I'm an only child and sometimes it's like all their hopes are pinned on me. If I fail, then what else have they got?' The weight of her secret was etched on Sophie's pale face, outlined by the dark circles under her eyes. Ella knew that feeling only too well. Being the centre of your parents' world was a gift and a burden, all at the same time. If you ended up letting them down, exactly like Sophie felt she had, there was no backup plan. Ella's parents had forgiven her for every mistake she'd ever made and there was every chance Sophie's parents would too. Sometimes the hardest part was forgiving yourself.

'Just because you're having a baby before you might have planned to, that doesn't make you a failure.' Ella paused, struggling with how to phrase what she wanted to say next. 'Have you thought through all your options?'

'I'm not getting rid of it. I can't. I had an appointment at the clinic and everything, but I just couldn't do it.' She rested a protective hand on her almost invisible bump. The wonders of muscle tone on a young, first-time mum were helping to keep her secret, but that wouldn't last forever; especially as Sophie was so slim. Sooner or later she was going to have to tell people, or they'd guess for themselves and that usually made things much worse.

'Okay, it's good to know you've considered your options in that respect. But what about after the baby's born? Have you thought about whether you want to raise the baby yourself or—'

'I can't give it up. When I felt it move for the first time last week, I just knew I couldn't. It's probably selfish of me not to think about adoption when someone with their own house and more money could probably give it a better life, but I want to keep it.'

'It's not selfish and there's lots of help out there. I can refer you to some other service providers who can help with things like housing and what grants and benefits you'll be entitled to. If you think you'd find it useful to talk through how you're feeling, I can refer you for some counselling too.'

'I just want someone to tell me how to break the news to Mum and Dad.' Sophie used her sleeve to wipe her eyes, and Ella handed her some tissues.

'I'm sure the counsellor can work through some strategies with you, but you need to tell your parents before they start to suspect for themselves. If they confront you, I think you'll find it harder. If you can go to them with a plan of how you're going to raise this baby and maybe even how you can combine that with studying to be a teacher, they might find it easier to come to terms with.'

'Do you really think I could still go to uni?' A shadow seemed to lift from Sophie's face as she looked up, and Ella nodded.

'You might decide it's best to delay it for another year, but I've had lots of my ladies continue with studying. Some of them were still at school when they were pregnant, and they managed to carry on to university. It's about getting support from the services available, but also from your family and friends. Whatever you decide about the future, there doesn't need to be anything that's closed off to you for good just because you're having a baby. Right now, the priority is to make sure you and your baby are healthy. And the stress that keeping this secret is causing you isn't going to help with that. Are you living at home with your parents?'

'No, I'm working at the caravan park on the Port Kara road. I get free accommodation as part of the deal. It's okay for summer, but I wouldn't want to bring a baby back there, even if I could. My parents are in Somerset , and the sort of hours I'm working mean I don't go home all that often, but sooner or later they're going to find out.'

'What about the baby's father? I take it you aren't still with him?'

'He lives in Scotland. We were working together at a kids' holiday camp up there over Easter, before I came down to work in the caravan park over the summer, and that's when this happened. I thought getting work experience would look good on my uni application, seeing as I want to be a primary school teacher. And I wanted to prove to myself that I could get by living away from home because I was supposed to be going to uni in Essex. Euan is studying medicine, but his parents own the adventure centre where the camp is, so he helps out when he gets a break from uni. It was just a three-week thing and I don't want to ruin his life as well as mine, or make him feel he's got to be involved. We only did it twice and I still can't believe this has happened.'

'Hopefully talking to the counsellor will help you make up your mind about the rest and then you can decide when you're ready to tell your parents. But in the meantime, I'm here for you whenever you need me to be.' Ella was going to push as hard as she could to make sure Sophie got an appointment as soon as possible, but in the meantime she had a job to do. 'Shall we get you checked over? We'll listen to baby's heartbeat and measure for growth, and then we can do your blood pressure and check whether the iron supplements have stabilised your anaemia. If you can hop up onto the examination table, we can see what baby is up to.'

'Thank you.' Sophie reached out and touched Ella's arm. 'When I spoke to the midwife before you, she just kept saying I needed to tell my mum. But you've made it feel as if I don't have to give up on university forever because of the baby. I think if I can make Mum and Dad understand that, they'll be much less upset. I just need to find the right moment, that's all. I'm even starting to feel a bit excited about it now, because of you.'

'I haven't done anything special. You had the ability to deal with this all along. It just helps to talk sometimes.'

'Will you be my midwife all the way through? I really hope so.' Sophie gave her another beseeching look and Ella nodded. The baby wasn't due for almost five months, so he or she might not arrive before the end of Ella's contract, but Sophie had more important things to worry about for now. Hopefully, by the time Ella left, she'd be back with her parents in Somerset anyway.

'We're in this together.'

'That makes me feel so much better.' Sophie grinned as she lay down on the examination table. 'And I'm so glad you decided to come and work in Port Agnes.'

'Me too.' Ella retuned her smile. It really was good to be home. Having the chance to be part of these women's lives during one of the most important times, was a privilege. Ella had been lucky enough to fulfil the dreams she'd had when she was Sophie's age and she was determined to remember that, whatever else might not have worked out as planned.

5

'I'm sorry I had to make our meet-up earlier. I'd forgotten all about going out for Anna's birthday tonight.' Ella drew the teaspoon through the love heart shape the barista had made from a dusting of chocolate on the top of her latte. She'd been careful not to use the word 'date' and she felt guilty when she looked up at Brae, who was probably the nicest person she'd ever been out for a drink with. It really was great to have a friend to talk about old times with, too, but there just wasn't a spark. They were on their sixth 'meet-up' and it still felt like she was out with the big brother she'd never had. Thank God she'd been as honest as she could with him in the end and explained it was only a couple of months since Weller had ended things. She'd even confessed to being jilted on the steps of the registry office and if Brae had already known about it, then he'd done a good job of acting surprised. He'd also been really sweet and said it was no reflection on her, but it was much more difficult to believe Brae than it was to like him.

'It's no problem at all. I just like hanging out with you, you know that.' Brae grinned.

'I like spending time with you too.' The third time they'd got together, they'd happened across an elderly lady who'd come back to her car and discovered it had a flat tyre. At that precise moment the heavens had opened, and Brae had insisted on Ella taking the woman to the café opposite, pressing a ten-pound note into her hand to pay for tea and cake. The rain had been coming down so hard it was bouncing back out of the puddles that had already formed on the pavement by the time Ella got the old lady inside the café. They watched Brae through the window as he changed the tyre, water dripping off his beard and other cars saturating him as they raced through the puddles in the road. He was an old-school gentleman, with the emphasis on gentle, despite him being at least six foot five.

'So what are you up to for Anna's birthday then?' Brae picked up the huge mug of hot chocolate he'd ordered, the tiny marsh-mallows sliding down the whipped cream towards the rim of the cup.

'Casa Cantare apparently.' Ella pulled a face. An Italian-themed wine bar was one thing, but one where you were expected to get up and join in with the karaoke was quite another. 'I can't sing to save my life, but I'm hoping the others will take over and I'll just be able to stand at the back, doing a couple of doo woops, or la la las, if they force me to join in.'

'I can't imagine Casa Cantare being Anna's sort of thing. She was my sister, Morwenna's, midwife and she always seemed a bit shy to me the times I met her. I was staying with Morwenna at the time and trying to make myself useful by taking her to some of her appointments.' Brae laughed. 'Although I suppose the shyness might just have been me, I can be a bit intimidating with this beard and this much bulk.'

'You're not intimidating at all, you're lovely.' She'd been about to add that he reminded her of a big teddy bear, but it probably wasn't a comparison anyone wanted to hear. 'Anna's very professional when she's at work and I suppose it might come across that she's a bit reserved. Although I'm not entirely sure that Casa Cantare is her idea of fun, any more than it's mine. Jess has taken over the organisation. So I think we're getting the birthday celebration of her dreams, rather than Anna's.'

'From what you've said, Jess sounds a lot of fun.'

'She is and basking in the glow of the first year of marriage from what I'm told.' Ella's mind was working overtime. Jess might not be available, but there had to be someone at the unit who'd see Brae for the wonderful person he was. If Ella achieved nothing else in the next few months, then finding Brae the woman of his dreams would make it all worthwhile. She was pretty sure that Penny, the unit's receptionist, was single, after another break-up with her on-again, off-again boyfriend, and she'd said she was coming along to the birthday celebration. Anna had been off work for her birthday, the day before the karaoke marathon, to spend it with her boyfriend, Greg, who she'd admitted she was hoping might mark the occasion with a proposal. So Ella and the others were expecting her to roll up with a big sparkly rock on her finger. With that sort of romance in the air, then maybe the stars could align for Brae and Penny. 'Actually, if you're not doing anything, why don't you pop by Casa Cantare later on and come and see what idiots we're all making of ourselves?'

'Really?' Brae looked ridiculously pleased as she nodded, and guilt stabbed at her stomach again. If it worked out it would all be worth it though.

'It'll be good fun and I'd like you to meet some of the others.'

'I've got Pete and Linda working in the shop tonight anyway, because I thought we were going out later. So at least I won't have to go back now and send them home!'

'Great! I think it would be good for you to meet a few more

people. You hardly ever go out, working all hours in the shop. It's about time you widened your social circle.'

'You're right. I actually tracked Dan Ferguson down online too and sent him a friend request.' Brae shook his head. 'God, that really makes me sound desperate! But seeing you again has got me in the mood for nostalgia, and me and Dan used to be on the rugby team together.'

'Have you heard back from him?' Ella tried to keep her tone light. If Dan got in touch with Brae again, he might well tell him what a bitch Ella had been to him since she'd been back in town – criticising his work, and the sort of brother and uncle he was, without any real evidence for either.

'Yeah, he got back to me straight away and we're going to meet up next week. I thought maybe you'd like to come too?'

'I, er—' Ella suddenly seemed to lose the power of speech.

'No hurry, it's next Wednesday, just let me know between then and now.'

'Okay.' Ella could definitely come up with a plausible excuse between now and next Wednesday. There was no way she could spend a whole evening in the pub, sitting so close to Dan that she'd be able to smell the sandalwood aftershave he'd been wearing every time she'd seen him since she'd been back in Port Agnes. She was supposed to be focused on helping Brae find his way out of the friend zone, not thinking about Dan Ferguson – which was a hell of a lot easier to do when he was as far away as possible.

* * *

'We're engaged!' The diamond was every bit as big and sparkly as Ella had expected, it just wasn't on the right person's finger. Penny had rushed into the separate restaurant area of the wine bar fifteen minutes late, shouting her news and waving her newly adorned hand in the air, before anyone had been able to warn her that now might not be a good time.

'Congratulations.' The collective response was muted but Penny didn't seem to notice, despite Ella's attempts to signal with her eyes that sharing her news so enthusiastically was going to feel like a massive foot-in-the-mouth moment later on.

'Come on then, Anna, let's compare rings and we can see which of our boys did the best job at picking out something we'll be happy to wear for the rest of our lives!' Penny sat down in the empty seat opposite Anna with a thud, thrusting her hand towards her boss and making the ring catch the light.

'Greg didn't propose, Penny, but congratulations.' Anna's voice was tight and, even if her eyes hadn't been glassy, it would have been obvious she was working hard to contain her emotion.

'Oh God, I'm so sorry, I should have thought—' Penny looked mortified.

'It's not your fault, it's not anyone's fault. I just read the signals wrong, that's all. Really, really wrong as it turned out.'

'We can fill Penny in later if you don't want to go through it all again.' Ella spoke softly, aware of how hard it had been for her boss to be so open with all of them the first time she'd recounted the story, but Anna shook her head.

'I can sum it up in one sentence anyway.' Jess pulled a face. 'The man's an idiot, that's all Penny needs to know.'

'It's fine.' Anna sighed, despite her words. 'I might as well tell Penny now, seeing as the rest of you know already. He doesn't want any of the things I do.'

'He didn't finish with you on your birthday, did he?' Penny widened her eyes, looking like she'd be ready to hunt Greg down and cause him some serious harm if that's what had happened. Toni and Jess had already threatened as much, so there was quite a posse in the making.

'No, he bought a very nice present. Three weeks adventure

trekking in South America, but when he realised how disappointed I was, everything came out. He wants to spend his life seeing the world whenever we've got the time and money. But I want a wedding, kids and a dog. The whole cliché of family life, which according to Greg always turns into a miserable grind in the end.'

'Oh Anna, I'm sorry. And you had no clue he felt like this?' Penny asked more or less the same question Ella had when Anna had broken the news to the rest of the team. After all, she knew only too well what it felt like to have no idea what was going on in your partner's head.

'No idea, I thought we wanted the same things. I'd talked about kids right from the start, and he'd never said no to the idea before. I was thirty when we met and I'm thirty-seven now. But the person I thought I was going to start a family with in the next year or two, wants to backpack across the Andes instead and then give up everything we've got here to do what he calls "proper travelling". Maybe he's right, maybe I am boring for going for the safe option that almost every other person takes, but the thought of delivering all those babies as a midwife and never having a child of my own... I don't think I can do it.'

'You should never compromise on something that means that much to you.' Ella was only too aware of the sacrifices her parents had made for her, but they hadn't once given her any indication that they regretted it. Ruth was always telling Ella that she was their everything and, if Anna felt the same about having children, trying to convince herself that she wanted Greg enough to give up that dream would only lead to heartbreak.

'He wants to sell the cottage so we can buy a campervan and go travelling for a few years, without having to work. Ferguson Conversions made him a crazy offer, more than twice what we paid for the cottage, to turn it into two flats, but what Greg doesn't understand is how much I love my job and Port Agnes.'

'Ferguson's Conversions!' Frankie screwed up her face. 'Businesses like that have pushed the prices up so much around here that it's no wonder people like my daughter and her family had no choice but to move away and settle somewhere they *can* afford to buy a house.'

'That's Lissy's brother, Dan, isn't it? You went out with him when you were at school, didn't you?' Anna looked at Ella and she felt herself go hot. A big part of her wanted to leap to his defence for some reason. He was running a business and what did the others expect – that Dan could just give properties away to locals like he was some sort of charity? Another part of her wanted to pretend she had no idea what Anna was talking about. Between looking after Lissy and listening to her dad's rants about all the developments springing up locally, Dan's name seemed to come up far more often than was comfortable. Maybe she could brazen it out, just this once.

'Who told you that?' Lissy had spilled the beans to Jess when they'd been at the house together, but Ella hadn't expected it to be a topic of conversation with the other midwives.

'That'll be me.' Gwen held up her palms. 'Your mum *might* have mentioned it when I popped in for some split cream buns and I *might* have mentioned to Anna that reigniting that particularly flame could convince you to stay in Port Agnes for good. I mean, who wouldn't want a bit of that? Never mind cream buns, those are some buns I'd definitely queue up for!'

'Gwen, for God's sake!' Frankie pulled a face. 'We're talking about the man who drove my daughter out of Port Agnes.'

'It still doesn't explain why she chose to get as far away from you as New Zealand, though!' Gwen gave her friend a playful nudge and Frankie laughed, her face losing all of its tension. Unfortunately, it was just another reminder for Anna of what she'd lost.

'New Zealand was on Greg's list too, after three years of seeing

Europe in the campervan.' Anna sniffed. 'The best I can hope for now is that I'll be able to afford to buy him out of the cottage, but with what he's been offered by Ferguson's Conversions, I don't know if I'll even be able to do that.'

'Can I take your orders now?' The waiter who'd been hovering, waiting for the arrival of the last member of the party, suddenly appeared at Bobby's side.

'We'll have six bottles of wine to start, I think. Two white, two red and two rosé.' Bobby looked around the table and everyone nodded.

'The house wine, sir?'

'Whatever's got the strongest alcohol percentage!' Bobby dropped a wink in Anna's direction and Ella was relieved to see her smile. She'd said she wanted to get it all out in the open, so if she suddenly burst into tears over her chocolate brownie later on, or in the middle of a rendition of 'I Will Survive', they'd know why. Hopefully she wasn't going to regret being so open the next day, especially as it was obvious she'd already had a drink or two for Dutch courage before she'd arrived.

'And your food order?' The waiter held up his notepad, but Bobby shook his head.

'Give us ten more minutes and some wine first please and I think we'll be ready.' Bobby closed the menu to emphasise the point. 'I think it's going to be one of those nights when we all need to get horribly drunk.'

'If I can still remember any of this in the morning, I'll have considered you all to have failed and I'll need to take note for your performance reviews.' Anna laughed for the first time as Bobby saluted, the atmosphere seeming to lighten a little. God knows what state Brae would find them all in when he arrived later on, but either way he wouldn't be getting together with Penny, and Ella couldn't help worrying that she was going to end up making Brae feel rejected all over again. Bobby was right, it was definitely going to be one of those nights.

* * *

Ella was at the back of the group in Casa Cantare, pretending to join in with their rendition of Ariana Grande's 'thank u, next', when she spotted Brae leaning on the bar, watching them. Anna was giving it her all, with strong support from Jess and Toni, so thankfully none of them seemed to notice that Ella was lip-synching about as convincingly as a badly dubbed martial arts movie. As soon as the song ended, she headed over to Brae and he already had a drink waiting for her.

'You're the best.'

'I do my best.' Brae smiled. 'You and your friends look like you're really going for it up there!'

'Let's just say a lot of wine has been drunk, although not enough for me to do anything but mime.' Ella glanced over her shoulder to make sure that Anna wasn't within earshot. 'It hasn't been the best of birthdays for our boss, though, so I was even prepared to pretend to harmonise to make her smile.'

'I know the feeling. Last year I was still posted overseas and I think the highlight was opening another plaid shirt that my mum had sent me.' Brae laughed. 'Just because I look like a lumberjack, it doesn't mean I want to dress like one!'

'Things will get better this year, I'm sure of it.' Ella squeezed his hand, just as Penny came hurtling towards the bar.

'Ooh, look at you two, all loved up! You've kept that quiet, Ella.'

'This is my *friend*, Brae.' She put emphasis on the word, rather than attempting to explain to a very merry Penny that she and Brae weren't a couple. 'And Brae, this is Penny, she's our receptionist at the unit.'

'Yes, you've mentioned her.' Brae grinned as Penny lurched towards him, planting a kiss on his cheek as if they'd known each other years.

'Brae! I know you from somewhere, don't I?' Penny narrowed her eyes, swaying slightly from side to side.

'I've got the fish and chip shop on the harbour. You've probably seen me in there?'

'Oh yes, that's it!' Penny slapped her palm against her forehead. 'Me and my boyfriend, Joel, come into your place all the time. Best chips in Cornwall, Joel says.'

'Your boyfriend sounds like a wise man.'

'Actually, he's not my boyfriend any more, we're engaged.' Penny waved her hand in front of Brae's face, like Cornwall's answer to Beyoncé. 'But shush, we can't mention it, not in front of Anna. All she got was a backpack!'

'Well she looks like she's enjoying herself.' Brae gestured towards the stage, where Anna and Bobby were doing a very loud and largely tuneless rendition of 'Don't go Breaking My Heart'.

'It's just a façade.' Penny slurred the last word. 'She's gutted, cos he won't let her have babies either.'

'Penny!' Ella's tone was sharp, but broadcasting Anna's business for everyone to hear was out of order and Penny wouldn't have done it if she hadn't drunk the biggest share of the wine Bobby had ordered. 'I'm going to get you a coffee.'

'Okay, maybe it's a good idea. I'm starting to feel like I'm on a boat.' Penny grabbed hold of the corner of the bar.

'I'll get it.' Brae held up a hand when Ella started to protest. 'What sort of coffee would you like?'

'I'd like a latte, but you'd better make it a black Americano I think.' Penny screwed up her face.

'Can I get you anything else, Ella?'

'I'm fine, but thank you.' She touched his arm again, wishing she could tell him how lucky the woman he ended up with was going to be, but she didn't want Penny picking up on it and starting to ask Brae awkward personal questions.

'He's really nice. Why don't you ask him out?' Penny was still swaying, her eyes slowly opening and closing, as she spoke.

'Because we're old friends from school and that's it. I'm only in town for a few more months anyway.'

'Not everything has to be long-term.' Penny dropped an exaggerated wink, letting go of the side of the bar and almost falling over.

'Come on, I think you ought to sit down.' Hooking her under the arm, Ella helped Penny to a seat at one of the tables closest to the bar.

'Too much excitement. That's all.' Penny was slurring her words again. 'Yesterday morning I thought me and Joel were finished for good. I mean we're always rowing, splitting up and then getting straight back together again, but this was a biggie! He accepted a contract to go to Scotland in the new year to work at a fishery up there and I thought he'd decided that was going be his clean start, but then he phoned and told me he'd found a house online to rent in Aberdeen and that he wanted me to go with him. By lunchtime we were at the jewellers in the high street, choosing this! It's amazing how much can change in a day, isn't it?'

'Sometimes one day really can change everything.' Ella could name at least three that had changed her life beyond all recognition. 'How are you feeling about relocating to Aberdeen, you've only just started at the unit?'

'We only came to Port Agnes a few months ago, when Joel took a job on one the trawlers and I worked in a gift shop until I got the job at the unit. The idea of moving again was the reason for all of the rows we've been having lately, but when I thought he was really going to go to Aberdeen without me...' Penny blinked again, several times. 'I didn't even think about it when he asked me to go. Wherever Joel is, is where home is. When you love someone, you'd go anywhere for them, right?'

'Right.' Ella swallowed hard and, as she looked up again, Brae was walking back to the table with Dan right behind him.

'Look who I found over at the bar!' Brae gestured towards Dan, as if Ella might not have noticed him standing there.

'You're gorgeous and if I hadn't just got engaged...' Penny waved her hand in the air, the diamond catching the light, as she stared at Dan.

'Here's your coffee, Penny.' Brae caught Ella's eye as he set the drink down on the table and rolled his eyes. 'After that, I think it might be a good idea if you call that fiancé of yours and get him to come and pick you up.'

'Good idea.' Penny was blinking again. 'Joelly would do anything for me and I'd follow him anywhere. Because we're in love! But you might have to call him, because I can't really see the numbers.'

'No problem, give me your phone and I'll do it for you.' Brae laughed again. 'But I think we're going to have to take the phone outside for you to be able to hear him. There's so much noise in here. Do you think you can make it outside?'

'You look strong enough to hold me up, if I need it.' Penny swayed again, as she got to her feet, but she was soon making a wobbly path towards the front door. 'Come on.'

'I can go with her if you want, she's not your responsibility.' Ella moved to get to her feet too, but Brae shook his head. Penny really wasn't his problem and, if anyone should have been helping her out it was Bobby, after he'd plied her with so many celebratory drinks. Ella would happily have taken on the task, though, if it meant she didn't get stuck waiting at the table with Dan, trying to make polite conversation without raking up the past.

'It's fine and Penny's right, if she falls down, I'll be much more likely to be able to pick her up again. That's one benefit of being built like a barn door.' Brae shrugged. 'I'll be back soon, though, so don't go anywhere and don't start the reminiscing without me!'

'There's not much chance of that.' Ella mumbled under her breath, as Brae disappeared outside with Penny, before looking up at Dan. 'Are you going to sit down then, or just stand there like you're waiting for a bus?'

'Well with an invitation like that, how can I refuse!' Probably the second most annoying thing about seeing Dan again was that he didn't seem to be bothered by the fact that she was constantly sniping at him. The most annoying thing was that she couldn't seem to stop herself from doing it.

'So were you here drinking on your own?'

'I met a friend for dinner and then we came in here for a drink.' Something about the way he said it convinced Ella that he was talking about a woman, long before he confirmed it. 'Her taxi turned up just as Brae came over to the bar.'

'So you don't drive your dates home after dinner?'

'It depends how well the dinner went.' He was laughing again and there was no way she was going to give him the satisfaction of rising to the bait.

'What about you, how are you getting home?'

'Is that an offer? Have you still got your Beetle? I seem to remember some very memorable lifts home in that old car.'

'I got rid of it in the last year of uni. It had sat unused for long enough by then.' She gave him a pointed look, but at least she stopped short of telling him that he'd have known that if he hadn't ducked out of her life.

'That's a shame, I loved that old car.' He held her gaze for just a second more than was comfortable and she tried not to think about how many times they'd sat side by side in Betsy, which was the name they'd given the car her parents had bought her for her seventeenth birthday. There'd been hundreds of goodnight kisses and hours of sitting, parked up at the lookout point on the Port Agnes road, planning their future. Together. One of the reasons she'd ended up having to get rid of Betsy was because, every time she'd come home from uni and seen the car parked up on one of the side roads leading away from the harbour, the old car had looked abandoned and Ella had known exactly how that felt.

'She was past her best a long time ago and I don't think she'd have been able to get up the hill to The Old Stables at Six Acre Farm.'

'I don't live there at the moment. I'm renting it out and staying in one of the cottages on Mercer's Row. So even if Betsy was still on the scene, my walk home wouldn't really warrant a lift.'

'Just as well I wasn't offering you one then.'

'I suppose it is.' Dan was still looking at her, in a way that made her want to stare at the specials menu, the floor, or even her shoes – as long as she didn't have to hold his gaze. They'd had so many dreams of things they were going to do together and nothing that had happened instead had ever lived up to that. Although, even if they had done all those things, the reality would probably never have lived up to what they'd imagined, sitting side by side, in that old car. You weren't supposed to be able to grieve for what you'd never had, but she missed having that much hope, feeling that excited about what the next phase of life might bring. And Dan was still just watching her, as if he could read her mind, the lull in the conversation making her desperate to fill it with something, anything that broke the tension.

'Why didn't you come with me?' Even as the words came out, Ella hadn't known she was going to ask the million-dollar question that had been on the tip of her tongue every time she looked at him.

'Things were complicated, the timing wasn't right and I didn't feel like I could just leave Lissy to it and follow my dreams, but if we could have just waited, then maybe—'

'Maybe what?' For the first time she looked at him the way he'd looked at her, searching his face to see if she could work out what he was thinking, but he'd closed down again.

'I don't know. Who knows what would have happened? The thing is you're home now and it's been good to see you again.'

'Has it?' Ella wasn't sure it was the word she'd have used to describe seeing Dan again. It was one of those words, a bit like 'nice' or 'fine', that was non-committal enough not to mean anything much at all. He could have said amazing, or incredible, but those words wouldn't have been right to describe Ella's feelings either. They were all too one-dimensional. She'd have gone with confusing or difficult; even terrifying came closer than 'good'. Seeing him again brought up emotions she'd buried so deep she'd forgotten she could even feel them. And that didn't feel good to Ella, not now, not when the most comfortable thing would be to feel pretty much nothing at all.

'I missed you.' Dan was the first one to drop his gaze this time. 'And I always hoped that one day we might be able to be—'

'Friends?' She cut him off before he could get to the word she knew had been coming. Weller had said pretty much the same thing to her, in the series of texts he'd sent to try and excuse what he'd done and persuade her to accept his apology. All aimed at making himself feel better, no doubt. She didn't want to be Weller's friend and she wasn't sure she was capable of being Dan's either.

'That would be something.' For a second or two Dan looked like he was going to say something else, but then he gestured towards Penny's abandoned coffee cup. 'Your friend looks like she's had quite the celebration.'

'You could call it that!' Ella was grateful for the change of subject; if they had any chance of being friends, the less time they spent going over the break-up, the better. 'She got engaged today and she's moving up to Aberdeen for her fiancé's job.'

'That's a big move.'

'Not for Penny, she didn't even have to think about it.' If he saw the parallels between himself and Penny, and how different their decisions had been, his face gave nothing away.

'That was a bit of luck.' Brae came back into the wine bar without Penny. 'Joel was already outside waiting for her. Apparently she'd forgotten all about the fact that she'd arranged for him to pick her up at ten. It still took both of us to get her into the car, it was like her bones were made of jelly!'

'You're a star.' Ella smiled up at him, pushing the image of Betsy sitting abandoned in the side street, slowing falling to bits, out of her mind. 'Let me get you a drink as a thank you.'

'I'll get the drinks.' Dan got up on his feet, before either of the others could protest. 'What can I get you?'

'Just a beer for me, please.' Brae took the seat that Penny had been using.

'What about you, El?' No one but Dan had ever called her that and she wasn't sure she liked the fact that he was doing it again, now. Suddenly Ysella seemed a much better bet.

'Just a sparkling water, thanks.'

'No problem, very sensible.'

'What else would you expect from our head girl?' Brae winked as he looked at her and she suddenly had a horrible feeling that Dan and Brae had been talking about her behind her back. She'd had enough of that back at school, admittedly never from either of them, but there'd been more than enough other people to poke fun at the fact that she always tried so hard at whatever she did. Apparently that had been akin to a crime at Three Ports High. Ella Mehenick, the baker's daughter, who had ideas above her station, with her plans to go off and study in

London, and who didn't mind how hard she had to work to prove her doubters wrong.

'Actually, cancel the water. I think I'm going to head home.'

'Are you okay?' Brae had instantly flushed red, obviously mortified at the thought he might be behind Ella's change of heart. But none of this was his fault, or even Dan's.

'I'm fine, just a bit tired, that's all. And my bed is calling me.'

'So we'll see you on Wednesday night instead then?' Brae had such an eager look on his face, she couldn't bring herself to give him an outright refusal.

'I'll have to check the shift patterns at work and let you know. Thanks for a lovely evening, Brae.' Leaning forward, she planted a kiss on his cheek, before turning back to Dan. 'And thanks for the offer of a drink.'

'No problem. Hopefully we'll see you on Wednesday then.' Going out for a drink with Dan would make it feel like a step closer to being friends and that still felt like too much of a leap, so the best she could offer him for now was a non-committal shrug.

'Like I said, I'll make it if I can, but I'll let Brae know either way.' Getting up, Ella headed back towards where the rest of the midwives seemed to be practising some kind of dance routine, ready for their next turn on the karaoke machine. If she could persuade whoever was rostered on call for Wednesday night to swap with her, she might even be prepared to give the karaoke one more try before she headed home.

6

Ella pulled into the driveway outside Lissy's house, not sure if she'd be able to get her little Fiat 500 out of the farmyard again. The rain on the way up to Liberty Farm had been lashing the window so hard that the windscreen wipers had barely been able to keep up and she'd been through a huge puddle that had splattered the window with what Ella could only hope was mud. Peering through the windscreen, she could see the sky had turned gunmetal grey and, even though it was only four o'clock, it was almost dark outside – until a crack of lightning lit up the sky for a split second as it seemed to make contact with the ground on the far side of the farm. The weather had been wild all day and the waves were already crashing against the harbour wall when Ella had left for work that morning. As a low rumble of thunder echoed down the valley, it was starting to feel almost apocalyptic.

Running for the front door, Ella was relieved to see Lissy already standing there, waiting to let her in.

'I've just put Noah down for a nap and I was watching out of the window to let you in as soon as you got here. It's horrendous, isn't it?'

'I've had to change my shoes three times already today, it's like we've had six months' rainfall in a day. I wouldn't be surprised if I had webbed feet by the end of my shift!'

'That could come in handy if you wanted to enter the swimming race at the Silver of the Sea festival.' Lissy laughed. 'Come in, I've already got the kettle on and I'm expecting Dan to turn up at any moment looking like a drowned rat.'

'I thought he'd be working on the renovations to Mercer's Row.' Ella had been counting on it. Having to try and navigate through the feelings that her history with Dan brought up when she was supposed to be concentrating on work, wasn't her idea of fun. If she hadn't been Lissy's midwife, it would have been quite easy to avoid Dan if she really wanted to, even in Port Agnes.

'I invited him over for lunch, it's nice to have some adult company every now and then. But just as he was leaving, the cows started thundering down towards the bottom field after they got spooked by the lightning. I was going to go down with the Land Rover and try and round them up, but he wouldn't let me.'

'He's absolutely right, that sounds pretty dangerous.' She just about stopped herself from asking if Lissy was sure Dan should be doing it either. The idea of trying to herd massive free-range cows, and ending up being the one getting chased across the field, sounded like a nightmare to Ella. She'd have been worried about anyone doing that, not just Dan.

'It's one of the downsides of having a completely free-range farm, but it was Mum's dream and she always ended up agreeing to go along with Dad's ideas instead. So I had to go for it once I got enough land. We couldn't do it at Six Acre Farm. The farmhouse here might be much uglier, but we've got nearly ten times as much land.'

'How are you going to manage all of that when the baby

arrives? I'm guessing that Dan can only help out every so often?'
Ella followed Lissy into the kitchen.

'He's been amazing. Not just since I got too big to do much
around here either.' Lissy filled the teapot with boiling water.
'Since Niall started his job, I wouldn't have been able to manage
the farm without Dan, but he's the only person who really under-
stands why it's so important to me.'

'Dan got the start he needed for his business too, because you
kept Six Acre Farm going after your parents died, and you got
him through the end of school. I imagine he feels he owes you a
lot after all of that and you should be really proud of yourself for
holding the family together the way you did.'

'Not quite, I made a lot of mistakes.' Lissy let go of a long
breath. 'I had no idea what I was doing when they died. There
was an insurance payout, but it didn't even cover the mortgage on
the farm and there were some other debts Dan and I hadn't
known about. Mum and Dad still weren't breaking even when
they died and it turned out that farming organic garlic wasn't
going to make us millionaires either.'

'Don't be so hard on yourself, it must have been so difficult
and you were so young.'

'Dan was still in school, but even then he knew better than
me. When I said I wanted to take out a loan to convert the stables
into a farm shop to sell the garlic, he wanted us to convert it into a
house instead and sell it to pay off the debts.'

'That doesn't surprise me, given what he's ended up doing.
There won't be an original barn left on the Atlantic coast if Dan
gets his way!'

'I just thank God he had an eye for it.' Lissy poured milk into
the mugs. 'The farm shop was too far out of town to be of interest
to the tourists, and the prices were too high for any of the locals
to pay. All it did was get us in more debt and, by the time Dan was
leaving school, I really thought we were going to lose the farm. If

he hadn't spent the next year working every hour that God sent, I don't know what we'd have done. He spent five days a week working for Three Ports Construction, learning all the skills he could and earning enough to pay the bank loan and the mortgage, while I kept up the garlic farming, which just about covered the rest of the bills. Then every weekend he was working to convert the farm shop into accommodation for holiday lets. The only time he ever took off was when you came back from uni.'

'He never told me things had got that bad.' The skin on the back of Ella's neck prickled. She'd been so wrapped up in the plans they'd made, she hadn't even considered that Dan might not have had a choice when he'd changed his mind about joining her in London.

'We didn't want anyone to know. I felt like I'd let Mum and Dad down and you know what Dan's like, he didn't want to have to ask anyone else for help. Especially when there were still people in Port Agnes who'd have been only too happy to see the back of incomers like us. You were the only one who ever made Dan feel like he really belonged here and without you, I think he wanted to prove it to himself, as well as to everyone else.'

'I wish he'd felt like he could talk to me, even if I was away at uni.' Ella took the mug of tea that Lissy had handed her, trying to ignore the twist in her gut that felt a lot like guilt. Looking back she wasn't sure that she'd given him the chance to talk to her. He'd kept saying that he needed to wait, but she'd just assumed it was an excuse. She hadn't asked why when she could have done, which would have given him the opportunity to tell her why he couldn't leave. It wasn't all on her, he could have told her if he really wanted to, but maybe – just maybe – it wasn't all on him either. 'If I'd known, maybe I could have helped.'

'I think that's what he was most afraid of. He always said you were the most driven person he'd ever met and he didn't want to hold you back. He'd never have forgiven himself if you'd given up your dreams on his account. You were definitely the only teenager I'd ever heard of with a five-year plan!'

'Back then, there was no midwifery unit in Port Agnes, and I didn't think there was any way of really making something of myself if I stayed here.'

'But now the unit's here, you could move back for good?'

'Maybe.' Ella gave an almost involuntary shake of her head. She'd been so determined that she was only back for six months, but all of a sudden she wasn't so sure six months would be long enough. For the first time in a long time, she had no one to answer to but herself and there might just be a chance she'd stay a bit longer after all. If she stayed, it would have nothing whatsoever to do with Dan. If she told herself that often enough, it had to be true. 'And what about you, how's the farm working out for you now?'

'It's good, we're finally starting to do a bit more than break even. That's not to say it isn't still incredibly hard work.' Lissy ran a hand over her baby bump. 'But you'll be pleased to hear I've got two new part-time farm workers starting next week. Dan sorted that out too.'

'That's great.' Dan would probably have had a halo to polish if his sister could have arranged it and, from what Lissy had said, Ella could understand it. But it didn't change the fact that he made his living from ripping the history out of Port Agnes, selling it to the highest bidder and pricing the people who'd lived there all their lives out of the market. Until that changed, he'd always have more enemies than friends among the locals, however honourable the original reasons for starting his business had been. For a long time she'd held on to a lot of resentment towards Dan as well, but there was a chance she might have had that wrong too. It was possible there were worse reasons for staying on in Port Agnes than finding out if she'd judged her first love far too harshly. If she was wrong about Dan, then maybe she could believe it was wrong to give up on the idea of love altogether after what had happened with Weller. Just maybe.

* * *

Lissy's check-up had been straightforward with nothing to flag any concerns and Ella had been keen to get off the farm before the driveway got even more churned up by the rain, which was still falling relentlessly from an iron-grey sky.

Just as she'd been about to open her car door, a huge black and white cow had come galloping past, flattening her against the side of the Fiat and making her scream.

'Jesus Christ!' Ella screamed again, as three more cows came thundering up the driveway. They were absolutely huge close up and they seemed to be in a big hurry to get wherever it was they were going. They probably weren't enjoying the torrential rain any more than Ella was and her hair was already plastered to the sides of her head. But she didn't care what she looked like, as long as she survived what was beginning to feel like a stampede.

'Are you okay?' Dan suddenly came sprinting down the path, with three more cows just ahead of him. 'I was just rounding up the stragglers that I couldn't get back up here with the Land Rover, but I thought you'd still be inside with Lissy. I'm really sorry if they scared you.'

'Is that definitely the last of them?' Ella finally peeled herself away from the side of the car, as the three cows Dan had been following charged past her towards the barn.

'I promise.' Dan drew level with her. He was absolutely soaked, the shirt he was wearing clinging to his chest; all those years of working in construction had clearly broadened his physique. 'You didn't get knocked by them, did you?'

'Thankfully they just wanted to get past me.'

'Why don't you come back inside and get warmed up for a bit. You're soaked.'

'It's fine.' Ella pushed her hair away from her face, as another memory flashed into her head. It had been the day after their A-Levels had finished and Dan had suggested going to Ocean Cove, a sheltered bay that most tourists never found out about. They'd been walking along the water's edge, when she'd suddenly slipped and ended up almost as wet as Dan was now. He'd helped her up and then jumped straight into the waves with all his clothes on, just so that she didn't feel stupid. 'I've got to get going anyway and the longer I stand out here, the more my hair's going to look like an old mop head.'

'I always liked your hair best when you let it stay curly.' For a moment she thought Dan was going to reach out, like he had so many times before, and tuck a stray strand of hair behind her ears, but he just smiled. She tried to ignore the fact that her body had immediately gone onto high alert, all her senses heightened in anticipation of his touch. If he wasn't interested then she wasn't going to give even the slightest hint that she was either.

'You better get going then, but I just wanted to ask how Lissy and the baby are doing?'

'Everything looks great.' Ella opened the car door as she spoke. 'But she's desperate for Niall to come home and I know she's hoping things will change and he'll be around a bit more when the new baby comes.'

'I'll be having words with him if he doesn't.' Dan sounded more like Lissy's dad than her brother, but they'd had to fill that role for one another since they'd barely been more than kids.

'I think she'd appreciate that.' Ella got into the car. 'I'll see you around then.'

'Bye, El.' He held up a hand as she pulled the car door closed and she silently prayed she'd manage to pull off Lissy's driveway without skidding in the mud and, worse still, having to ask Dan to move the car for her. For once luck seemed to be on her side, even if the weather still wasn't letting up, and the little car coped surprisingly well.

No one could make hot chocolate like Ruth Mehenick, and Ella could almost taste it, as she thought about getting back to the bakery. It might still be summer, but the weather definitely called for a hot cup of home comfort. Turning out of Lissy's driveway and onto the Port Kara road, which dipped down into the valley at Port Agnes before leading up to the neighbouring town, the road looked more like a stream. The windscreen wipers of the car were struggling to keep up with the deluge all over again, and Ella could so easily have missed the flash of white in the ditch about half a mile from Liberty Farm. The car was almost obscured by the thick hedgerow lining the ditch, but Ella could just about make out the back wheels and rear windscreen of the hatchback.

'Oh no, please.' Her hands were already shaking, as she pulled into the passing place, just past the site of the crash. Whoever had crashed the car probably got straight out and was already back home, thanking their lucky stars that things hadn't ended up anywhere near as badly as they could have done.

'Help!' Ella heard the shout as soon as she started towards the car. Any hope she had that this might be nothing more than a car stuck in a muddy ditch, disappearing.

'I'm coming.' Reaching the hedgerow, she wasn't sure things were going to be that easy. There was barely any space between the back of the car and the thorny hedgerow to see what she was even dealing with. Ignoring the thorns tearing at her clothes and into her cheek, she squeezed through a tiny gap just up from where the car had crashed through the hedge. It was a small three-door hatchback with the driver's window half open, but she couldn't make out how many people were in there. 'Are any of you hurt?'

'There's only me and I don't think so.' It was a woman's voice and she sounded young, almost childlike; she was probably terrified.

'Can you get out?'

'Neither of the doors will open and the window will only open halfway down, the car's wedged in so hard against the side of the ditch.' The girl's words were punctuated by a shuddering sob, as Ella attempted to inch closer to the car to try and see her. 'I'm such an idiot. I only glanced at my phone for a sec, but the road was so wet and I lost control. I can't even see my phone now and I thought no one would ever come. If something happens to the baby, it'll be all my fault!'

'*The baby?*' Despite how worried Ella had been that the car could suddenly start to slide and crush her, the knowledge that the girl in the car was pregnant pushed all of that aside.

'I'm five months pregnant.' The girl had completely given into crying now and Ella was finally close enough to see her.

'Sophie, is that you?'

'Oh my God, Ella!' Last time Ella had seen her, Sophie's biggest concern had been telling her parents about her unexpected pregnancy. Now she looked absolutely terrified; her tear-stained face just visible over the half-open window.

'It's all right, sweetheart, I'm going to get you out of there.'

'I'm going to be in so much trouble. I've ruined everything and I don't want to end up in prison!' Sophie was sobbing so hard now, Ella had to strain to hear her.

'None of that matters. A car can be replaced, but you and the baby can't. I'm going to go back to my car, grab my phone and get you the help you need.'

'I'm scared.'

'I know you are, sweetheart, but I'll be right back, I promise.' Scrabbling back up the side of the ditch, Ella had to reach out and a grab a handful of the hedgerow to stop herself sliding back down again, the thorns ripping into the flesh on the palm of her hand. By the time she got back to the car and got her phone, her hands were almost too wet and bloodied for her to press the keys. When she eventually got past the security code, it took less than a second to realise that she wasn't going to be making an emergency call. There wasn't even one bar on the mobile signal, for either calls or the internet. Even if she managed to get an emergency call through, it could be ages before they got here. But Liberty Farm was only half a mile away, and Dan had a Land Rover.

'Sophie!' Ella called out, as she squeezed back through the hedgerow.

'Are they coming?'

'I can't get a signal, sweetheart, but my friends have got a farm just up the road from here. I'm going to run down to them and they'll be able to get you and the car out of the ditch much more quickly than if we wait for the fire brigade anyway.'

'Please don't leave me again!'

'I promise I won't be long and it'll be the last time. I'll stay with you then, until you're out again and safe, and we can get you and the baby all checked over.'

'Please hurry up!'

'I'll be right back.' Ella didn't even feel the branches tearing into her flesh again, as she scrabbled back out of the ditch and seconds later she was running towards Liberty Farm, not sure if the tightness in her chest was down to fear, a lack of fitness, or the combination of the two. Things only got harder when she reached the driveway of the farm and her shoes completed disappeared beneath the deep tracks of mud left by her car, and whatever other vehicles had gone up and down since the storm had broken. By the time she got to the door of the farmhouse, the mud was splattered up as far as her waist. Hammering on the door, she held her breath, terrified that Dan might already have left and headed in the other direction.

'Oh my God, Ella, are you okay?' Lissy answered the door, with a still sleepy Noah on her hip.

'I am, but there's a young girl – one of my patients – who's driven her car into a ditch just down the road and she can't open the doors to get out.'

'I'll phone an ambulance.' Lissy was already turning to head back down the corridor.

'I think it'll be quicker if we can get her out and I can check her over straight away. She's panicking already and, if it takes them another twenty minutes to even get here, I'm worried about what the stress might do to her, and the baby. I thought Dan might be able to help?'

'Of course! He's upstairs, borrowing some of Niall's clothes to drive home in, but I'll go and get him. He'll definitely want to help.' Despite being pregnant, and carrying a toddler, Lissy had a remarkable turn of pace. She was heading up the stairs within seconds and, less than a minute later, Dan was following down behind her.

'Do you think the Land Rover will do the trick, or shall I go down to the bottom field and get the tractor?' Lissy had clearly filled Dan in, but he obviously hadn't had the time to change out of his wet clothes. Given the rescue attempt he was about to make, it was probably just as well.

'I don't want to leave it any longer than we have to.' Ella was still standing in the open doorway, but she barely even noticed the torrential rain any more. 'If we don't manage to move it with the Land Rover, at least I can sit with Sophie while you go and get the tractor. I think we should call 999, just in case we can't do it on our own. If they get here quickly enough, we might not even have to worry about getting the tractor if the Land Rover doesn't work.'

'I've just got to grab some tow rope and I think there are some traction tracks in the barn that Niall bought when his car got stuck in the top field last year.' Dan turned to his sister. 'Can you call 999, please?'

'Of course, be careful. Both of you.'

'I'm going to run back down to Sophie, while you get what you need. I don't want to leave her.'

'I'll be there as quick as I can,' Dan called out as Ella made her way back down the farm track, trying desperately not to fall over. She wouldn't be any use to Sophie if she slipped over in the mud and ended up as a casualty herself.

By the time she got back down to the car, Ella was really struggling to catch her breath. It had been a long time since she'd run for anything other than a bus.

'Sophie, help is on its way,' she called down from the gap in the hedgerow. She didn't want to risk Dan driving straight past them by climbing back down into the ditch, where he wouldn't be able to see her.

'I think I'm going to be sick and I can't stop shaking.' Sophie's voice was shaking too. 'I'm losing the baby, aren't I?'

'No, sweetheart. You're fine and the baby's going to be fine too... Just keep breathing nice and slow and steady.'

Ella didn't think she'd ever been so pleased to hear the chugging sound of an approaching vehicle as the old Land Rover came down the road towards them.

'My friend, Dan, is here now and he'll get you out. Just keep concentrating on your breathing. I'm just going to go and tell him what I think we need to do.' Ella turned towards where Dan had pulled up, after making a three point turn she wouldn't have even thought possible.

'I need to go down there and take a look at the position of the car to see if I think we can move it.' Dan jumped out of the four-wheel drive, which looked like it had been through its fair share of battles already.

'It looks like it's the front half that's actually wedged in.'

'How did you get down there?'

'There's a small gap, just there.' Ella gestured towards the hole in the hedgerow. 'It's a bit tight, though.'

'Are you calling me fat?' Dan raised an eyebrow and just the briefest of smiles crossed his face, before he disappeared through the gap in the hedge, leaving Ella to follow on behind him.

'What do you think? Do we need the tractor?' She'd barely given him a chance to get down there before she asked the question, but she was almost as desperate as Sophie was to get the car out.

'I'm going to put the tracks under the front wheels and then I think we can give it a go.' Dan turned towards the driver's side of the car. 'How are you doing, Sophie? Are you ready to get out of here?'

'Definitely.' Ella still had to strain to hear the younger woman, but her voice already sounded a bit calmer.

'Okay, I'm going to grab the tracks, tie the tow rope to the car and then I'll be back.' Unlike Ella, Dan managed to get out of the ditch without needing to grab on to every branch in the hedgerow.

'Do you really think we can do it?' As he nodded in response, Ella's shoulders started to relax too.

'We can. You're going to need to pull the Land Rover forward, but all you need to do is keep it slow and steady.'

'I think you'd be better at it than me.'

'You'll be fine and I need to be down in the ditch to make sure the tracks don't shift, and if I push the car from the front it'll help keep it moving in the right direction.'

'What if I do something wrong and the rope snaps? The car could roll back down and—'

'You can do this, I promise. You've never failed at anything you put your mind to and I trust you to do it right, you always do.'

'Are you sure it'll be okay?' She wanted to confess that it wasn't just Sophie she was worried about, that she couldn't bear the thought of anything happening to him, not after finding him again after so long. But if he'd responded with even a hint that she still mattered to him too, it might lead to something she couldn't control, to taking the risk of getting hurt again. Suddenly the prospect of towing a ton of metal out of a ditch seemed like the easy option.

'Absolutely.' Dan moved past her to get the tracks out of the Land Rover, his arm inadvertently brushing up against hers and for a split second the urge to hug him almost overwhelmed her – the slightest of touches triggering a muscle memory that actually made her arms ache for him. But she barely even had time to process the thought. Within minutes, he'd knotted the rope on the back of the Land Rover and attached the other end to a hook on the back of the car, just below the rear bumper.

'When shall I start towing?'

'Just wait until I get the tracks in place and we'll be good to go. If you stand by the gap in the hedge again, I can call up when we're ready.'

'Okay.' Ella watched as Dan pushed himself back down into the ditch, not once but twice. The first time, he had to get himself down the impossibly small gap on the left-hand side of the car to position the first track before coming back up and doing the same on the other side. If the conversion work ever dried up, he'd have made a pretty good fireman.

'Right, we're ready for you to do your bit now, Ella. Remember, just slow and steady. If you pull away in second gear and release the clutch slowly, it'll give you much better traction than first gear and the engine will rev less.'

'How will I know if I need to stop?'

'Just keep going until you see the car come up onto the road. Don't stop until you do.'

'Dan, I'm sorry.' She had to say it, just in case one of the scenes that were running through her head, where Dan ended up crushed by the car, somehow came true.

'For what?'

'For giving you such a hard time lately about helping Lissy, when she'd said you've been great, and, well, just for, you know.' The truth was, she wasn't even sure herself exactly what she was sorry for. It could have been for not making him feel like he could talk to her about the real reasons why he couldn't follow her to London, or for acting as if their break-up had been ten days ago, instead of ten years, or for taking out her bitterness about Weller on Dan. Either way, it felt good to get it off her chest.

'Anyone who looks out for my sister the way you do can nag me as much as they like. I know this isn't the right moment, but a situation like this makes you realise that tomorrow isn't promised to any of us and I think we've got things we need to talk about. Or at least things I should have told you a long time ago. But for now let's get this done.'

'Okay.' There were things Ella wanted to say to him too, now that she knew the sacrifices he'd made. But if she hesitated for a second longer, she was never going to hold the nerve she needed to try and move the car. Turning around, she ran towards the Land Rover with legs that felt as if they were made of jelly.

'Right, second gear, slowly release the clutch...' Ella talked herself through the process, praying that nothing would come down the road in the other direction. She had no idea what she'd do if that happened. Although anyone who had a choice probably wouldn't choose to be out driving around in weather like this. She couldn't even work out how to turn the windscreen wipers on and she daren't look down to try and figure it out. She just had to keep going until she saw Sophie's car in the rear-view mirror. She could feel the resistance even before the engine started to rev hard, despite the advice that Dan had given her.

This wasn't going to work, the rope was going to snap and it would all be her fault. They should have just waited for the fire brigade. It felt like hours had gone by as the Land Rover strained to pull Sophie's car out of the ditch, but all of a sudden she saw the shape of the little hatchback emerging and the Land Rover shot forward as the tension relaxed.

'Oh, thank God.' Ella kept moving forward until she was sure the car was clear of the ditch. Pulling up the handbrake so hard it hurt her hand, she jumped out and ran back towards the ditch. Dan was already helping Sophie out of the car, but he was covered in mud from head to toe. The last time she'd seen him looking anything like that she'd been standing on the sidelines of a rugby pitch and Dan had just scored the winning try to secure the Three Ports rugby team's win in the under-18s Cornish Cup. He'd been everyone's hero that day and it seemed nothing much had changed on that front either.

'Thank you both so much.' Sophie's eyes were like two dark pools in the pallor of her face, but she managed a wobbly smile, as she kept hold of Dan's arm.

'We're just glad you're okay.' Dan turned towards Ella. 'But I definitely think you should get checked out and there's only one person here who's got the skills to do that.'

'I don't want to go to the hospital. They'll ask what happened and I'll have to tell them about looking at my phone.' Sophie suddenly looked terrified again.

'If it's okay with Ella, I can tow your car up the road to my sister's farm and Ella can check you over there, while I have a look at your car. Then maybe, if everything looks okay, one of us can drive you home.'

'Can we do that, Ella, please?'

'Okay, but if there's any sign that you or the baby need checking over in the hospital, then we're going and neither Dan nor I will tell anyone how the accident happened.' Ella paused for a moment. 'As long as you promise never to look at your phone while you're driving again.'

'I promise!' Sophie's face immediately lost some of its pinched look. Thanks to Dan, it really did look like everything was going to turn out okay and Sophie had learned a lesson she was never going to forget. Ella could only hope that she'd learnt just as much from her own past mistakes, but every time she looked at Dan she was less and less sure. Without him there, she wasn't sure she'd have had the courage to do what she'd done and she'd forgotten how he'd always had this innate belief in her ability to do anything, much more belief than she'd ever had in herself. When she was with Dan, she'd never had to be that girl striving to prove to everyone – including herself – that she was good enough. If her biggest mistake from the past had been to love Dan so wholeheartedly that it could never be replicated, there was a very good chance she hadn't learned anything much at all.

7

Both Sophie and her baby seemed to have got away from the accident unscathed. The check-up that Ella had given her hadn't raised any cause for concern; the baby's heartbeat had been loud and regular, and even though Sophie's heart rate and blood pressure had been slightly raised at first, by the time Lissy had cancelled the 999 call and plied them all with cups of tea, even that was back to normal. The car had skidded into the ditch, rather than crashed, and Sophie had insisted that it had almost stopped before it slid off the road.

Ella had still suggested that Sophie went for a scan, but as her twenty week appointment was due in less than forty-eight hours' time, Ella had eventually backed down. Dan had been more insistent about getting her car checked over by a specialist before Sophie got back on the road and, before the young woman had the chance to protest, he'd arranged to take it to a garage in Port Kara and then drop it back to Sophie once it got the all clear. Ella had given her a lift back to the caravan park and made Sophie promise to call her if she was even the tiniest bit worried about herself or the baby.

There hadn't been time for Dan to tell her whatever it was he'd decided he needed to get off his chest just before she'd moved the car. Ella hadn't particularly wanted an audience for that conversation anyway; with Lissy fussing around them, and Sophie still recovering from the shock, the timing had been all wrong. When Ella had thanked Dan again for his help, just as she was leaving with Sophie, he'd made a joke about her owing him a drink and she'd promised to make good on it by meeting him in The Jolly Sailor one night the following week. They could talk then, presuming he still wanted to, and at least she could deliver the apology she felt she owed him.

Sophie hadn't texted until the day of her scan and then only to let Ella know it had all gone okay, but two days later she had a check-up booked in at the unit and Ella was desperate to see how she was doing. Sophie was another patient who Ella was seeing more often than the guidelines dictated, but she'd cleared it with Anna and they'd both agreed she needed the extra support because of her circumstances. As Jess had said, when Ella first joined, that sort of flexibility was one of the benefits of community midwifery in a place like Port Agnes.

'This is for you.' Sophie peered over the top of the potted pink orchid that she was holding in her arms, as she came into the room.

'That's so lovely, but you really didn't need to.'

'Yes I did, in fact I wish I could buy you something much better. I don't know what would have happened to me if you hadn't come along when you did, and if Dan and Lissy hadn't been just up the road.'

'It's beautiful. Thank you.' Ella took the plant and set it down on the desk.

'And did you notice the colour?' Sophie couldn't keep the smile off her face.

'It's a girl?'

'Yes and I'm so relieved.' Sophie sat down on the chair opposite Ella's. 'If it's going to just be me and the baby, then I'm glad it's a girl.'

'Have you thought any more about telling your parents?' Ella didn't want to pressurise her, but she'd arranged for Sophie to have some counselling sessions to talk things through. That way, even if she decided she really didn't want to break the news to her parents, she'd at least have a plan.

'I keep picking up the phone to call them, but I just can't go through with it.' Sophie bit her lip. 'I think Mum would be okay, but she'd want to tell Dad and I just can't face it.'

'Are you worried he'll be angry?'

'It'll be worse than that. He'll be disappointed.'

'Maybe you need to give him a chance.'

'If it was just him, it would be okay, but everyone back home will be talking about it. That's what happens when you're the vicar's daughter.'

'I can see how that could make things difficult.' Ella hadn't known that Sophie's father was a vicar, but she could easily imagine how that might make Sophie's every move a focus of interest in her home town. Jago might not be a man of the cloth, but he was the chairman of both the residents' and retailers' associations, as well as a parish counsellor, and almost everyone knew who he was. The thought of disappointing him had always been one of Ella's biggest fears and there'd have been an all-too-willing queue of people waiting to fill him in if she'd ever put a foot wrong. Poor Sophie would have the whole congregation sharing their opinions – good or bad – even though it was none of their business.

'Thank God I didn't have to ring them and tell them I'd written off the car. Dan was worried that the accident might have bent the chassis, but his friend said it was fine. He's been amazing.' Sophie smiled and her whole face seemed to relax into an almost dreamlike expression. 'When he brought the car back, he was a bit shocked about the state of the caravan I was staying in I think. The windows started leaking in the storm and there was a bit of mould on the walls from the last time it leaked; he said I shouldn't be staying somewhere like that while I was pregnant.'

'I've got to say I agree with him, if the caravan isn't even keeping the rain out.' This was yet another time that Ella wished she could wave a magic wand and solve Sophie's housing problems herself. She'd worked with some expectant mothers in London whose accommodation issues had been much worse than Sophie's and it had broken her heart every time when there was so little she could do to help. Social services had often had to step in and arrange emergency accommodation, which was almost always pretty grim, and Ella was really hoping that Sophie would find a way to talk to her parents before she went down that route. 'Have you spoken to the caravan park, to see if they can sort it out?'

'They'd already told me that if I wanted on-site accommodation, they could only give me one of the old caravans that aren't up to standard to rent out to holidaymakers and all the staff caravans are pretty grotty. It's supposed to be a perk of the job and we get a lower hourly rate because of the free accommodation, but Dan was worried that the mould might be bad for the baby.'

'Is there any chance you could afford to rent somewhere else, even a room, if you decide you really can't face going home?'

'That's what Dan asked me and, when I said there was no way I could afford it, he offered to let me stay at his place.'

'*In his house?*' Ella's scalped prickled. Even if Dan's intentions were entirely honourable – which she hoped to God they were – the offer could easily be misconstrued, especially by someone as vulnerable as Sophie.

'No! Well, it is his house, but he's not living there. He gave me the choice of two places, one used to be a telephone exchange apparently and he said I was welcome to stay there as long as I didn't mind the estate agent showing people around every now and then, but there are no neighbours nearby and I thought I might get nervous when it gets dark.' Sophie pulled a face, suddenly looking even younger than her nineteen years. 'I felt awful, turning down such an amazing offer, but Dan was lovely. He said I could stay for free in one of the cottages that he's converting down by the harbour, as long as I didn't mind hearing a bit of building work next door. I was hardly going to complain about that! And I definitely feel safer knowing that he's staying in a cottage at the other end of the row.'

'That's really nice of him. How long can you stay?' Ella hadn't seen that coming. According to most of Port Agnes all he cared about was profits. That wasn't the Dan Ella had known all those years ago, but she'd let herself believe the rumours and assume he'd changed for the worst. This was the Dan she remembered and maybe he hadn't changed that much after all. She just hoped Sophie wouldn't see the temporary solution as the answer to all her problems. She was still going to need her family's support, but Ella knew how easy it could be to believe Dan could solve anything. She'd been about the same age as Sophie when she'd thought the exact same thing.

'The caravan park closes on the first of November, so I'll have to go back home to Somerset then. There's no way I'll be able to live on my own and pay the bills when I'm not working. But Dan said I can stay until then and the reason he won't take any rent is because there'll be too much building work going on in the other cottages for him to be able to rent it out properly. I'm so glad you went and got him instead of calling the fire brigade. It's like I've got my very own hero!'

'Have you had your first appointment with the counsellor yet?' The more Sophie said, the more Ella was starting to panic that she was forming a worrying attachment to Dan and the counselling appointments suddenly seemed more important than ever. He was being so lovely to Sophie, and Ella had to admit now that she'd definitely misjudged him, so there was every chance that Sophie could misread his motivations too. There were people in Port Agnes who'd be only too willing to believe he had an ulterior motive, but Ella didn't believe that for a second, even if the idea of Sophie falling for him made her jaw clench.

'I had my first session yesterday.'

'Did it help?'

'We mainly talked about Euan, the baby's father, and deciding whether or not to tell him that I'm pregnant.'

'And have you made any decisions?'

'The counsellor asked me if I'd want to know if our situations were reversed and I had to admit I did. If he doesn't want to be involved, that's fine, but I know now that I do need to tell him.'

'I think you've made the right decision. At least you can explain things to your little girl when she's older, if she wants to find him later on.' Ella really was doing her best not to give advice, but she definitely agreed with Sophie's counsellor on this.

'He calls or messages me to see how I am quite often, and he was pushing to meet up before the end of the summer, saying he'd drive all the way down here if I wanted him to, so it's not like he's forgotten me.' Sophie shifted in her seat. 'It's just that if Euan reacts badly, I think it's going to make it even harder for me to be brave enough to tell Mum and Dad.'

'Try not to worry about things that haven't even happened yet. I know it's hard when you're doing all of this on your own.'

'I don't feel so much like that now I've got you and Dan on my side.'

'You've made a lot of progress after only one counselling session, so I know you'll do the right thing for you and your little girl, whatever that might be.' Ella metaphorically crossed her fingers that working with the counsellor would stop Sophie from fixating too much on Dan, but she wanted to warn him too. She'd have to speak to Anna first though, and find out how much she could say without risking patient confidentiality. 'Okay then, shall we have a listen to what your baby is up to in there?'

'Yes, please!' Sophie got herself onto the examination table and pulled up her top and within seconds Ella had picked up the sound of the baby's heartbeat on the Doppler.

'Her heartbeat sounds perfect.' Smiling, Ella measured Sophie's bump. 'And she's right on track for your dates too.'

'See, she's perfect already.'

'She's doing brilliantly, you both are, but I want to do your bloods once more, just to check that your iron levels are still stable, and we'll do a urine test at the same time.'

'Thank you for looking after me.'

'I'm here for you any time you need me, even if you're worried about something that's got nothing to do with the baby.' Ella helped Sophie sit back up and tried not to hear Jess's warning on her first day ringing in her ears. There were some things that a midwife couldn't take responsibility for, but with Sophie's vulnerability and her growing reliance on Dan, her young patient wasn't the only person Ella felt she needed to protect. She still hadn't agreed which day she could meet Dan for a drink, but she was going to have to put her worries about raking up the past to one side and get on with it. She needed to find a way of warning Dan to tread carefully, without making him think she had any doubts about his motives, and meeting him for a drink would provide the perfect opportunity. Suddenly it mattered – as much as it had more than a decade before – that Dan knew she believed in him too.

* * *

Ruth grabbed the letter she'd been reading off the table and shoved it into the handbag on the chair next to her, but not before Ella had spotted the red letters spelling out that it was an overdue payment notice.

'Do you want me to make you some toast before you head off to work, my love?' The crease between Ruth's eyebrows didn't relax, even as she smiled at her daughter.

'Let me make you some breakfast for a change, Mum, you look worn out.' Ella flicked the kettle on and turned to face her mother. 'Is everything okay?'

'Yes, I'm just not sleeping all that well lately.'

'If you've got something on your mind, you know you can always tell me, don't you?'

'Thank you, darling, but I'm fine honestly.' Ruth picked up the handbag she'd stuffed the letter into and put it into the bottom of the Welsh dresser. Ella knew her mother well enough to know when the subject was closed. Offering her parents money to help them out if they were struggling wouldn't work; they were far too proud to ever accept. Ella was just going to have to find some other way of figuring out what was going on with her parents' finances and persuading them to let her help sort it out.

'At least let me make you some breakfast.' There was an uncut wholegrain loaf from the bakery already on the chopping board. 'Scrambled eggs and mushrooms on toast?'

'Perfect, but you'd better put some on for your dad too, because he'll probably be starving when he gets in; he was up at half four baking. It's always been part of the job, but I think he's finding the early starts a bit tougher now he's getting older. Although I'd better not let him catch me saying that!'

'I wish neither of you had to work so hard.'

'The bakery is your dad's life and you know he wouldn't have it any other way.' Ruth's smile didn't quite reach her eyes.

'What about you, though, Mum?'

'I love it too and I don't want you worrying about us, things will turn out fine, they always do.' This time when Ruth smiled, it looked much more genuine. 'After all, I got you when I never thought I would, so I know things always come right in the end.'

'Looks like I'm just in time for breakfast.' Jago opened the door from the courtyard into the kitchen and Daisy shot into the room, immediately taking up residence by the oven and giving Ella the sort of wide-eyed look a puppy would have been proud of.

'I'm making scrambled eggs and mushrooms on toast, Dad, if that sounds good?'

'Throw in a slice or two of bacon for your old dad and you've got yourself a deal.' Jago sat down next to his wife, blowing his daughter a kiss as she handed him a mug of tea so strong it was the colour of mahogany. Just the way he liked it.

'Did Daisy try to kill any seagulls while you were out?' Ruth dropped a lump of sugar into her tea, as she spoke.

'Not today, but she managed to knock over a stack of lobster pots at the side of Mercer's Row.' Jago turned towards Ella. 'That Dan Ferguson came out to help stack them all up again. If he thinks that makes up for what he's doing to those cottages, he's got another think coming.'

'Have you actually seen any of the houses he's worked on?' Ella whisked the eggs with the fork a bit more vigorously than she needed to. Her father hadn't been keen on Dan when they were dating, but that might not just have been down to the fact that he was from a family of incomers. He hadn't liked the idea of his teenage daughter dating anyone. But ever since Dan had become a developer, renovating properties in and around the Three Ports area, he might as well have been an armed robber as far as Jago Mehenick was concerned.

'I don't need to, I know his type only too well. Those places would make lovely homes for people like you, who've grown up in Port Agnes. But by the time he's finished turning them into soulless renovations, they will be out of the price range of anyone who doesn't earn London money.'

'Apparently he converted the old telephone exchange and it's lovely. He's saved the old windows and even put a reclaimed parquet floor down. I don't think he's in the business of soulless renovations. He's been really kind to a patient of mine too, letting her live rent-free in one of the cottages on Mercer's Row until she gets back on her feet.'

'It'll be a tax dodge or something, you mark my words! I suppose next you're going to tell me he's not in the business of making money either?' Jago shook his head.

'Doesn't everyone have to do that to get by?' Ruth took the words out of Ella's mouth.

'There's making money and then there's making money at the expense of others. That's why I went into buying The Old Forge with Clem and Jack.'

'You bought The Old Forge?' Ella couldn't believe neither of her parents had thought to tell her that they'd invested in another property. When she'd visited the previous Christmas, she'd noticed the auctioneer's notice nailed to the wall, which had probably become a structural support, given how much work The Old Forge needed. Jago was already working six days a week, seven if you counted the time it took to do the accounts. So when he thought he'd ever have the time to work on the building was anyone's guess, even if he'd had the skills to do it.

'I went to the auction with Clem and Jack because we were sick to death of people like Dan Ferguson buying up all the properties round here and, between the three of us, we just about scraped enough money together.'

'*Just about* is right.' Ruth rolled her eyes and Ella felt her pulse quicken. Her mother might be trying to pass it off as just another of her father's whims, but as far as she knew there were no savings to scrape together. And if her father had got into debt to try and prove a point, it could put her parents under a lot of strain. The fact that her mother was hiding final demands suggested it might already be happening and what Ruth said next did nothing to reassure her.

'Never mind that you've no money left to do the place up, at this rate we'll have a very expensive pile of bricks where our savings used to be. Every time we build up a nest egg it seems to disappear.'

'When we sell the place, *to a local*, we'll more than make our money back.'

'I won't hold my breath.' Ruth's face had that pinched look again.

'I'm sure you'll find someone local willing to take it on.' Ella kept her tone as even as she could. If she got a job in Plymouth, she might be able to share a nurses' flat at the hospital until she'd finished her teaching course and use the money she'd saved for a deposit with Weller to buy her father out of his investment, or at least cover his share of the renovation costs. Maybe then her mother would stop feeling like she had to hide the overdue payment letters. It had to be worth a try.

8

There were three midwives and Frankie, one of the midwifery care assistants, on duty in the unit, but it was strangely quiet. There'd been no call-outs for assistance with home deliveries, and no one had rung to say that their contractions had started, or that they were in established labour and heading into the unit.

'Isn't it qu—' Anna had barely opened her mouth to speak before Gwen cut her off.

'Don't you dare say quiet! You know what will happen if you do, all hell will break loose.'

'Sorry, I was hoping it was going to be really busy tonight and that I wouldn't have time to think about anything else or worry about whether I can afford to eat next week, now that I'm paying the mortgage all on my own.' Anna sounded exhausted.

'You've finished things with Greg then?' Gwen leant forward and Ella wondered if she should excuse herself and let them talk in private, but Frankie had no such qualms and had pulled her chair closer to where Anna was sitting.

'If I didn't do it, I think we'd have ended up hating each other. I'd have resented him for taking away my chance to be a mum, and he'd have resented me for holding it against him. Luckily the bank is lending me enough to buy him out of the cottage and at least he took the estate agents' valuation. It makes the break-up really easy in that respect, but suddenly it's all happening so quickly, and I just don't know what I'm going to do.'

'You'll be fine without him. You don't need a man, nobody does!' Frankie punched the air, like the warm-up act at a female empowerment rally, trying to get a lacklustre crowd on message.

'I do if I want a baby.' Anna pulled a face. 'And that's what I'm grieving for, not so much Greg but the chance to be a mum. I'm thirty-seven and the clock's not just ticking, it's ringing the bell for last orders!'

'I had a mum on my ward once who was forty-nine and having her first baby without any fertility treatment.' Ella gave her friend a reassuring smile. She didn't add that the woman had spent the last four months of her pregnancy on bed rest, after nearly losing the baby. It was so hard to know what to say to someone who desperately wanted a baby, despite what her mother had been through. She'd been about eight years old when she'd found the memory box her mother kept on the top shelf of the wardrobe after a desperate search to try and uncover her Christmas presents. There was paperwork in there from the fertility clinic and polaroid photographs of the building where her mother had all her treatments, along with hospital wrist-bands from Ruth's admissions and a couple of grainy scan photos from the two occasions she'd been pregnant. One was from when she was carrying Ella, and the other from an early loss she'd had the year before, after her sixth round of IVF. When Ella had pressed for information about what it all was, Ruth had explained it to her in words an eight-year-old could understand. Her mother had gone to great pains to express how thrilled she'd been to finally hold her daughter in her arms, but Ella had still walked away feeling sad for all Ruth had been through and with a new awareness of the burden that being a longed-for only child could carry. It had never really left her, even more than twenty years later.

'See, it's never too late!' Frankie tapped the side of her nose. 'And so what if you haven't got a man? There's plenty of places you can get a donation, if you know what I mean!'

'You mean a sperm bank?' Anna looked doubtful.

'Well, yes, but I was thinking more about Casa Cantare at closing time on a Friday night. All you'd have to do is wear that black sparkly top you've got, you know the one that makes your boobs look like an eighteen-year-old's, and you'd be laughing.' Frankie gave Anna a knowing look. 'You'd be fighting them off with a stick.'

'I can't even hear the name Casa Cantare without feeling like I've got a hangover all over again.' Anna pulled a face. 'And as for getting pregnant by a drunken stranger on a Friday night, I think I'll give it a miss.'

'In Port Agnes you'll be lucky to find a stranger anyway, unless you want a bloody emmet to father your baby. And I'd rather take my chances with a turkey baster than that!' Gwen folded her arms across her chest. The fact that she was nearly sixty, about to become a grandmother for the second time, and had actually been born in South Wales, didn't stop her having an opinion.

'Well if you don't want to do any of that, why don't you just start dating?' Frankie raised her eyebrows. 'Be honest and tell the guys you meet that you're looking for something serious that could lead to marriage and a family. You could always set yourself a cut-off point of forty. If you haven't met someone by then, you can take Gwen's advice and buy a turkey baster instead!'

'I've been with Greg so long I wouldn't even know where to start with dating now. I just don't think I could do it even if I wanted to, which I don't.'

'If it wasn't for the baby thing, you could afford to leave it. But if you're insistent on doing it the boring old-fashioned way and finding a father you actually want a relationship with, then you've got to get your behind in gear.' Frankie fixed Anna with a stare. 'You've just got to get straight back out there. Hold your nose and dive in. After all, if Ella can do it after getting jilted, you certainly can.'

'Frankie, for God's sake, we agreed not to talk about that!' Gwen elbowed her in the side. 'And I was the one everyone thought would blab about it. You know Ella doesn't want it mentioned.'

'So everyone knows?' Ella looked at the others, who slowly nodded in response. 'And you made some sort of pact not to mention it, because it's such an embarrassment?'

'It wasn't like that.' Anna put a hand on her arm. 'We just wanted you to be able to put it behind you. I thought if you wanted to talk about it, that should be your choice not ours.'

'I'm sorry, Ella, it's just me and my big mouth.' Frankie bit her lip.

'It's fine. I know it was big news in Port Agnes when it hit the papers; my parents have kept all the clippings. I'm just thankful that they didn't put them up in a frame behind the counter, like they did with my degree certificate.' Ella managed a smile at the thought. 'It's just my luck to get publicly dumped on the day two social media celebrities were getting married and for it all to go viral.'

'Are people on social media really celebrities?' Gwen wrinkled her nose.

'They're some of the biggest names around nowadays, especially with teenagers.' Ella shrugged. 'But I'd rather people talked to me about it, if they want to ask what happened.'

'I'm sorry, Ella, we really weren't doing that. I spoke to everyone about it when you took the job, because it had been in the local paper and I thought it might get mentioned. But you've moved on and so should everyone else.' Anna squeezed her shoulder.

'That's what I was getting at.' Frankie looked from Ella to Anna, and back again. 'I was just trying, in my usual clumsy way, to make the point that you've moved on really well and got your life back together. So there's no reason why Anna can't do the same. Especially as your break-up was far more...'

'Humiliating?' Ella laughed. Poor Frankie was just digging herself a deeper hole, but it didn't matter any more. Most people went through a break-up at some point and just because Ella's had been more public than most, it was no different. Frankie was right, she'd moved on. Coming back to Port Agnes had proved what she'd always known deep down, that her feelings for Weller had never been strong enough to match what she'd felt for Dan. She'd told herself it was because first love always felt different – idealised and untouched by the reality of past relationship failures – but it was more than that. If she ever considered committing to spending her life with anyone again, it would need to outstrip what she'd felt for Dan; to push him into second place. But she was in no hurry and she certainly wouldn't go looking for all of that. She was already in a much better place than she had been – on the brink of settling for second best.

'Do you still have feelings for Weller?' Anna had a glassy look in her eyes as she asked the question.

'I think if I'm really honest I had a few niggling doubts about getting married too, but I put them down to the usual pre-wedding jitters, or the influence of my dad constantly telling me that Weller wasn't the man for me.' Ella looked at her friend, knowing she was only revealing part of the story. 'But humiliation was higher up on the list of emotions than heartbreak when we split, and according to Mum that means I never really loved Weller; not like you're supposed to love the person you've agreed to spend the rest of your life with.'

'I still love Greg, but not enough to give up the idea of being a mum.' Anna sniffed. 'The trouble is, just because we're finished, there's no guarantee I'll be able to do that anyway – either on my own, or in a relationship. And what if I've given up on him for something that's never going to happen?'

'If you really want a family, you'll find a way, whatever route that takes.' Frankie gave her a hug, but Anna frowned as she pulled away.

'I know it probably sounds vain, but I want to give birth to my own baby, one that's biologically mine, and to go through the agony and ecstasy like our ladies do every day. I know it's not what being a mother is about at all, but I can't help it. I blame the job!'

'It's not egotistical at all.' Ella paused. 'You're just being honest, and you've been honest with Greg too, which must have been hard.' It was obvious from Anna's face the toll it had taken. There were dark circles under her red-rimmed eyes.

'My daughter had a friend in your position and she put pinpricks in the condoms. She's got a little boy now – and a divorce!' Gwen winked. 'So things could definitely be worse.'

'Maybe I should give it another year or two with Greg. He could still change his mind?' As Anna spoke, her phone pinged. Picking it up, she smiled. 'If I believed in signs, I could definitely take this as one. That was Liz Johnson, one of my mums-to-be. She's gone into labour with her first baby and she's forty-three. She's on her way in now. So that gives me five years to change Greg's mind.'

'Would you really want to do that, though?' Frankie grimaced. 'Grind Greg down until he agrees to be a dad? Having a new baby is hard enough on a relationship, even when both parents want it. We see it all the time, don't we?'

'That's true.' Gwen put her hands on her hips. 'My daughter's friend – the one who put holes in the condoms – split up from her husband when their baby was six months old. He said he couldn't take playing second fiddle to his son and now she's a single mum anyway. She'd have been better off going to a sperm bank in the first place.' Gwen and Frankie were brave enough to say what Ella had been thinking. If she'd begged Weller to go through with the wedding and he'd agreed, deep down she'd have known he didn't really want to be with her. That would have been much harder to live with than the temporary humiliation, however painful it had seemed at the time. And if Anna took Greg back, just so she wasn't on her own, things wouldn't turn out any better.

'I don't suppose trying to force him into it would be a good idea.' Anna sounded as if she was trying to convince herself, and Ella just hoped something would happen to make her realise she was worth more before it was too late.

By the time Liz Johnson arrived at the midwifery unit half an hour later, Frankie was assisting Gwen with another birth. It meant Anna and Ella were both free to support Liz and her wife, Trudy, with the delivery of their first baby, and both mothers-to-be were beyond excited.

'I can't believe this is finally happening!' Liz grinned at her wife, looking remarkably serene for someone in labour, with bright red lipstick that appeared to have been freshly applied.

'I know, babe, me neither.' Trudy squeezed her hand and Ella looked up at them both, after examining Liz, while Anna monitored the baby's heartbeat.

'Well it's definitely happening.' Ella grinned. 'You're already nine centimetres dilated and, if I was a betting woman, I'd say the baby will be here by half past nine.'

'Can Trudy cut the cord?' Liz looked at her wife. 'This was all her idea, and I might have carried the baby, but if it wasn't for her, we'd never have been having Monty.'

'Of course she can, as long as nothing unexpected happens.'

Anna's tone was warm. 'So you know you're having a little boy then? Last time I saw you, you hadn't found out.'

'It was one of the debates we kept having throughout the pregnancy.' Trudy laughed. 'We didn't find out at any of the hospital scans, but we decided to have one of those 4D scans, where you can see the baby moving. They said they could hide the gender if we wanted, but for once we were on the same page. We wanted to see everything and there he was; our little miracle, Monty.'

'Well he's certainly keen to get out here and meet you both.' Ella had looked at the notes before Liz arrived, and the couple had been through a long process of fertility treatment to get to this point. Having had such a battle to become parents, they were clearly making the most of every moment.

'Almost as keen as his mums are to meet him. It's been a long time coming.' Liz couldn't stop smiling.

'I didn't think I'd ever be a mum and I didn't want to be until I met you.' Trudy kissed her wife's cheek. 'Then when we were told the odds of conceiving at our age, it seemed even less likely.'

'But we struck lucky on our third round of treatment!' Liz's face suddenly changed, pain twisting her features. 'Although it doesn't feel quite so lucky right now... Argh! Oh my God, this is agony!'

'Is she okay? Is it supposed to hurt that much?' Trudy's eyes widened in fear, as Liz screamed again.

'It's perfectly normal, but because she's progressing so quickly it can intensify the pain too.' Ella checked the tracing of the baby's heartbeat, and Anna examined Liz again.

'Okay, I can see the top of his head. Do you feel ready to start pushing?' Anna looked at Liz, who had slumped back down against the pillows.

'I've never felt pressure like that down there. It's incredibly strong even when there's no contraction.'

'You've never tried to push something the size of a melon through your hoo-hah before, have you darling?' Trudy stroked Liz's hair. 'But you can do this.'

'Easy for you to say!' Liz tensed her body again. 'There's another contraction coming.'

'Right, use this one to push then.' Anna kept her focus on Liz, as Ella moved to the side of the bed opposite Trudy.

'Can you support my legs?' Liz spoke through gritted teeth, the red lipstick now long gone. 'I feel like I could give it a bit more welly if I've got something to push against.'

'No problem, I can take one side and Trudy can support the other one.' Ella braced her body against Liz's right leg.

'I'm having another contraction!' Liz dropped her chin to her chest and made a low growling sound.

'He's got black hair, darling, like you!' Trudy almost dropped her wife's leg, as the baby's head was suddenly clearly visible. It was definitely progressing more quickly than most labours, especially first ones.

'Okay, his head's completely out now. Don't push for a minute, just take little breaths for me.' Anna shot Ella a look and she didn't need to say anything. The cord needed to be unwrapped from the baby's neck. It was something that happened a lot and, as long as Anna could loosen it and slip it over the baby's head before Liz pushed again, it shouldn't cause a problem; but in Ella's experience, parents were inclined to panic when they were told the cord was around their baby's neck, so if Anna didn't have to tell them, she probably wouldn't.

'Is everything okay?' Trudy could see what was going on and she looked up at Ella; the terrified expression back on her face.

'It's fine. We just need to get everything ready for Liz to give one final push.' Ella nodded and Trudy let out a long breath as Anna expertly looped the cord over the baby's head.

'Okay, Liz, you can push with the next contraction and, if you get his shoulders out, that should be it.' Almost as soon as Anna said the words, Liz's face contorted again and within seconds baby Monty emerged into the world, straight into Anna's capable hands. Just moments later, the baby was lying on Liz's chest and both his mums were crying.

'Thank you so much.' Trudy hugged Anna and Ella in turn, her face still wet with tears.

'It was Liz who did all the hard work.' Ella smiled. She wouldn't swap these moments for anything; watching a new family spend their first moments together was the most incredible privilege and, when she looked across at Anna, there were tears in her eyes too. If Ella's route to becoming a midwife really had been mapped out before she was even born, she was glad of it.

'I want this.' Anna mouthed the words to Ella as Trudy and Liz gazed at their newborn son, and Ella nodded in response. She just wished she could promise her friend it would happen, but nobody knew what was around the corner.

9

Work had been crazy; three of the other midwives had come down with a sickness bug and Ella had ended up having to cover quite a few nights on call. It meant she'd been forced to cancel her meet-up with Dan in The Jolly Sailor and she still hadn't had a chance to speak to him about letting Sophie stay in one of his cottages, rent-free. When she'd spoken to Anna about it, they'd both agreed that she needed to tread carefully when she did speak to him. Sophie was old enough to make her own decisions and Ella couldn't risk letting Dan know how potentially vulnerable she might be without telling him that neither the baby's father nor Sophie's parents knew she was pregnant. If she bumped into him when she was up at Liberty Farm for a home visit, she was going to have to find a way of talking to Dan on his own, but the prospect of revealing too much about Sophie's situation wasn't the only reason that made her nervous. The more the old Dan had revealed himself to still be very much in existence, the harder it had been to suppress all the good memories of when they were together. It had been much easier when they'd been buried under the resentment she'd felt about him breaking his promise to come to London with her, when she'd still had no idea why.

Pulling into the farmyard, she spotted Lissy up ahead attempting to catch a chicken that was doing a passable impression of Roadrunner from the Loony Tunes cartoons. She had Noah by the hand; he was wearing red wellingtons and a determined expression as he tried to slip out of her grasp.

'Afternoon, Lissy, can I help?' Ella called out as she shut the car door.

'Definitely! Although I can't decide if I've got more chance of catching Flo or holding on to my son.'

'You keep hold of Noah and I'll try to catch the chicken.' Ella put her bag down on the bonnet of the car and attempted to approach the chicken slowly, but intent on escape, it ran straight through her legs. Doubling back on herself, she decided the softly-softly approach wasn't going to work, so she gave chase.

'You won't need to go to the gym tonight, Ella. Sorry about this!' Lissy laughed, as Ella ran past her for a third time. Finally, she managed to corner the chicken, grabbing hold of it and gripping on as tightly as she dared. There was no way she was letting the flipping thing go again, even if it was trying to peck a hole in her hand.

'Where do you want her?'

'I'll put her in the barn, if you can keep an eye on Noah. Sorry, I thought his dad was going to be home in time to keep an eye on him so I could get some jobs done on the farm in peace. But something's come up and he can't get back after all.'

'Does that happen a lot?'

'It's just his job; when we first started, we couldn't keep the farm going without it and I think he's still a bit nervous about risking putting all of his eggs into one basket. If you'll pardon the pun!' Lissy laughed, taking Flo from Ella. 'I'll be two minutes and then we can have a cup of tea. I've been dying for one for hours and it'll be great to have an excuse to sit down.'

'You've got to start looking after yourself, too, Lissy. Going hours dying for a drink isn't good for you.' Ella took hold of Noah's hand, before he made a dash for it.

'You sound just like Dan! I know you're right, but it won't be for much longer, Niall's promised he'll be around a lot more when he finishes the big contract he's working on and the farmhands Dan organised are increasing their hours from next week.'

'Has Dan been able to help you much?'

'He's been working twelve-hour days down at Mercer's Row, but he helps out whenever he can.' Lissy shrugged. 'One of the benefits of having known my midwife since we were kids is that I feel like I can ask you a really cheeky question.'

'Go on.' Ella braced herself for the question she'd been dreading and expecting in equal measure, but now that it looked as though Dan's sister might finally be about to ask if Ella still had feelings for him, she realised she didn't know what her answer would be. Ever since Lissy had told her the reasons behind Dan's decision to stay in Port Agnes, she'd felt as if she owed him an apology for resenting the choice he'd made, when all he'd done was the right thing. But when Lissy asked her question, it had nothing to do with Dan.

'Can you take Noah inside and flick the kettle on, please? I'll be as quick as I can.'

'Of course.' Heat flushed Ella's cheeks as she turned away. Lissy probably hadn't even given Ella's relationship with Dan a second thought. It was so long ago and just because being back in Port Agnes full-time had made it feel to Ella like the clocks had been wound back more than a decade, it didn't mean anyone else felt the same.

By the time Lissy got into the house, Ella had made the tea

and Noah was busy throwing plastic bricks into a storage box, then turning it over to empty out the contents before starting all over again.

'You're an angel. Sorry it took longer than I said, but I thought I'd check on the cows quickly while I was out there.'

'How are things, apart from you being run off your feet? Pregnancy can be a strain, even without the added stress of running a farm.'

'I'm okay, but I'll be glad when I've got my body back. I was pretty small last time, right up until the end, but this time around I'm struggling to do my shoelaces up. Thank God I spend my life in wellington boots.'

'When's Niall going to be home?'

'He's promised he'll come back next weekend for a couple of days and he daren't break that promise after letting me down this weekend. Dan's taking Thursday off to have Noah overnight and take him to the seal sanctuary, to give me a bit of a break. He'll probably have to work all weekend to make up for the lost time, but I could have worse little brothers.' Lissy smiled. 'Although I think Uncle Dan might be more excited about going to see the seals than his nephew, given that Noah thinks all animals are dogs. Dog and Dan-Dan are about the only words he can say!'

'Dan certainly puts the hours in.' Ella wasn't going to confess that she'd spent far too long looking out of her bedroom window and watching Dan working on the outside of the cottages. He'd repointed the walls, replaced some roof tiles and that morning he'd been doing something to one of the windows. He had an impressive suntan as a result and Ella had noticed a group of teenage girls who were suddenly very interested in hanging out by the side of the harbour, sunbathing on towels spread out in full view of Mercer's Row. There was a beautiful sandy beach less than a hundred metres away, so there was only one explanation for why they suddenly preferred the concrete of the harbour wall.

'He's determined to get the cottages looking how they used to when we were kids. He spent ages doing research on the history of Mercer's Row and applied to get the cottages recognised as buildings of historical significance, even though that'll end up making the renovations more expensive. He just wants to make sure, if he sells them, that they won't end up being changed beyond all recognition.'

'Is he like that about all the properties he works on?'

'Not all of them, but if anywhere around Port Agnes comes up for sale he always goes for a viewing and some places he just has to have. Although not even Dan always gets his way. He desperately wanted The Old Forge, but there was a group of investors who must have wanted it just as badly and the price went way beyond what Dan was willing to pay.'

'So there was a bidding war?' Ella definitely wasn't going to share that with Jago. If Dan had just stepped aside, her parents' finances might not have been in the state they were, but she could hardly blame him for that. She knew that many of the locals had Dan all wrong. Anyone who was prepared to lose profits by applying for listed building status definitely prioritised tradition over money.

'He was gutted about it, and when he thought it might get knocked down and replaced I was worried he'd end up chaining himself naked to the front of the building when the bulldozers pulled up.'

'You really think he'd have gone that far?' Ella was desperately trying not to picture it. There were already enough women in Port Agnes imagining what Dan Ferguson looked like without his clothes on.

'I don't know, but he'd probably have considered it to get maximum publicity for his cause. You know, like those women from the WI, or the firemen and farmers who do it to raise money from calendar sales?' Lissy laughed again. 'Now I'm picturing naked firemen, God help Niall when he gets home. I think the pregnancy hormones are getting to me; I might be exhausted, but I'll be jumping on him as soon as he gets through the door!'

'If that doesn't persuade him to spend more time at the farm nothing will!'

'What about you? Are you ready to start dating again?' Lissy squeezed her arm. 'It must be hard after what happened with your fiancé, but you can't let that stop you moving on.'

'You know about Weller?' Ella's face went hot as Lissy nodded. 'Does Dan know?'

'Oh sweetheart, everyone does. You know what Port Agnes is like and the story made the front page of the *Three Ports News*.' Lissy squeezed her arm again. 'But you've got nothing to be embarrassed about. Weller's the one who should be ashamed.'

'I hate being that person, the one everyone feels sorry for, and I hate being the centre of attention.' Ella pulled a face. 'What did Dan say?'

'I showed him the paper and all he said, when he'd finished reading the article, was that Weller was an idiot.' Lissy smiled. 'You know you're the reason he wanted to buy The Old Forge, don't you?'

'He said that?'

'No, but it was obvious.' Lissy shrugged. 'He told me when you guys were still at school that you'd talked about what sort of house you wanted to buy and that you'd told him you thought The Old Forge could be converted into a lovely house. I don't think he ever forgot it.'

'I haven't thought about that in years and it would be way too big and expensive to have as a single house. If I remember rightly, I said I'd buy it if I ever won the lottery! We talked about a lot of stuff back then that was never going to happen.' Ella's words came out in a rush, like she was running and struggling to hold a conversation at the same time. But the truth was, she *was* fighting to catch her breath. Dan had remembered too and, despite everything that had happened between them, he'd wanted to buy the house they'd fantasised about sharing. Maybe it had nothing to do with his decision to buy the house, but maybe, just maybe, it had.

'Perhaps you coming home is the universe's way of giving you both a second chance?'

'I think we've both changed far too much and had too many reality checks to believe in any kind of happily ever after with someone we went out with when we were still at school.' After what Weller had done to her, Ella couldn't imagine ever letting another man back into her heart – least of all someone who'd already broken it once. At least not until just lately. If she was really honest with herself, there'd been moments – ever since Lissy had revealed why Dan had stayed, and especially since the rescue with Sophie – when Ella had pictured what a life with Dan might be like. She hadn't wanted to, and the rational side of her had screamed that you could never go back, never recreate the intensity of that first love. Except her brain didn't always play ball when it came to being rational, especially not where Dan was concerned. She could say the right words, though, tell Lissy what she thought was the sensible answer and the rest she would just keep to herself. It would pass eventually, it had to.

'Oh I don't know, maybe the fact that you've both changed means you wouldn't repeat the same mistakes this time. Dan's not as bad as he used to be about trying to solve all his problems without letting anyone in.' Lissy smiled. 'Go on, Ella, give him a chance, you know you want to!'

'It's only a few months since I split up with Weller and, even if I did think me and Dan had a shot, I'm nowhere near ready.' It still felt more like Ella was trying to convince herself than Lissy. The gossips of Port Agnes would love that, Ella Mehenick hooking up with her childhood sweetheart so soon after being jilted. She'd had more than enough of being the centre of attention to last her a lifetime and, if she ever did risk another relationship, it certainly wouldn't be in the full glow of the Port Agnes spotlight.

She had no idea if Dan would be interested, even if she was prepared to go with her heart instead of her head. All she could do was keep reminding herself that you could never go back and, if that didn't work, at least she had an ace up her sleeve. She was leaving Port Agnes at the end of her contract and putting as much distance between herself and Dan as possible was one way of making sure that the battle between her head and her heart went the right way. Once and for all.

* * *

Ella scrabbled around in the bottom of her handbag trying to find her phone before it stopped ringing. She'd only put it in there a few minutes beforehand, with the intention of leaving early to have a walk along the coastal path before work. It was a mystery how such a large object could do such a good job of disguising itself so quickly amongst the half-eaten tubes of Polos and packets of tissues that lined the bottom of the bag. But just for once she managed to find it before it stopped ringing.

'Hi Ella, it's Jess. Sorry, I know you're not due in until ten.' It sounded as if the night shifts Jess had recently started volunteering to cover were taking their toll.

'No problem, what's up? You sound worn out.'

'We had two deliveries last night. Both of them went fine, but it was just a bit of a long night.' Jess yawned as if to prove the point. 'God, sorry, I can't seem to get used to the night shift! I was just calling because Sophie Brighouse has been on to the unit in a bit of panic and she wanted to know if she could see you when you came in, but you've got back-to-back appointments this morning.'

'I could pop across to Mercer's Row and see her at home, if that would work?'

'I'm sure she'd really appreciate it. She said she just doesn't feel quite right. The exact word she used was *weird* and I think she just needs a bit of reassurance.'

'I've got her number, so I'll give her a call and see if it's okay for me to go over.' Ella caught sight of her reflection in the mirror, and the sudden urge she had to put on a bit more make-up had absolutely nothing to do with the fact that she might bump into Dan. 'Will you still be at the unit when I get in at ten?'

'No. I'm heading off at nine, just in time to miss Dom heading off to work. We're like ships in the night at the moment.'

'You know I'm always happy to cover for you if you need a bit of time off. You've been working so many hours lately.'

'Thanks Ella, you're a star, and that's why the rest of us are already petitioning Anna to find a way to keep you on at the end of the six months. It's not that we don't like Sadie, but we love you!' Jess laughed and Ella couldn't stop herself from smiling. If she could find a way of doing her teacher training in Plymouth and working part-time at the unit in Port Agnes, she'd definitely be willing to consider it, but only if she was sure her parents didn't need her help to get their finances back in the black. Either way, it was nice to know that the other midwives wanted her to stay.

* * *

There was no sign of Dan outside the cottages when Ella headed across to Mercer's Row, so it was just as well the extra layer of mascara she'd applied wasn't for his benefit.

'Thanks so much for coming over and I'm really sorry I'm

such a pain.' Sophie was pale-faced as she opened the door to her cottage.

'It's no problem and of course you aren't a pain. You know I said you could call my mobile any time you're worried.'

'I know, but I thought I should go through the unit and book an appointment. But when they said you didn't have any I got really worried and the other midwife said she'd see what she could do. I called in to work sick this morning, I just can't face it, but they've told me if I'm not back tomorrow that I needn't bother coming back.' Sophie bit her lip, stepping aside to let Ella into the cottage.

'They can't do that, don't worry.' Ella knew the family who owned the holiday park and they had a reputation for employing people who were desperate enough to accept low wages and poor working conditions. She might not be able to solve all of her young patient's problems, but if Sophie went back home to her parents, the first thing Ella would be doing was to find out if there was any way she could stop the Tredinnick family treating their staff the way they did.

'I don't know, the manager seems to fire staff all the time, so I can't see him making an exception for me.' Sophie sighed. 'But at least I've got this place and they can't come knocking on my door to check if I'm really sick. I don't know what I'd have done without Dan and I still can't believe he's letting me stay here for free.'

'It's lovely in here. I've got to admit I thought it would be more of a wreck.' If Ella had seen the interior of the cottage in an advert for a high-end holiday brochure, it wouldn't have looked out of place. It was fully furnished too. She'd expected an armchair and a TV at best, given that Mercer's Row was midway through being renovated. Instead it had all of Dan's trademark touches, the same attention to detail that she'd seen in the Old Telephone Exchange. The walls were mostly whitewashed, but he'd taken the plaster back in parts to reveal the beautiful Cornish stone underneath and the piles of old carpet in the skip outside had obviously been pulled up to reveal the original flagstones beneath. Dan had created a nook in the space under the stairs, which led straight up from the living room. He'd created bespoke shelving to fit the quirky dimensions of the space and there was a squashy two-seater sofa where Ella could just imagine spending a lazy afternoon reading with her feet on Dan's lap. Shaking herself to get the unwanted image out of her head, she turned back to Sophie. 'I'm amazed at how much Dan has already done.'

'Me too!' Sophie smiled for the first time. 'But he said this one needed the least work out of the four, so his team did this one first and he was staying here himself until I moved in.'

'And the furniture's his too?'

'He said he didn't want to get it ruined by moving it to the cottage at the other end of the row where he's staying now. Although he stays up at the farm with his sister quite a lot too, so he's not always around much.' There was a definite note of regret in Sophie's voice.

'Let's sit down and you can tell me what's been worrying you.'

'I met Mum for dinner last night after work. She said she was driving down to Port Agnes to see me and I had to tell her that I wasn't staying at the caravan park any more. I tried to come up with an excuse why I couldn't meet her, but I couldn't come up with any I hadn't already used.'

'How did it go?' Sophie's baby bump was fairly obvious now, so hiding it would definitely have been a challenge.

'She hugged me and two seconds later her arms dropped to her side and she said: you're pregnant, aren't you?' Sophie's voice shook as she recounted the story. 'And I just burst into tears.'

'Oh sweetheart, that must have been hard for you.' Ella put an arm around the younger woman's shoulders. 'How did your mum react?'

'She cried too and at first I thought it was because she was so angry with me, but she said it was because she was so sad I didn't feel like I could tell her as soon as I found out.'

'That's really good news! Do you feel better now that she knows?'

'A bit, but now she's got to tell Dad.' Sophie's voice caught in her throat. 'And I've always been his little girl. He'll be so shocked and it will make life really awkward for him with some of his parishioners.'

'Don't worry about what everyone else thinks, as long as your mum and dad are on your side that's all that matters.' Ella knew better than anyone that it was easier said than done and she still struggled to take her own advice every day.

'I think that's why I feel so weird today, because I know Mum could tell Dad at any minute. My stomach won't stop churning and I feel like I want to be sick, but I know it's all in my head.'

'Think about how worried you were about telling your mum and how well that turned out.' Ella squeezed her hand. 'Do you know when she's planning to tell him?'

'She said as soon as she finds the right moment and she wanted me to go home with her, but Dan's said I can stay here until I'm ready and I don't want to go back until Dad's had some time to process it all. Mum offered to pay Dan to cover my rent, but he said it helps him out having someone stay at either end of Mercer's Row, as it makes it look like the whole terrace is occupied. Mum's paying the money into my account anyway, so at least I can still buy food and run my car if I get the sack from the caravan park. If Dad takes it okay, I'll be going home soon anyway, but not even Mum seemed sure how he'd react.'

'How does she feel about you staying here?' Ella was worried that Sophie's attachment to Dan was only going to get stronger all the time she was thinking about her parents rejecting her and she'd noticed that she'd stopped even mentioning the prospect of telling the baby's father.

'She said Dan's a real-life Good Samaritan, you know, like the story from the bible? I used to tell it to the kids at Sunday school and look at me now, pregnant and still a teenager! But helping out there is what made me want to be a teacher in the first place.'

'You've got nothing to be ashamed of, Sophie, and I'm sure your dad will agree.' Ella squeezed her hand again. 'I'm almost certain the weird way you're feeling is just down to nerves, but let's just get you and the baby checked over to make sure.'

'Thanks, Ella. I feel better already just talking to you.' Maybe Sophie just needed to take things a step at a time and Ella just hoped that Dan's act of kindness wouldn't end up making things more complicated, but she definitely needed to talk to him about it. She just had to work out if there was anything else she needed to talk to him about, or whether the old adage was right and that some things were just better left unsaid.

* * *

'Ella!' Dan called out from the upstairs window at the far end of the terrace as she walked past after checking Sophie over. Thankfully there'd been no sign she was suffering from anything more than nerves. 'Hang on a sec and I'll come down.'

'Okay, I need to talk to you anyway.' Ella ran a hand through her hair, as she waited for him to open the front door.

'Is Sophie okay? She got herself in a bit of state last night after her mother left and I told her to give you a call.'

'She's fine and it sounds like you were quite the hit with her mum for letting her live in the cottage rent-free.'

'Do you want to come in?' If Dan didn't want to have the conversation on the doorstep, he must have realised how it might look to others.

'I haven't got long...' But even as she started to protest, Ella found herself crossing the threshold of the cottage. The inside was minimalist to say the least, but she could already imagine how good it was going to look when it was finished. Dan was halfway through ripping up a layer of laminate flooring – the same sort of shade as Donald Trump's fake tan – exposing more beautiful flagstones underneath. There was an open sofa bed squeezed up into one corner of the room and not much else.

'Sorry, I needed to do some prep work upstairs before the plumbers get here and I haven't got round to making my bed.'

'So you're living like a squatter and you've got a nineteen-year-old sleeping in your bed at the other end of the terrace?'

'You make it sound really dodgy! I know things haven't always been great between us, but I hope you know me a bit better than that.'

'I do, Dan, but you know what it's like round here. There are people who'll be only too willing to think the worst of you.'

'Including your dad?' Dan didn't wait for her to answer. 'If I cared about what people thought I'd have left Port Agnes years ago. I'll always be an outsider to some of them and most of the others seem convinced that all I want to do is ruin the town and drive all the locals out.'

'If people knew you'd applied to make Mercer's Row a protected building and that you're helping Sophie, and having to live like this as a result, maybe they'd realise you're not who they think you are.'

'I'm not doing any of it to impress anyone else. I do the things I do because they matter to me.' Dan met her gaze and something in his face softened. 'Anyway, the cottage at this end has always had a special place in my heart.'

'And mine.' The words had come out before she'd been able to stop them and she had to drop her gaze. The cottage had been where they'd shared something they'd never be able to share with anyone else and the fact that it had apparently meant as much to him as it had to her mattered more than she'd ever have believed. 'I'm just worried about how vulnerable Sophie can be and she might read more into your kindness than you realise.'

'I'm not doing anything to give her the wrong idea, El, I promise, but if you'd seen the state of that caravan she was living in and the working conditions up there. There was no way I could let her stay there, especially not after the accident.' Dan sighed. 'Now that she's back in touch with her mum I'm sure it'll sort itself out before we need to start worrying.'

'I know you offered Sophie the cottage for all the right reasons, and it was really kind of you. I just hope her mum doesn't wait too long to tell her dad, so Sophie can go home.' As Ella looked up again, the realisation that Sophie wasn't the only one in danger of getting a dangerous attachment to Dan Ferguson suddenly hit home. It was no good trying to convince herself that her head might still win the battle, it was already too late.

10

Ella was debating between a Starbar and a mint Aero in the newsagent's on Paradise Lane – halfway between the midwifery unit and her parents' house – when the newspaper headline caught her eye.

JED HARRIS AND PETRA ALEXIA EXPECTING TWINS

Then in slightly smaller text beneath it:

YouTube stars to live stream birth!

'Can you imagine anything more undignified than being filmed giving birth? Even those awful documentary programmes blur out some of the bits that not even your husband should see, but showing every minute of the whole thing?' Doris Myklow, who'd run the newsagent's for as long as Ella could remember, pulled a face as Ella put both chocolate bars and the newspaper onto the counter. 'Still I suppose someone like you would be used to all that mess.'

'To me it's always a miracle, otherwise I'd stop being a midwife and I couldn't get enough of those documentaries before I started the job. I can't say I'd want to have my own labour live streamed for the world to see, but for some people sharing every aspect of their lives is just what they do.' Ella shrugged. 'It's probably not even true, anyway. You know what newspapers are like.'

'As do you!' Doris rang up the prices on a till that wouldn't have looked out of place in a *How We Used to Live* museum. 'I thought they might have asked you to be their midwife, given the connection you've got.'

'We once bumped into each other on the steps of a registry office. I'm afraid that's it.' Ella shrugged again. According to Ella's mum, Doris had displayed billboards outside the shop for at least three weeks, bearing the headline:

LOCAL GIRL IN CELEBRITY JILTING SHOCK!

so it was no surprise that Doris was still harping on about it.

'I suppose you're going down to the Silver of the Sea festival?' Doris wrinkled her nose as Ella nodded. 'Place will be running alive with tourists and emmets, you wouldn't catch me down there.'

'Exactly how long does someone need to live in Port Agnes before they aren't an emmet any more, Doris?'

'They have to be born and bred, with parents who've lived down here full-time too. The children of those second-homers won't count, even if they're delivered up at your unit.'

'Good to know. So it wouldn't matter if someone moved down here, joined the lifeboat crew and rescued a local child from the sea? They'd still be incomers?'

'An emmet's an emmet, that's all there is to it. That's not to say they don't have their uses, some of those home and garden magazines they buy from here are almost five pounds each! More money than sense most of them.'

'I'll see you later, Doris.' Ella wouldn't be able to change the old woman's mind, whatever she said and, unlike Doris, she was really looking forward to the Silver of the Sea festival. She'd come home for it a few times over the years but it hadn't always been possible in the time she'd spent living in London. It hadn't been Weller's idea of fun and he'd always been more than happy to use it as an excuse to go to a gig or festival with Ste when she did come down. In the first few years after leaving home, she'd steered clear of the festival altogether, not wanting to risk bumping into Dan.

Things were different now, though. Jess, Toni and Anna all had the day off too and she was looking forward to spending some time with her new friends before giving her parents a hand in the bakery. The festival was always the busiest day of the year and the good weather was only going to make the event more popular.

Walking back down towards the harbour, the appeal of the festival was obvious. All of the fishing boats had been decorated for the event and there'd be a flotilla out to the Sisters of Agnes Island, which lay just off the coast and was cut off from the mainland at high tide. The boats would circle the island three times and come back into the harbour. It looked like the crews had gone all out this year too, with fancy dress outfits spanning everything from pirates to mermen and there was a real carnival atmosphere, with the Port Agnes folk singers already performing on the harbourside.

'Excellent timing, Ella. You're just in time for a champagne cocktail!' Jess uncorked the bottle as she called out to her. 'We've got our own picnic table and enough champagne to sink the flotilla.'

'What are we celebrating?' Ella asked, as Jess poured the champagne into a jug filled with clear liquid, ice and mint leaves.

'Girl power.' Jess stopped pouring just as the champagne threatened to spill over the sides of the jug. 'And no better way to do that than with champagne mojitos.'

'Sounds a bit dangerous to me!' Anna pulled a face. 'I better just stick to the one. I'm on call tomorrow and I'm at the age where a hangover lasts a lot longer than it used to!'

'Well I've got three days off and if I can still remember the row I had with Dom this morning by the time I wake up tomorrow, I'll be asking for a refund on this champagne.' Jess was already topping up the glasses.

'You might forget the things he said to you, but I won't.' Toni spoke through gritted teeth. 'Especially when the reason all his mates know he might have a problem is down to him, not you.'

'Dare I ask? Or would you rather not talk about it?' Ella took the glass that Jess passed to her.

'We've been waiting for tests to see why we haven't had any luck falling pregnant, now that we've been trying for over year, since before the wedding.' Jess's attempts to look casual were ruined when her eyes filled with tears. 'He got drunk at the rugby club and confided in one of his friends that he's terrified of finding out he's got a low sperm count and now they're all calling him Jaffa.'

'I still don't get that bit?' Anna looked at Jess, as she spoke.

'Because Jaffas are seedless oranges.'

'And he blamed you for that?' Ella's jaw had already tightened at the insult Dom's rugby mates had thrown at him. After everything her parents had gone through to have her back in the very early nineties, when the IVF success rate was even lower, it wasn't a subject she could laugh at. If Jess and Dom had to go through that too, it could end up breaking their hearts.

'He called her a stupid cow for *forcing* him into requesting the tests.' Toni looked like she'd happily push Dom into the harbour if he turned up. 'Apparently it's all Jess's fault that he got drunk because of the stress and blabbed his secret fears to a bunch of Neanderthals.'

'So the least you can do is drink with me, so I can forget for one day how much of a dick my husband is being.' Jess downed her first champagne mojito and topped up her glass straight away. At this rate, this year's Silver of the Sea festival was going to be memorable for all the wrong reasons.

* * *

'Do you think Jess is okay?' Ella made her way along the harbour-side with Anna, weaving in and out of the crowds. She had half an hour left until she was covering the bakery for a couple of hours with Maddie, while her parents had a bit of a break. She'd watch the flotilla head out for the first loop of the Sisters of Agnes Island and her parents would be able to watch the boats come back in before the swimming race took place. The bakery would close in time for the final parade, where the children of all the fishermen would lead the way up to St Jude's and the vicar would give a service of thanks for the bounty of silvery fish that gave them all their livelihoods. The annual Silver of the Sea award would then be presented to a local hero who'd done something to support the fishermen and helped keep the industry alive in Port Agnes, so that it retained a working harbour.

'I hope she will be.' Anna frowned. 'She and Dom seem to be having a tough time of things lately, that's why Jess has been volunteering for so many night shifts. I think she's trying to avoid the conflict at home.'

'Poor thing, they've not been married long, have they?'

'No, I think the Port Agnes midwifery unit might be cursed on the relationships front!' Anna's laugh was hollow. 'Greg handed in his notice and he's already halfway across Europe in the campervan he bought, and now I seem to be further away than ever from having a family of my own.'

'Have you thought about trying online dating?'

'I just don't know if I'm ready for all of that. I'd have no idea what to write about myself in the profile for a start. Writing "*I want a baby within the next two years*" probably isn't going to cut it. Especially as most guys my age are looking for women ten years younger and, if I date someone in their forties, they'll probably already have children and have had the snip. So there's no way they'll be able to start all over again even if they wanted to.'

'What about a younger man?' As they walked past Brae's fish and chip shop, Ella caught sight of his distinctive red hair. He was seven or eight years younger than Anna, but he wasn't like a lot of men his age. He was definitely the settling down sort.

'Oh God no! Younger men want some kind of cougar when they're going out with older women. I'm far too self-conscious for all of that!'

'If you want a wingman for the online dating, I'd definitely be up for it.'

'We could both set up profiles!' Anna raised an eyebrow, but Ella shook her head so hard her sunglasses slipped down her nose.

'I'm definitely not ready for that. Being infamous in Port Agnes as a jilted bride would make any relationship I tried to have a subject of far more interest than it should be to anyone but me. I'm more than happy to steer clear of dating until I leave town again.'

'I hope you change your mind, because I'd still really like you to think about staying if Sadie decides not to come back after her secondment.' Anna stopped as they reached a stall selling paintings, ceramics and ornaments made by local artists. 'I mean, how could you leave a place like this?'

'I do love these paintings.' Ella looked at the painting Anna was pointing at. It was definitely the work of the same artist who'd painted the mural at the midwifery unit. 'And, wherever I end up, I'd love to have one hanging on the wall, I'll just need to save up first.'

'We've got a small one by Dan Ferguson for under five hundred pounds.' The young woman running the stall smiled at Ella, who stood there with her mouth hanging open.

'Did you say *Dan Ferguson*?'

'Yes.' The stallholder was still grinning. 'We could sell twenty times the number of his paintings if he could produce them quickly enough, but he doesn't get that much time, what with running his business. Although I'd happily give him a hand with anything he wanted!'

'They're so beautiful.' Ella looked at the painting more closely. It was a view down to Port Agnes and the Sisters of Agnes Island beyond it, which was the exact view Ella remembered from lookout point where she and Dan had spent so many hours sitting in her little VW Beetle planning their futures. Had Dan remembered any of that when he'd painted the picture? When they'd planned to move to London, Dan was going to go to art school, but she'd assumed he'd let go of his dreams of being an artist when he'd decided to stay in Port Agnes. Except it turned out that their home town had given him all the inspiration he'd needed and he was even more talented than she remembered. He'd found a way of achieving everything he'd ever set out to achieve, and more, without having to leave his family behind. Suddenly she felt like the one who'd made a huge and unnecessary sacrifice.

'You should treat yourself, you deserve it. When Dan painted the mural at the unit after his nephew was born, I thought we were going to have to take out extra insurance. So five hundred pounds is a real bargain.' Anna gave her an encouraging nudge, but Ella shook her head. She couldn't spend that sort of money until she was certain her parents didn't need her help, no matter how much she loved Dan's work. The fact that he'd painted a mural for Noah was just another indication of the man he was; he loved his family with the sort of devotion that instantly made Ella feel even more connected to him. He'd be an amazing dad one day too, because family ties meant the world to him, just like they did to Ella and her parents. It was all the more reason she couldn't risk letting them down by spending money that could help get them out of the financial hole they seemed to be in.

'We'd better get down to the other end of the harbour if we want to see the boats going out.'

'Come on then. There's always a chance there'll be a trawlerman dressed as Long John Silver – looking to settle down with a wife and family – who'll catch my eye.' This time when Anna laughed it was genuine and if anyone deserved to find her pirate prince at the Silver of the Sea festival, it was her.

* * *

Having failed to find the Long John Silver of her dreams, Anna had headed back to meet up with Jess and Toni again after Ella started her shift at the bakery. She'd given Anna some pasties and cream buns to take back to the others in the hope that it would soak up some of the mojitos that Jess had been knocking back so quickly.

After a bit of persuasion, her parents had finally set off to watch the end of the flotilla and Ella had been so busy serving the relentless stream of customers who'd come into the shop that the time had passed before she'd known it.

'We're completely out of pasties and we've almost run out of everything else.' Ella smiled as her parents came back into the shop arm in arm. They'd had their ups and downs and they could bicker for hours over the smallest of things sometimes, but they still loved each other after all these years.

'Well done, my love, it looks like you and Maddie have been busy.' Ruth smiled at her daughter.

'You didn't sell those cream buns I put in the cake box, did you?' Jago let go of Ruth's arm and came round the back of the counter.

'What, the one with "*RESERVED, DO NOT SELL*" in block capitals written across the top of the box?' Ella looked at her father. 'No, Dad, I didn't sell them.'

'That's good, because I've got Clem and Jack coming over in a bit to talk about the plans for The Old Forge so we can start getting an income from our investment.'

'That's great!' It would be a real weight off Ella's mind if her parents could get out of the financial hole Jago's investment had clearly put them in. 'Oh talk of the devil, here they are now.'

'I'll cover the counter now that it's quietening down and everyone's getting ready to watch the parade.' Ruth put an arm around her daughter. 'What would we do without your help, my love?'

'You'd probably have been able to retire by now.' Ella squeezed her mother's waist. 'I'll go and make some tea for dad and his friends and then I'll help you close up and we can watch the parade together.'

'You're an angel and I'll love you even more if you make your old mum some tea too.'

'I'd do anything for you, Mum, you know that.' For some weird reason, Ella's eyes suddenly filled with tears. Maybe it was the sentiment of the Silver of the Sea festival getting to her – giving thanks for the things that sustained the lifeblood of Port Agnes and, for Ella, that would always be her mum and dad.

They'd sacrificed so much to give her the life she had and they'd always been on her side, even when she'd made choices they must have found tough – like moving hundreds of miles away and getting engaged to Weller, who they could see wasn't right for her long before she realised it herself.

'Here you go.' Ten minutes later, she was back with a tray laden with mugs of tea. The shop was empty of both customers and stock, and Ruth had already turned over the closed sign on the bakery door and was busy clearing up, before they set off for the parade.

'Thank you, my love.' Ruth took a mug off the tray. 'I think you're just in time. Things are getting a bit heated over there.'

'What's Michael Tredinnick doing here?' Ella couldn't stop her lip from curling slightly. He'd gone to school with both her parents and, according to Jago, he'd always had a bit of a thing for Ruth. So he hadn't taken it very well when she'd started going out with Jago instead. He'd certainly taken every opportunity he could over the years to belittle the Mehenick family whenever he got the chance, asking how their *little business* was going and whether Ella was still playing doctors and nurses in London. Her mother had told her more than once that Michael made her flesh crawl and Ella didn't need to ask why.

The Tredinnick family owned the caravan park where Sophie worked, but also had several other businesses they ran out of Tredinnick Farm – the biggest of which was Dreckzel Developments. They'd been responsible for a series of new builds on the outskirts of Port Tremellien, which made up the third of the Three Ports coastal towns, with Port Agnes and Port Kara. They were exactly the sort of identikit housing estates that her father loathed, so it was a major shock to see Michael Tredinnick involved in the discussions about the future of The Old Forge.

'I didn't buy it to see it knocked down and have some shoebox apartments take its place.' Jago's raised voice would have made it perfectly clear how he felt, even if there hadn't been a muscle going in his cheek.

'We've looked at every possible way of getting our money back without selling it to Dreckzel Developments, but we're not going to get our original investment back, let alone find any way of making money off it. It needs far too much work and we over-paid because of that bloody Ferguson boy bidding against us.' Clem Verran was her father's oldest friend, so if anyone could persuade him to sell The Old Forge it would be him. 'And at least Dreckzel Developments is a local business and someone from Port Agnes will benefit if we sell to Michael.'

'And who's going to be buying these apartments? Will they be ring-fenced for locals or sold to yet more emmets?' Jago didn't even look at Ella as she set the mugs of tea down on the table in the corner of the bakery that was usually reserved for elderly or disabled customers to sit and wait while their orders were made up. She hadn't known Michael was there, so she hadn't made him a drink. Although even if she had, she wouldn't have wanted to make him any tea. Not after the conditions he forced Sophie to live in and threatening to sack a pregnant woman for having one day off sick.

'It's a business, Jago, although I know that's not really your field.' Michael had an incredibly patronising tone. 'So they'll sell to the highest bidder. I'm helping the three of you out and paying over the odds so you don't lose any money, but like Clem said, I can't make a profit on the place by renovating it. I can get six apartments on that footprint and that's the only way to make the investment pay.'

'Would it make a difference if at least one of the flats was ring-fenced for a local?' Jack Carew was another old friend of her father's and he was clearly trying to play the peacemaker, but Michael was already shaking his head.

'I can't do that and this obsession with ring-fencing the town will send us all bankrupt. The reason you boys need to stick to the sort of small businesses you run is because you've got no idea about property or supply and demand.' Michael turned and gestured towards where Ella was now standing, wiping down one of the surfaces and pretending not to be listening to every word that was said. 'The kids born here don't want to live in the town their whole lives, things have changed. Just take Jago's daughter, over there, she was so desperate to get out of Port Agnes that she headed to London as soon as she could and didn't come back until she was dumped live on the internet! She's only back here now because she's got her tail between her legs and wants to hide from the real world. That chance to escape from reality is the reason emmets love Port Agnes so much.'

'Michael, that's out of order, you can't—' Clem had started to protest, but Jago had already cut him off and got to his feet.

'Get out.' He pointed a finger at Michael, who started to bluster. 'Now!'

'You're making a mistake, Jago, and when you boys come back to me begging me to buy The Old Forge, you'll find the price has just dropped by fifty grand. And I suggest Clem and Jack take that off your share.'

'I'd rather end up on the street than sell the place to you.'

'It's your funeral.' Michael stalked out of the bakery, slamming the door so hard behind him it made the windows rattle.

Clem pushed his chair back from the table. 'Sod the tea, I'm going for a pint.'

'I'll come with you.' Jack got to his feet too. 'I daren't go back and tell Marion the deal's off before I have a bit of Dutch courage.'

'I'm sorry, lads, I just couldn't take that from him.'

'I know.' Clem patted his old friend on the shoulder. 'I just hope Tredinnick's not right about us all ending up on the street if we can't get our money back.'

'It won't come to that.' There was a definite note of doubt in Jago's voice and Ella felt sick to her stomach. It looked like her parents' one chance of getting back in the black had just disappeared and the thought that they could end up losing everything they'd worked so hard for was terrifying.

* * *

Watching the parade up to St Jude's was always emotional. The children of the crews who went out on fishing boats and trawlers, working ridiculously hard for up to eighteen hours a day, always made the most of their special day together and it never failed to move Ella to tears. There was always a point in the service at St Jude's where the vicar would pay tribute to those from Port Agnes who'd lost their lives searching for the silver of the sea, sometimes in the year since the last festival. It was why Ella felt so awful that her tears this time weren't just for the lost souls and the hard-working crews who made Port Agnes what it was, and who sacrificed so much for their families. She was crying for her parents, and for herself. She'd resigned herself years ago to being the Mehenick girl, with everything she said and did getting back to her parents and her actions reflecting on them as a family. But now she was the Mehenick girl who'd gone to London and made a fool of herself in the most spectacular way possible. To top it all, her father was so pig-headed that he was willing to throw away the chance to recoup their investment in The Old Forge just to save face. He might think he was doing it for Ella's benefit, but he couldn't have been more wrong. She had no choice but to learn to live with humiliation, but she couldn't live with the idea of them potentially losing their livelihood and their home with it.

She hadn't been able to face going inside St Jude's for the service. The church was always packed to the rafters anyway and the vicar's blessing was piped out over the speaker system to the crowd outside, who were mostly sitting in the paddock to the right of the church or perched on the wall that ran around the perimeter of the churchyard. The other midwives had gone back to Anna's cottage for a takeaway to try and sober Jess up a bit before she went home. Ella had insisted that her parents went inside St Jude's and she'd sat at the other end of the churchyard from the crowd on the stump of an old oak tree, where she could still just about hear the loudspeaker, but she wouldn't have to speak to anyone.

'Are you okay, Ella?' She'd just been wiping a fresh crop of tears out of her eyes when Dan had appeared out of nowhere, almost making her fall off the tree stump. 'Sorry, I didn't mean to scare you, but I just wanted to come over and make sure you're all right?'

'Why wouldn't I be?' Her tone was defensive, but if he was nice to her then she really was going to lose it.

'Because you're hiding at the back of a graveyard crying when you should be with your family joining in the celebrations.'

Ella looked at Dan for a long moment, still not sure if she could face being totally honest with him about why she was sitting alone in a mess of tears. But there was something so familiar in the way he looked back at her, such an echo of the past when she'd felt able to share all her dreams and fears with him, that the truth just came out. 'I'm a laughing stock and now I've probably put my parents' retirement back by another decade when I've already cost them a fortune over the years. I bet they wish they hadn't spent more than enough to pay off their mortgage on fertility treatment to have me.'

'You know that's not true.' Dan took hold of her hand, just the gentlest of touches still able to make her skin tingle and his kindness making it even harder to hold it all together. 'Do you want to tell me what's happened?'

'Dad got an offer from Michael Tredinnick to buy The Old

Forge from him and his friends, but because Michael said something about me being jilted, Dad chucked him out and now he's stuck with a massive debt and a building he can't do anything with. All because I'm one big joke.'

'Oh El, you're not a joke. Michael Tredinnick is a scumbag and you shouldn't give what he thinks a second thought.'

'But in Port Agnes I'm always going to be the girl who got jilted, aren't I?'

'Not to anyone that matters. To most people here you'll always be lovely Ella Mehenick, the girl who's still happy to muck in at her parents' bakery and serve people with a beautiful smile on her face, who also happens to be a brilliant midwife. But to me, you'll always be the first person I ever fell in love with and I think Weller was an idiot to blow his chance with you. I know what that feels like.'

'I wish you'd told me why you couldn't come to London.' Ella met his gaze. The truth was if he'd said even half of what he'd just said to her when she'd left for university, she'd have come straight back home to be with him. She'd spent over a decade thinking she'd been duped by the illusion of first love but, if she had, then Dan had too. It had been everything to both of them. 'You had so much talent and we had so many dreams, I couldn't understand why you'd chosen Port Agnes over me and then Lissy told me how close you'd come to losing Six Acre Farm. I'm so glad you're still painting and your pictures capture Port Agnes exactly the way I think of it.'

'I think about you every time I'm painting, everything in Port Agnes reminds me of you.' Dan put a hand under her chin. 'And there's never anyone who's come close to how I felt about you.'

'We were kids, we didn't know anything...' Even as she tried to protest, she knew it was pointless. And, if Dan didn't kiss her soon, she was going to launch herself at him.

'We're not kids any more.' Pulling her to her feet, he waited until Ella closed the gap between them, kissing him with ten years of pent-up emotion. Any pretence she'd tried to keep up that she'd lost the love of her life on the steps of a London registry office disappeared in that instant. It had always been Dan.

11

Walking back down towards the harbour, leaving the crowd at St Jude's behind them, the thoughts racing through Ella's head were keeping time with the rapid pace of her heart. The kiss had been everything she remembered, but as soon as she'd pulled away from Dan she started to question whether she'd been a complete idiot. Her contract in Port Agnes would be over before she knew it and she'd be leaving again. There was a good chance that Dan was every bit as tied to staying as he'd been more than ten years before; Lissy's family was growing and Dan clearly wanted to be a part of that.

If she let herself go into a relationship with Dan, both feet in, and allowed her heart to have its own way, then there'd be pain down the line. It was almost guaranteed. But now she'd opened the box where she'd locked up all those feelings, it was impossible to get the lid back on. She could ask Dan whether there was any chance he might want to leave Port Agnes with her this time around, but it would have been way too much too soon. It was like one of those dating shows that Ella couldn't stop watching, even when her toes were curling with second-hand embarrassment, after one of the couples had brought up the subject of having children with their date ten minutes after they'd met. Asking Dan if he was prepared to consider giving up his whole life in Port Agnes after one kiss would have been every bit as toe-curling, only this time the embarrassment wouldn't be second-hand.

'You look like you're a million miles away.' Dan turned her to face him, as they drew level with the wooden shelter where they'd caught the bus to school together all those years ago. He'd get up early and ride his bike down from Six Acre Farm, leaving it chained to the bike rack behind the shelter all day, just so that they could have the whole bus journey to school and back together. Their initials might still be in the wood at the back of the shelter; he'd carved them out with a compass – a sign to the world that their relationship was something permanent. It had all been so simple back then.

'I was just thinking about us.'

'Thinking tends to get *us* into trouble.' Dan's tone was gentle. 'Can't we just enjoy the fact that we've found each other again and not overthink what might come next?'

'Maybe we can, but once everyone finds out that there's an *us* in any sense of the word then we'll be bombarded with questions and expectations.' Ella took a deep breath, trying to phrase what she said next as perfectly as possible. 'Your sister will be so excited she'll be throwing us an engagement party in her head! And my parents will either freak out that I'm seeing someone again so soon after Weller, and another emmet come to that, or they'll assume it means I'm staying.'

'Is that still totally off the cards?' Dan's eyes searched hers and she shook her head, not wanting to admit how unlikely it was that she'd be staying when her contract was up.

'Like you said, we don't know what's going to happen next, but we'll have no chance of just enjoying the moment and keeping things casual as soon as anyone else finds out.'

'So what are you saying, that we keep it to ourselves? Meet in secret, like we did when we first got together, before your dad found out about us and threatened to string me up from the mast of one of the boats in the harbour?' Dan laughed and she nodded. Maybe it was stupid; they were grown-ups who could date whoever they damn well wanted and everyone else could just mind their own business. Except this was Port Agnes and they both knew the chances of that were almost nil.

'If you'd rather go back to us trying to be friends again...' Even as she said the words, deep down Ella knew she could never really just be Dan's friend. She could try and pretend, if that's what he wanted, try to control the way her body reacted to even the slightest touch of his hand. But he was shaking his head, thank God.

'I quite like the idea of meeting in secret, that way I get to keep you all to myself. If we were together officially, you're right, Lissy would be wanting us to go over for dinner parties with her and Niall, when he's back home. If it turns out we don't have that long together, if you still decide not to stay, then I want to make the most of whatever time we've got.'

'Me too and that way we both know where we stand. Nothing too serious, just making the most of it while it lasts.' Ella had stopped trying to convince Dan to keep things casual, because he seemed to be fully on board. It was just herself she needed to convince now and she had a horrible feeling that might turn out to be a hell of a lot harder.

* * *

Dan and Ella had left the churchyard before the Silver of the Sea award had been announced. This year it had been awarded to all the anonymous donors to the Port Agnes Fishermen's Bereavement Fund, and so the shops and restaurants that lined the harbour would take turns to display the sculpture of hundreds of silver fish in their shop windows. The honour for the first month had gone to Mehenicks' Bakery and it seemed to have given her parents something to smile about. Ruth had said if there were people out there generous enough to donate so much to the fund without wanting recognition, then she could believe that someone would eventually see the potential in The Old Forge and want to preserve its history. Ella had thought about talking to Dan, but her father would never had accepted an offer from him, even if he could pay enough to cover the debts.

The time seemed to be slipping by so quickly, and on the second Friday of September, Ella was on call for home deliveries. There were no due dates that day, but that didn't mean anything. Babies came when and where they were ready. Anna had been called out only the previous week to a mother who'd given birth in a phone box when she'd realised she was in labour and her mobile had died. She'd only felt five contractions and it made the speedy delivery of Liz and Trudy's baby look positively pedestrian. It was only thanks to the woman's leggings that her baby didn't land straight on the phone box floor. Apparently, Anna had got there in time to cut the cord, help mum and baby back inside, and wait for the ambulance to arrive. Things weren't often that dramatic, but life as a midwife was anything but predictable which was why Ella kept checking her phone hadn't somehow miraculously been switched to silent.

At seven thirty, Ella's phone started to ring, and she snatched it up straight away.

'Ella Mehenick speaking.'

'Hi Ella, it's Dan. Can you come over?'

'I'd would, but I'm on call.' Ever since the Silver of the Sea she'd desperately been trying to play it cool, but it was only because she was working that she wasn't already halfway to his place. The kiss in the churchyard had rekindled feelings she'd forgotten she was capable of, but she'd woken up at three o'clock the next morning wondering what the hell she'd done. Somewhere between then and the sun rising, she'd convinced herself that a passionate fling – which couldn't do anything but burn out when she left Port Agnes again – was exactly what she needed to get over being jilted. She'd got over Dan once and she could do it again, she was almost sure of it.

'No, sorry, I didn't mean to *my place*. I'm calling because Lissy's gone into labour.' There was a slight note of panic in his voice, which was more than enough to make Ella forget the heat that had risen up her neck when she'd realised Dan's only desire for her was in a professional capacity. 'Niall's due to fly into Exeter tonight and I'm supposed to be picking him up at ten. She told me not to call you yet because the contractions are still a long way apart, but I don't know if it's safe to leave her. Not that she'll want me there when she's actually giving birth.'

'Don't worry, I'll come straight over and see what's going on.'

'Thanks El. You're an angel and she'll probably kill me for calling you before she's ready, but the noise she makes when a contraction comes is like nothing I've ever heard before and I've got no clue if any of this is normal.'

'It'll be fine, but she needs you to be calm and to let her know it'll all be okay, because she's probably panicking that Niall won't be back in time. I'll be up to you within ten minutes.'

'I'll let Lissy know you're on the way, and Ella...'

'Yes?'

'I'm so glad it's you.'

She didn't get a chance to answer before he ended the call and, by the time Ella got up to the farm, Dan had inflated the birthing pool Lissy had hired and was already starting to fill it.

'I didn't know if I should do this or not, but I just wanted to keep myself busy, so I don't start panicking!' Dan offered the explanation as Ella followed him from the front door to the lounge. 'Lissy's just gone to get changed in case things start to happen. Do you want a drink?'

'Tea would be great.' She'd seen this reaction plenty of times before; the partners and loved ones of women in labour often wanted something else to do so that they didn't have to focus all their energies on worrying about the impending birth.

'Lissy and the baby are going to be okay, aren't they? It's not due for another two weeks.' Dan suddenly fixed her with a look that made him appear every bit as vulnerable as the sixteen-year-old boy she'd first met not long after he'd lost his parents. 'Lissy's all that's left of my family and the baby's not supposed to be coming this early.'

'It's really not that early. Any time from thirty-seven weeks is seen as full-term and Lissy's at thirty-eight now.' Ella reached out towards him and he grabbed her hand. She hated seeing him like this; he'd lost so much in his life already and sadly he knew that the worst really could happen; it was no wonder he looked so terrified. Dan had always been the one building her up, making her believe in herself, but this time she was on solid ground, doing what she knew she was good at, and it was her turn to support him.

'I know I probably sound dramatic when thousands of babies are born every day, but when you've lost people you love so unexpectedly the way Lissy and I did when we were kids, you can't help imagining the worst sometimes. Especially after how traumatic Noah's birth was and Niall needs to be here for this.'

'I'll be here the whole time and if there's even a hint that Lissy needs any help, we'll get her straight into the hospital.' She squeezed his hand again. 'It's going to be okay and, even if Niall doesn't make it home for the birth, all that will be forgotten once the baby is here and you'll all have another member of the family to love. It's not just you and Lissy against the world any more and I promise I'll be here for you both, until the baby arrives, however long that takes.'

'I know I've said it already, El, but I'm so glad you're here.' Dan brushed his lips briefly against hers. 'I know you'll do the right thing by Lissy and I'd be even more nervous if it was anyone but you supporting her. I'm just concerned I might make things worse if Lissy picks up on how worried I am about her.'

'It's lovely that you care as much as you do, and Lissy knows that.' He was right, though, the nervous energy he was giving off was palpable and the best thing he could do was keep himself busy, to distract both himself and Lissy from just how worried he was. 'I think making that tea you promised would help. After all, a cup of tea's the answer to everything!'

'Absolutely.' Dan nodded, the relief at having somewhere else to direct his attention showing on his face. 'If you can just keep an eye on the pool to make sure it doesn't flood the place?'

'No problem.' Ella couldn't help grinning. Dan definitely hadn't done this before if he thought there was any danger of the pool overflowing in the next couple of minutes. Just after she'd checked the water temperature was going to be okay, Lissy came into the room holding her back.

'I'm sorry, Dan shouldn't have called you out so early. I'll be ages yet. I was hours and hours the first time, even before things got tricky.'

'He loves you and he's just worried about you, that's all, and I'm glad he called me out, especially after what you went through with Noah.' Ella plumped up the cushions on the sofa and gestured for Lissy to sit down. 'Are the contractions still twenty minutes apart?'

'They're more like fifteen minutes now.'

'Is the pain bearable when they come?'

'Well, put it this way, I wouldn't want it to last too long, but I can handle it. I just don't want to have the baby before Niall gets back. I kept telling him not to leave it this close to the baby's due date!'

'Dan said he's due to pick him up from Exeter at ten?' Ella looked at Lissy, who nodded in response. 'That means he'll have to leave now if he's going to get there on time, and I'm going to stay here with you while he's gone, in case things start to happen.'

'What if you get another call-out?'

'It'll be fine, I've got colleagues on call too, if it happens. Is Noah in bed?'

'Uh-huh.' Lissy put her hands on her lower back again.

'Are you getting a contraction?'

'There's just a lot of pressure all the time.'

'As soon as Dan's gone, I'll examine you and we can check how many centimetres dilated you are,' Ella said, and Lissy's face relaxed, the back pain obviously easing off a bit.

'He still really likes you, you know?' Lissy smiled. 'I'm saying this now because neither of you can tell a woman in labour to shut up, so it's the ideal opportunity for me to talk sense into you both.'

'He's a nice guy.' Ella's voice barely sounded like it belonged to her, she was trying so hard to keep her tone casual. 'But I'm not here for that much longer and I've already started looking for another job.'

'All I'm saying is don't rule it out. I don't know how I'd have coped without Dan, he's done more around the farm than I could possibly expect while Niall's worked back-to-back contracts. It's given us enough put by so Niall can take a couple of months off and pay for the help Dan has organised to give us some time together with Noah and the new baby. We're going to use the time to decide if it's realistic for Niall to work full-time on the farm instead of working away again. I'm just hoping our gamble for him not to fly home until this close to the baby's due date won't cost him the chance of seeing it arrive. But if Niall comes home for good, then Dan can stop feeling like he needs to take care of me and, maybe this time, even if you decide to leave Port Agnes, it wouldn't have to be the end.'

'We're not even—' Ella had been about to protest that there was nothing going on between her and Dan, but Lissy had known her for far too long and she'd see right through the lie. Thankfully he came back into the room, giving her the perfect excuse not to finish her sentence.

'Here we go, tea for the workers.' He set down a tray of tea and biscuits. 'I've just checked the arrivals and Niall's plane is due to land on time, so I'm going to head off. Try not to have the baby before I get back.' He dropped a wink and Lissy rolled her eyes. He was much more like his old self now that he had a job to do, and collecting Niall would mean he didn't have to watch Lissy in so much pain.

'I'll do my best, but be quick, okay?'

'I won't let you down, sis.' He kissed her on the cheek. 'Anyway, from what I understand, it's really easy to stop a baby arriving until it's convenient!'

'Oh, shut up and get going!' Lissy pretended to swat him away and he did as he was told, heading out towards the front door.

'Shall we take a look at you then and see whether this baby is going to hold on for Niall?' Ella opened her bag and pulled on some gloves as Lissy positioned herself on the sofa ready for the examination. 'Okay, it feels like you're between two and three centimetres dilated.'

'What's the likelihood of me giving birth in the next three hours?'

'Most people take longer than that to get from three centimetres to pushing, but babies don't always follow the rules.' Ella smiled. 'I think the odds are on your side, though, unless the contractions really start to speed up. Five hours is about average for the first stage of labour with a second baby and then you've got to push. I'd suggest doing the opposite of what I usually recommend and avoid moving around so that gravity doesn't give the baby any extra help.'

'I read that being in the birthing pool can slow the labour down too, if it's still in the early stages; maybe we can try that?'

'Normally I wouldn't recommend getting in before five centimetres for that reason, but if you decide to get in the water I can't stop you.'

'Tea and biscuits it is then, followed by a wallow in the pool.' Lissy rearranged her clothes. 'Are you sure you won't need to go to another delivery, if there's someone further along than me?'

'It's all quiet out there tonight and it's fine for me to stay here unless there's an emergency, especially as you're on your own. I've let my colleague, Toni, know that you're in labour and she'll come over when you get a bit closer to the end of the first stage. Jess and Anna are both on call too, so I'm sure we'll cope between us and I'm all yours.'

'I really wanted a home birth, but suddenly it feels as if I'm being a real pain.' Lissy picked up the mug of tea her brother had made. 'It's just, after what happened with Noah, I wanted everything to feel calm and to have as little intervention as possible. But if things go wrong I'm going to cause even more hassle.'

'Try not to worry. We talked about the risks and we all agreed that a home birth was viable.' Ella swallowed the concerns she'd had about Lissy's plans before she'd met her. Lissy was made of tough stuff and if there was any sign of the baby getting into distress or the labour slowing down too much, then she'd take action early. Hopefully it wouldn't come to that.

'I'm really glad you're here with me. It's been so nice having you back in town and back in my life.' Lissy looked at Ella. 'And I'm not the only one who thinks so, however casual you and Dan pretend to be around one another.'

'Even if I was staying in Port Agnes, after what happened with Weller I'm not ready for anything serious.' Ella couldn't hold back the question she'd been fighting not to ask almost ever since she'd seen Lissy again. 'I'm sure Dan's had his fair share of relationships since we split up, so he's obviously not in any hurry to settle down with one person either.'

'He's had girlfriends, but he hasn't been as serious about any of them as he was about you. Although that didn't stop most of them falling hard for him. The more casual he is about things, the more they seemed to want to be the one girl who was going to change him.' Lissy shrugged. 'Either that or he's very good at attracting stalkers! There was one, about three years ago, who kept turning up here and begging me to ask Dan to propose to her on her birthday, when I knew it was never going to happen and he hadn't given her any reason to think it would.'

'Poor girl.'

'Poor Dan more like, she wouldn't take no for an answer and she bombarded him with thousands of calls and messages after they split and then, last year, there was DeeDee.' Lissy pulled a face.

'I take it you didn't like her?'

'She's a writer and they met when he was commissioned to design the artwork for her book cover. She decided to rent a holiday apartment in Port Agnes for the whole summer and they ended up going out to dinner a few times.'

'That sounds normal enough?' Ella could tell from the look on Lissy's face that there was more to come.

'Hmmm, maybe until I found her lying naked on Dan's decking.'

'You're going to have to finish that story!'

'He was still living at the converted stable block at Six Acre Farm at the time, but he'd gone to Redruth to source some slate for a job and he rang me to say he thought he might have left his wallet in his kitchen because he couldn't find it.' Lissy paused to take a sip of her tea. 'When I got over there, I went around the back, and all I can say is thank God Noah was at nursery.'

'She was just hanging around naked in Dan's back garden?'

'She was lying on the decking, wearing high-heeled shoes and nothing else, apparently waiting to surprise him when he got home. I don't know who screamed more when we saw each other.'

'Maybe she'd already arranged it with him?' The thought bothered Ella more than it had a right to. There was nothing serious between her and Dan, so what he got up to now was barely any of her business, let alone what happened in the ten years or so when they'd been trying their best to avoid each other.

'He was almost as horrified as I was when I rang up and shouted down the phone at him for letting me find a naked woman on his decking.' Lissy shook her head, looking around the room as if DeeDee might suddenly pop out from behind the sofa. 'He'd already asked her not to keep turning up at his place unannounced, but I think she thought he might change his mind if he found her there naked. Apparently she was acting out a scene she'd written in one of her books... She writes *erotica*.'

'Oh God, a Fifty Shades of Grey sort of thing?' Ella suddenly felt more vanilla than ever; she and Dan hadn't even slept together yet. It wasn't that she didn't desperately want to, but it was another line to cross that would make it even harder to convince herself they could keep things casual. But it was only a matter of time and the thought that he'd been with women like DeeDee in the years they'd been apart was more than a bit terrifying. How the hell was she supposed to compete with someone who knew enough about sex to make a career out of writing books about it?

'I read one of her books and it was enough to put me off sex – and DeeDee – for life. Especially when I knew by then that she'd set her sights on Dan. I kept imagining Dan in her secret pain room in her holiday apartment.' Lissy burst out laughing, spraying tea all down her front. 'I honestly don't think Dan was remotely into her, or all the stuff she wrote about. At least I hope not, he's my little brother and just... yuck!'

'You never know what goes on behind closed doors. In this job, nothing surprises me any more.' The idea of Dan being DeeDee's muse might have been amusing to his sister, but it was doing absolutely nothing to calm Ella's nerves and it was definitely time for a change of subject. 'Right, I'll go and check on the birthing pool. It should be full up by now and then you can just try to relax.'

'I'll try, but I'm having another contraction.' Lissy had stopped laughing, her mouth forming an O shape instead, as she attempted to breathe through the pain.

'Let me know when it's passed and I'll set a timer, so we can see if they're getting any closer together.'

'Okay, I think that's it.' Lissy sat back against the cushions and Ella started the timer. Slow and steady, that's what this labour needed to be. But all either of them could do was wait and hope that Dan would get Niall home in time.

* * *

Three hours after the birthing pool was filled up, Lissy's contractions were coming fast and she was almost ready to push. There was still no sign of the men, but Niall had rung twenty minutes earlier to say they were only ten minutes away.

'Where are they? They should be here by now!' Lissy thumped a fist against the side of the birthing pool.

'I'm sure they'll be here any minute.' Ella looked at Toni, who'd arrived half an hour before, and held up crossed fingers. It wouldn't be long now, no matter how much Lissy wanted to hold on.

'You said that ten minutes ago!' Lissy growled the words as another contraction took hold. Seconds later her body relaxed. 'I'm sorry, I know it's not your fault, but I just want him to get here so badly.'

'Don't worry, I've had a lot worse than that thrown at me before now! I'm just going to check the baby's heartbeat again.' Ella picked up the waterproof device she'd been using every five minutes to check the baby's heartbeat, to make sure it wasn't getting into distress.

'Is it okay?' Lissy bit her lip as another pain came, but so far she'd refused the gas and air, which was the only pain relief she could have in the pool.

'It's fine. Are you sure you don't want something for the pain?'

'I've come this far, so I'm going to try not to now.' Lissy grimaced. 'Oh God, I think my body wants to push.'

'If the urge isn't overwhelming, try to take short breaths. But, if you're really ready to push, nothing's going to stop this baby from coming.' Ella put her hand on Lissy's arm. She'd tried so hard to hold on for her husband, but there were some things no one could control.

'I can see car headlights!' Toni suddenly shot towards the window. 'I think they're here.'

'Oh please, hurry up!' Lissy yelled the words this time. 'I can't slow this down any longer.'

'Don't try then.' Ella stroked Lissy's hair away from her face. 'When you get the next pain, take a long breath, and push down into your bottom.'

'It's coming!' Lissy did as she was told, and Ella used a mirror to check on her progress. 'I've got to push again.'

Toni positioned herself at the opposite end of the birthing pool as Ella continued to talk Lissy through the process.

'Oh baby, I'm so sorry.' Niall ran into the room, throwing his case onto a chair and immediately kneeling down beside his wife. 'I thought I was going to miss it.'

'Me too.' Lissy smiled for the first time in about an hour. 'I don't think it's going to be long.'

'It certainly isn't.' Ella needed Lissy to keep her focus. 'The baby's starting to crown, so you need to give it everything you've got with the next push.'

'Where's Dan?' Lissy turned her head. 'I don't want him to see me like this.'

'It's okay, he's gone up to check on Noah and he's going to stay out of the way until the baby's here and you're decent again.' Niall laughed, but seconds later it was drowned out by the sound Lissy made as she pushed again. Despite Lissy's panic about not being able to hold on, it took another ten minutes before she gave the push that finally delivered her baby. And as she turned for Ella to lay the baby on her chest, she looked the personification of exhaustion.

'Do you want to see what you've got, Dad?' Ella turned to Niall while Toni checked the baby's cord to make sure it was safe to delay clamping.

'Wow! We've got a little girl! Look at her, she's beautiful, just like you.' Niall was really emotional, but Lissy barely looked as if she was taking it in and Ella touched her shoulder.

'Are you okay, Lissy?'

'I'm just really tired.' She'd gone very pale, which could have been down to exhaustion, but Ella couldn't risk waiting to find out.

'Okay, let's get you and baby out of the water now so we can check you over properly.' Ella looked at Toni who nodded, clamping and cutting the baby's cord in an almost seamless movement so she could take care of the baby while Ella checked Lissy over. With Niall's support, they helped Lissy to the daybed that had been set up in the corner of the room. Examining her, Ella breathed out. There was no sign of a haemorrhage and her blood pressure was in the safe range, but at least now she could monitor Lissy until she was sure everything was okay and the third stage was over.

'Here you go, here's your little girl. I've checked her over and she looks completely perfect.' Toni passed the baby to her mother, and Niall put his arms around them both.

'I can't wait for Noah to meet her in the morning. Our little family's complete.'

'I couldn't agree more.' Lissy, who was finally getting some colour back into her face, smiled. 'I'm not sure what Noah is going to make of her, but I think it's time her Uncle Dan met her.'

'I'll go and get him.' Niall looked back at his wife and daughter at least three times, before he finally left the room. Less than thirty seconds later he was back with his brother-in-law in tow.

'Are you both okay?' Dan's eyes widened as he looked at his brand-new niece. 'She looks just like you, Lis, which is lucky given her dad's ugly mug!' Dan was obviously joking, and Niall roared with laughter.

'Agreed. She's beautiful, isn't she?' Niall's eyes were shining, as he spoke.

'She certainly is, mate. Have you got a name for her?'

'We're thinking of Tegen. It's Cornish for pretty thing.' Lissy looked at her brother.

'Sounds very fitting to me.' Dan nodded. 'I put some champagne in the fridge earlier so we could wet the baby's head and toast the brilliant midwives.'

'We'd better not in case we get another call-out and we're both driving anyway. Maybe we could do our toast with another cup of tea?' Ella looked at Toni.

'Yes, and a biscuit. I gather I missed out earlier?'

'Can I give you a hand, Dan?' Ella told herself she was only offering to give the new parents some time with their daughter, while Toni kept an eye on Lissy and the baby. But that wasn't the whole story; she wanted to spend a bit of time on her own with Dan, even if it was only five minutes.

'That would be great, thanks.'

'Was there a lot of traffic on the way back from the airport?' Ella put the teabags into the pot, as Dan took a bottle of champagne out of the fridge and she tried not to picture how many women like DeeDee he'd been involved with over the last ten years. Standing in the confined space of the kitchen, it was easy to imagine how DeeDee and the girl who'd been desperate for Dan to propose had fallen as hard for him as they obviously had.

'There was a broken-down car on the road up from Port Agnes, and we had to help push it out of the way. I felt a bit guilty about leaving the driver waiting for the AA, but Lissy had to take priority.' Dan turned to face her, his eyes suddenly taking on a glassy look. 'I'm just so glad she's okay. When I picked Niall up, he started talking about how touch and go things had been when Noah was born. I kept trying not to picture us turning up here and finding out that something had gone badly wrong and that she'd had to be rushed to the hospital. I knew I'd be crying like an idiot, but thanks to you they're happy tears.'

'I always wanted a brother or sister and when I see you and Lissy together, that's exactly how I would have wanted it to be. Your parents would be so proud of the two of you and the way you look after each other. Even now.'

'Lissy was my whole world after Mum and Dad died, and putting her first was always so easy because she did the same for me. The only time I've ever felt a shred of resentment for doing it was when I lost you.'

'You did the right thing, I just wish I'd known why.'

'Do you think things would be different now if I'd told you?'

He looked at her and she gave an almost imperceptible nod, before she could stop herself.

'I don't know, we were so young... It probably wouldn't have worked between us anyway.'

'But it might have done?'

'Anything's possible.'

'Do you really mean that? Is there a chance you could end up changing your mind about leaving Port Agnes?' Dan held her gaze again and she tried to shrug, but for some reason her shoulders refused to cooperate.

'I can't see me staying here, but given that Lissy's been trying to persuade me that I should, I wouldn't rule anything out because she's pretty single-minded when she puts her mind to something. I really didn't think she was going to be able to wait to give birth until Niall got here, but she was so determined.'

'I told you. When she makes a decision about something, there isn't much that can stand in her way.' Dan turned towards her. 'A bit like someone else I know.'

'I'll definitely take being compared to Lissy as a compliment.'

'All the important women in my life have been strong women and, thanks to you, I've now got a niece who I'm sure is going to be every bit as determined.'

'Lissy did all the hard work, believe me.'

'Selling your achievements short is the only thing I've ever wanted to change about you and I wish you could see yourself the way other people see you.'

'What, the girl whose fiancé—' She'd been about to come out with her standard line again when Dan kissed her, stealing the words from her mouth. The truth was, when she was with Dan, she forgot all about what other people thought. And that was going to make it harder than ever to say goodbye when the time came.

12

'Woah, it's starting to get really windy out there.' Ella shut the back door of her parents' cottage as she came into the kitchen. It was almost October and the leaves had been dancing on the breeze when she was out walking with Daisy. The bakery shut at three on Saturday afternoons and her mum was sitting at the kitchen table soaking her feet in a bowl, with a cheese and pickle sandwich in front of her: Ruth Mehenick was planning to relax.

'I know. Morag Taylor came in for a white cob and said one of her fence panels had blown into her husband's koi pond. It was a proper to-do apparently.'

'Were the fish okay?' Ella laughed. What passed for drama in Port Agnes usually sounded like something out of a seventies sitcom. No wonder the town had made the most of her fifteen minutes of fame.

'Apparently they're in the bathtub while John sorts out the damage. Morag's got to go next door if she wants a shower.'

'We should count ourselves lucky then.' Ella grinned. 'Where's Dad?'

'He's next door talking to Brae.' Her mother paused for a moment, searching Ella's face. 'And he's got Weller with him.'

'What?' Ella pulled out a chair, suddenly feeling an overwhelming need to sit down before she fell down. The idea that Weller was in Port Agnes was shocking enough, but the fact he was with her father – and apparently still breathing – was far more of a surprise.

'He turned up just as we were closing for the day. I thought your dad was going to burst a blood vessel at first, what with his blood pressure the way it is. I was worried I was going to come through and find Weller knocked out cold. Then your dad walked back into the shop with Weller following him, and announced they were both going next door to see Brae.'

'Why on earth would Dad take him to see Brae?' If her mother's cheese and pickle sandwich had suddenly morphed into a Victoria sponge, she'd hardly have been more surprised.

'He probably wants Weller to see that you've moved on by introducing him to your new boyfriend. It'll save him getting any ideas about winning you back.'

'I have moved on, Mum, but not with Brae. How many times do I have to tell you we're just friends? Brae's happy with that, so why can't you be?'

'Your dad and I were friends at first, when we were at school. That's all I'm saying.' Ruth laughed at the look that must have crossed Ella's face. 'That's not the point anyway. Your dad wants to make Weller *think* that Brae is your new boyfriend, to rub his nose in what a stupid mistake he must already know he's made. The fact that you and Brae aren't really together is neither here nor there!'

'I've got to get next door before Dad makes things even worse than he already has.' Ella got back on her feet, her mind racing at a hundred miles an hour. What the hell did Weller want anyway? He'd hated visiting Port Agnes even when they were together.

Unlike her mother, Ella was certain of one thing: Weller wasn't here to say he'd made a mistake. She'd looked into his eyes on the steps of the registry office and he'd meant every word.

'Why don't you just wait until they come back?' Ruth looked up at her. 'I'll make you a sandwich.'

'I'm not hungry, Mum.' Ella was already halfway out of the door and her feet couldn't cover the ground quickly enough, even though the thought of seeing Weller again made her stomach churn.

'Dad!' Ella called out to her father, who was sitting at a table in the fish and chip shop, opposite Weller and Brae, while the two young girls who worked weekends took care of the customers. It was the lull between lunch and dinner, so the shop was relatively quiet.

'Hello, my love, what are you doing here?' Jago Mehenick smiled at his daughter as if it was the most natural thing in the world to find him sharing a plate of chips with her ex-fiancé.

'I might ask you the same.'

'Hi Ella. You're looking great,' Weller interjected before her father had a chance to reply, and Ella automatically wrapped her arms around her body.

'Weller. It's... good to see you.'

'Is it?' He narrowed his eyes and she shrugged, not wanting anyone to know quite how toe-curlingly awkward she was finding all of this.

'Well, I've got to admit I'm surprised to see you.'

'Weller's got something he wants to talk to you about.' Jago gave her a warning look. 'But before you hear what it is and make any hasty decisions, I wanted him to meet Brae – so he could see how happy you are now.'

'I'm not here to cause any trouble or stir things up, Jago. I keep telling you that.' Weller's tone was reasonable, but her father clearly wasn't buying it.

'Tell him how close you and Brae have been getting.' Jago looked at her, but Ella's gaze flitted towards Brae, who looked as uncomfortable as she felt. God knows what her father had forced him to say to Weller, but the last thing she wanted to do was embarrass her friend.

'We spend a lot of time together and I love Brae's company.' It was all true and maybe it would give Jago false hope, but that was his own fault for putting her in such a difficult position.

'See, I told you, they're together all the time.' Jago looked horribly smug, but if this stopped him landing a punch on Weller's nose then it was worth it. 'And you adore Ysella, don't you, Brae?'

'Like I said before, she's great company and the prettiest girl in Port Agnes.' Brae gave her an apologetic smile; he was just as cornered as she was. Although in his case, he was literally wedged up against the wall with Jago blocking his chance of escape.

'That's good to hear. I've always thought Ella's beautiful, so I'm glad she's found someone to really appreciate her. But that's not what I came to talk about.'

'If everyone's finished talking about me like I'm not here, then maybe we should go and have a chat elsewhere?' Ella turned to her ex-fiancé. 'Unless you'd rather finish your chips?'

'It would be good to talk.' Weller looked different somehow, but she couldn't quite put her finger on what had changed. Despite her desire to distance herself from him, she hadn't been able to resist checking the social media sites for his record company every now and then. With the new signing of The Undermods, the label seemed to be going from strength to strength.

'Don't you think you should check with Brae first?' Jago was serious. 'Not a lot of men would want their girlfriend going off for a private chat with her ex. I wouldn't stand for it if it was your mother.'

'For heaven's sake, Dad, this isn't the nineteen fifties!'

'It was nice to see you again, Mr Mehenick, and good to meet you too, Brae.' Weller nodded at them both. Despite being with Ella for years, he'd never progressed beyond calling her father Mr Mehenick, which said a lot about their relationship.

'Nice to meet you too, Weller.' Brae was too polite not to respond, even as Jago shot him a death stare.

'I'll ring you later, Brae.' Ella turned towards her dad. 'And don't even think about following us, Dad. I'm nearly thirty years old and I don't need a babysitter.'

'If you're not back in half an hour, I'm going to come looking.' She might as well have saved her breath for all the notice Jago had taken.

When she closed the door of the fish and chip shop behind her and stepped outside behind Weller, she half expected to see her father's face already pressed up against the window.

'So where are we going?' Weller stopped as they reached the harbour. 'I was relieved to get off as lightly as I did with your dad, but I need to brace myself if you're going to shove me off the harbour wall.'

'Don't worry, I'm not going to hurt you.'

'You'd have every right after what I did.'

'Let's go to the café on the high street. It's too windy to just wander around.' Ella didn't acknowledge his comment; it was easier on both of them that way.

'Fine by me, I'm just pleased that you're willing to talk to me.'

'Have you lost weight?' Looking at him closely for the first time as they waited for a table in the café, the hollows in his cheeks were obvious and even his skinny jeans weren't clinging to his legs in the way they should.

'Probably, but it's not the only thing I've lost.' Weller paused as a waitress came over and handed them both a menu.

'Would you like the table in the window? I've just cleared it.' The waitress gestured towards the stripped pine table, which had a heart-shaped tea light holder at its centre. The perfect spot for lovers to hold hands and make plans. It would have to do for them as well.

'That's great, thanks.'

'Do you want something to eat?' Weller looked up from scanning the menu after they'd taken their seats.

'No. You?'

'Not after all those chips.' He laughed. 'Pot of tea for two then?'

'Yeah, let's go wild.'

'I meant what I said, Ella, you look really good.' He moved to put his hand over hers, but she snatched it away.

'Don't.'

'It's okay, I'm not going to ask you to get back with me. I don't think you'd want that any more than I do, would you?'

'No. But it doesn't do much for a girl's ego to hear you haven't come to tell me how much you miss me.'

'I do miss you.' Weller paused again as the waitress came back to the table. 'Just a pot of tea for two for now, thank you.'

'That's all?' The young woman probably wouldn't have given them the best table in the café if she'd known they were going to be so cheap, but she shrugged when Weller nodded and disappeared without even bothering to write down their order.

'You were saying you missed me?' Ella fiddled with the position of the tea lights. It was weird to be so uncomfortable with someone she'd been so intimate with. They'd shared a flat and a life, but it was as if that had happened to someone else.

'I do. I miss your friendship.'

'That's what we should always have been, shouldn't we?'

'You know, don't you?' Weller looked across at her and she shook her head.

'Not exactly, but I guessed that there was someone else and that was the reason you decided to call off the wedding. I was probably just behind my dad in the queue to punch you after you left me on those steps. But when the anger subsided, I had to be honest with myself. I'd had doubts for a while too and I know you wouldn't have wanted to hurt me on purpose. I buried myself in work to push my doubts to the side, and you were so focused on the record label and planning the wedding, but both of us were trying to ignore the elephant in the room.'

'How did you know there was someone else in my life and that I didn't just have the same sort of doubts as you?'

'Because you'd have gone through with it otherwise, like I was prepared to. I think we'd fallen out of love a while before, if we ever really were in love. But when you announce you're getting married, it sort of takes on a momentum of its own, doesn't it?' She gave him a half smile and he nodded in response. 'I didn't want Dad to say that he'd told me so if I called off the wedding, and I convinced myself it was just nerves. But you were brave enough to call it off at the last minute and face the fallout. There had to be a reason and I figured it must be love.'

'You're right, but I'd been trying to fight it. *For years.*' Weller swallowed so hard she could hear it. 'It's Ste. I didn't want to feel the way I did about him and neither did he. I kept thinking the feeling would pass, I mean I'd never been attracted to a man before in my life. Then, on the morning of the wedding, he told me he loved me and that he always had, and he asked me if I really wanted to get married and walk away from the possibility of a life with him. It was then that I realised I didn't. I also knew, even though I was going to hurt you, that it was the only way to be fair to you too. I did love you, though, Ella, just not in that way.'

For a second or two Ella could hardly breathe, but even as her brain struggled to process the information, she could see that Weller and Ste had always been meant for each other. They'd been best friends and Ste had been Weller's sidekick for years. She had no inkling that they had romantic feelings for each other, but, looking back, it had always been obvious they were soulmates.

'Do you hate me?'

'No, why would I?' Ella put her hand over his this time and, unlike her, he didn't pull it away. When she'd kissed Dan in the churchyard, the last bit of resentment she might have been harbouring towards Weller had evaporated. Kissing Dan again had forced Ella to admit to herself that she'd never felt that way about Weller. Marrying him was a step closer to giving her parents the grandchildren they so desperately wanted. She'd been worried about leaving it too late because of her parents' fertility problems, and that if she didn't have children by the time she was thirty-five, she might never have them – leaving her parents with another broken dream. If anything, she was the one who should be apologising to him.

'Because my own parents hate me, so why wouldn't you? When I finally got up the courage to tell them, my father told me to get out of their house and never come back. Even my mum said I'd made things worse and that she could have found a way to live with it if I couldn't help myself, but "choosing" to love a man was something she could never accept.'

'Your tea,' the waitress interrupted just as Ella was struggling to find the words to respond. Weller mumbled his thanks as emotion threatened to get the better of him. As much as Jago and Ruth had their own hopes for Ella's life, she knew they'd never turn their back on her whatever she did. Weller deserved the same from his parents and her heart went out to him.

'I'm really sorry. That must have been so painful. I honestly can't believe there are still people who think like that.'

'Some might call it karma after what I did to you.'

'I'd much rather you did what you did, when you did it, than go through the divorce that would inevitably have followed. I was as much to blame for what happened as you, we should never have got engaged and I'm honesty grateful now that you broke things off.' She wanted him to believe everything she said because it was true. 'Even if I could have done without the whole thing going viral!'

'I'm so sorry it happened the way it did. I've been wanting to come and tell you about me and Ste for a long time, and to apologise for everything I put you through. But I only got the courage in the end because otherwise you're going to read about it sooner or later anyway and that really wouldn't be fair.'

'Why would I read about it?'

'Because of how well the label has been taking off since The Undermods joined us, and Ste and I have stopped trying to hide who we are. It hasn't taken much for the music journalists who follow the band to work out that we're a couple and, when one of them dredged up the video of us at Petra and Jed's wedding, I guess they figured there was a story in it. After all, there had to be a pretty big reason why anyone would give up the chance to marry someone as wonderful as you. God knows how my parents are going to react when the news gets out.'

'I'm so sorry they've reacted the way they have. If you and Ste love each other, and it's obvious that you do, whatever anyone else thinks that's all that really matters.'

'That's good advice and I promise I'll try to listen to it, but only if you do too.'

'What do you mean?' Ella tried to read the expression on Weller's face, but she still had no idea what he was talking about.

'Being back in Port Agnes definitely suits you, but—'

'But, what?'

'Forget it. I've got no right to say it.' Weller dropped his gaze to the cup and saucer in front of him.

'I want to know. *Please.*'

'After all I put you through, I'd hate to see you settle for something less than you deserve. It's obvious Brae's a lovely guy, but he's not right for you, Ella.'

'What makes you say that?'

'I can see by the way you look at him.' Weller shook his head. 'You can tell me to mind my own bloody business, but I want you to have what I've got with Ste. When I look at him, everyone else disappears. You deserve that, Ella, more than anyone I know.'

'Maybe I do feel that way, just not about Brae.' She bit her lip. She should probably have told her ex-fiancé to mind his own business, but it was a relief to finally admit it, even to herself.

'There's someone else?' Weller was suddenly animated. 'Does Brae know?'

'It's not anything serious, just the idea of what might have been if the last ten years or so hadn't happened, I suppose. But that's first loves for you, isn't it? They don't often stand up to the test of time or the reality of life. As for Brae, we're just friends, and he knows that as well as I do. It's just my parents who won't accept it and Brae's far too nice to put them straight.'

'Don't be too hard on them, Ella. They love you.' The shadows were back on Weller's face. 'And they'd never reject you the way my parents have. Be grateful for that, even when they're driving you mad.'

'I am and I'm more grateful than they'll ever know for what they've done for me, even if my attempts to show them that sometimes means I make decisions they don't understand.' Ella squeezed his hand again. 'Surely your parents will come round in the end and see how ridiculous they're being?'

'I'm not even sure I want them to any more. It nearly broke me and Ste, and I couldn't eat or sleep for weeks after Dad threw me out of their house.' He sighed. 'But you can have everything you deserve, Ella. A career you love, a family that adores you and the one person in your life who lights you up. I want that for you, I really do. So promise me, whatever happens with this other guy, that you won't settle for anything less?'

'I promise.' Looking at him again, she felt a surge of affection for Weller that she'd never expected to feel again. He'd set her free when he could have used her to cover his secret. Now she owed it to them both to make the most of it.

13

If Ella had been staying in Port Agnes, the cottage Anna had shared with her ex-boyfriend was exactly the sort of place Ella would have wanted to buy. It had thick stone walls that had stood up to over four hundred years of gales blowing along the Atlantic Coast and hitting land at Port Agnes. It was cosy, with a woollen rug in front of an open fireplace and two squashy sofas that faced each other. There was a big bookcase on the other wall, where photos interspersed the novels; every one of which Anna said she had read.

'You've got such a lovely home.' Ella spoke as Anna topped up their wine glasses again. The curry had been ordered from the only place that delivered in Port Agnes, and it was nice to have the chance to get to know Anna a bit better. There wasn't anyone in the team who Ella didn't get on with, but from the start Anna had been the one she'd connected with most. Even if they hadn't had their occupation in common, Ella was sure they'd have been friends.

'Thank you. It still feels a bit strange living here without Greg. When I bought him out, I got most of the furniture as part of the deal. But I'm beginning to wonder if keeping all those memories was such a good idea. I lost both my parents before we even met, so there were things of theirs that it was very important for me to keep, but I really should have tried harder to get rid of the things that remind me of Greg.'

'You were together a long time, weren't you? I know what it's like when something ends like that. Cheesy as it sounds, you have to rediscover who you are on your own.' Ella was doing it again – giving out the sort of advice she'd never found it easy to live up to, but it was always easier to offer good advice than act on it. Almost all the decisions she'd ever made had been an attempt to live up to someone else's expectations.

'I know, but if I'm really honest, I don't want to be on my own. I haven't got any family left and sometimes I don't feel as if I've got anyone or anything to anchor myself to without Greg.' Anna took a sip of wine. 'Would you give Weller a second chance if he asked?'

'No, and I really mean it when I say I'm glad it happened. He's found someone else now anyway and I'm genuinely happy for him.'

'You're a better person than me then.' Anna shook her head. 'Greg's already met someone apparently. He's coming back to Port Agnes in a couple of weeks for his sister's wedding and bringing his new girlfriend with him. I've been invited too.'

'Are you still going?'

'I don't know. Part of me wants to rock up there in the most expensive outfit I can find and show him what he's missing, but a bigger part of me wants to stay here, get blind drunk and cry mascara all over the cream cushions we bought together.'

'Would you take him back?'

'It was me who finished it, and the reasons I did haven't changed. I want a family and he doesn't. But I won't lie and pretend it doesn't hurt like hell that he's moved on so quickly.'

'So how's the internet dating going?' Ella looked across at her friend, just in time to see her grimace. The last time they'd spent the evening together, Anna had finally decided to take the plunge and put the profile that Ella and the other midwives had written for her up on a dating website, but by the look on her face it wasn't going that well.

'Let's just say not many of them are looking for a serious relationship, but there's always an upside. I could put on my own art exhibition in Pottery and Paper, with a gallery of all the willy pictures I've been sent! I never knew they could come in so many shapes and sizes, and there are enough variations in colour to rival a Dulux paint chart.'

'Oh Anna, I'm sorry but that's hilarious.' They both started giggling and by the time Anna showed her some of the photos she'd been sent, Ella was crying with laughter.

'Why do men think we want to look at those? I spend most of my day looking up lady bits as it is, I don't want to come home and look at that!' Anna took another swig of her wine. 'After the year you, me and Jess have had, maybe I should cut my losses and realise I might be better on my own anyway.'

'Is Jess okay, I thought she was coming tonight?'

'I think things are still really difficult between her and Dom.' Anna sighed. 'Last time she went out for the evening he wasn't there when she got home and he didn't come back until the next day. Apparently he'd got drunk with his mates and ended up sleeping on one of their sofas, but she said it makes going out feel like hassle she doesn't need. It's like a light has gone out in her lately, she was always the one organising our nights out and being up for a party.'

'I do sometimes wonder why people stay with the partners they do. Would you want to have a baby with someone like that?' Ella tried not to think about the fact that she'd been planning on starting a family with Weller. She'd known she was making compromises by settling down with someone she didn't love, and yet she'd still been prepared to have children with him. It hardly gave her the right to judge.

'Jess is really close to Dom's parents from what I can gather and, because she was fostered, I think she just craves that sense of being part of a family. She and I are both missing that in our lives, even if it's for very different reasons.'

'I think I'd rather take Gwen's suggestion, and try out a sperm bank, than be with someone who wanted to punish me every time I went out.' Ella frowned. 'Although you should probably ignore everything I say. I'm the least qualified person to be handing out advice to anyone else.'

'Maybe I should ring up Three Ports Radio. It's their agony aunt phone-in tonight, isn't it?'

'I'd almost forgotten they did that and God knows why anyone in the Three Ports area would want to spill all their problems to Dr Jenny. I'd bet my last pound she's not a doctor and they don't even try to disguise people's voices. Although I don't know why I'm laughing, they had a phone-in after my video went viral apparently to ask other people to share their stories about being dumped!'

'Oh come on, let's do it. Who knows, it might even make us feel better. Maybe there's someone out there whose relationship history is even more disastrous than ours?' Anna grinned.

'I doubt it, but let's listen anyway. Maybe we'll recognise one of the callers!'

'Alexa, play Three Ports Radio.' Anna gave the instruction and it was a bit of an anti-climax to hear Tina Turner belting out the tail end of a song. But then the DJ came on.

'That was Tina Turner with "Nutbush City Limits", and now back to our regular phone-in this Saturday night with Dr Jenny, who's telling us how to move on from heartache.'

'Thanks Robbie.' Dr Jenny sounded as if she was doing an

over-exaggerated impression of Nigella Lawson. 'It's all a state of mind really and loving yourself is the only true path to happiness.'

'Oh, for God's sake!' Ella picked up her glass of wine, fighting the urge to tell Alexa to play anything but Three Ports Radio.

'The problem is, Robbie, that lots of people find it difficult to practice self-love.' There wasn't a hint of amusement in Dr Jenny's voice, so maybe it was just Ella who thought self-love sounded like a euphemism and had to fight the urge to giggle like a schoolgirl as a result.

'And can it be dangerous?' The DJ paused for effect. 'If you don't learn the art of self-love?'

'Too much self-love can make you go blind.' Ella hadn't been able to stop herself from saying it and Anna nearly choked on her wine from laughing so much. All of which meant they missed out on Dr Jenny's no doubt revolutionary advice.

'And what about you, Dr Jenny, have you ever had any difficulty making relationships work?' The DJ lowered his voice, as if they were having a private conversation, instead of live streaming the show.

'Only once, Robbie, and it was my relationship with myself. I had to let go of all my insecurities and the false truths I'd built up about myself and it took a lot of therapy. Doing that is so much harder than people think and it was the most difficult thing I've ever done.'

'How can he stop himself from laughing when she says that sort of stuff?' Ella looked over at Anna, but she didn't get a chance to answer before the DJ announced that the lines were about to open for the phone-in.

'Based on the number of texts and tweets we've had so far, there are plenty of listeners out there who need Dr Jenny's help.' Robbie sounded far too upbeat about the prospect of so much heartbreak. 'Shall we take our first call?'

'Absolutely!' Dr Jenny mirrored his enthusiasm, her attempt to impersonate Nigella Lawson temporarily forgotten.

'Hi there, thanks for calling the Robbie Tremain show on Three Ports Radio, who have we got on the line?'

'It's, er, Brian.'

'Hi there, Brian. Can you tell us a bit about why you're calling our phone-in tonight about relationship disasters and loneliness in the Three Ports area?'

'They might as well call it the losers' hotline!' It was Anna's turn to shout at the radio and Ella pulled a face. She just hoped that the dubious Dr Jenny and her local DJ host weren't going to end up making their callers feel even worse about themselves, especially if they were somehow deemed to have failed at Dr Jenny's holy grail of so-called self-love.

'I'm calling because I want to know if there's anyone else out there like me.' Dr Jenny wasn't the only one doing impersonations. Brian sounded as though he was trying for Prince Charles, but couldn't quite disguise his Cornish accent.

'What do you mean by that, Brian?' Dr Jenny asked the question and for a moment there was silence, followed by a long sigh.

'They say there's someone for everyone, but I really don't think there is for me.'

'So you've never had a serious relationship?' Robbie posed the question this time.

'I had one when I was serving in the forces. We were supposed to be getting married when I came out. But once we were together all the time, she decided she didn't want to be with me any more.'

'And since then?' It was Robbie again.

'I've dated, but after a few dates it's always the same story. They like me, but only as a friend.'

'And how does that make you feel?' Dr Jenny's question

sounded like it came from page one of the psychologist's handbook.

'Depressed. I got in contact again recently with a girl I knew at school and we got on so well I thought maybe it might lead to something – especially as I get on really well with her parents too – but I was friend-zoned again.'

'Oh my God.' Ella muttered the words and Anna looked over, but she shook her head. She'd had a suspicion from his second sentence that Brian was actually Brae, but now she was certain. She didn't want to tell Anna, though. If Brae wanted to go by a different name, and disguise his accent, then she wasn't going to be the one to out him.

'Have you thought about speed dating?' Dr Jenny spoke as though it was a revolutionary idea. 'It's a good way of knowing whether you've got an instant connection with someone, and it sounds as though you're trying to form relationships with women where there's no chemistry.'

'Maybe it's just me. Maybe I'm incapable of making someone feel that sort of connection.'

'Of course you're not!' Ella hadn't even realised she'd said the words out loud, until Anna's eyebrows shot up in response.

'It could just be that you need to change your image a bit.' Robbie had suddenly got very animated again. 'Maybe we could organise a makeover?'

'I'm not sure I'd want to do that. I hate having my photo taken at the best of times.' In his panic, Brae had forgotten to try disguising his voice and there was no doubt in Ella's mind now that it was him.

'A Three Ports Radio speed dating event and singles party would be a great idea; we could broadcast live from the venue!' Robbie's voice had taken on a shouty tone, as if he was already trying to be heard against the background noise of a party, instead of the silence of a soundproof studio.

'That's a brilliant idea!' Dr Jenny's response was equally loud and they both seemed to have forgotten that Brae was there. Never mind preaching about 'self-love', they had a potential ratings winner in their sights.

'Is that something you'd be up for, Brian?' Robbie finally remembered he had a caller on the line.

'I think I'd be better off accepting that I'm supposed to be single forever and concentrating on my business and the friendships I've made.'

'There are far worse things than that, Brian.' At last Dr Jenny had said something sensible, even if it might not be what Brian/Brae wanted to hear.

'So that's really it for me?' There was such a sadness in Brae's voice, Ella wanted to run straight over to his place and give him a hug. Dr Jenny had been every bit as useless as Ella had thought she'd be.

'Remember what I said at the start of tonight's show. The most important thing of all is to learn to love yourself and, once you've done that, the rest will follow.' Exactly how Brae was supposed to achieve that remained a mystery, as Robbie had clearly decided the first call had run its course.

'Thanks for calling, Brian, and good luck! Right, then, let's move on to caller number two. Thanks for calling the Robbie Tremain Show, who's on the line?'

Just as the caller started to speak, Anna's mobile rang.

'Alexa, stop.' Anna picked up her phone as soon as the radio stopped playing, but Ella could still only hear one side of the conversation. 'Hello? Yes, that's right. Oh dear, well it can't be helped. As long as he's okay, that's the main thing. Okay, I'll check the bank tomorrow and let you know if there's any problem.'

'Everything okay?' Ella asked, as Anna disconnected the call.

'That was the Star of Bengal. The owner's son, who's also the delivery driver, was involved in a minor crash. That was one of the waiters letting me know they've shut down the restaurant and the kitchen for the evening, so we won't be getting our order.'

'Like you said, as long as he's okay, that's the important thing.' Even as she spoke, Ella's stomach grumbled in protest.

'Absolutely and I could knock us up an omelette, or there's probably a pizza in the freezer.'

'No, don't cook, I know somewhere we can get something to eat.' Ella was already on her feet, grabbing her coat.

'If it involves finishing off the leftover stock from your mum and dad's bakery, then I might just love you forever.'

'There's a tiny chance it could work out even better than that.' Ella smiled and metaphorically crossed her fingers that it would. Move over Dr Jenny, this was how to do it.

* * *

'Is Brae around, Pete?' The brightness of the lighting inside the fish and chip shop was making Ella's eyes sting. Anna was already sitting at the only empty table in the small dining area. If she was disappointed about where Ella had brought her, then she wasn't showing it.

'He's been out the back most of the evening.' Pete was Brae's cousin and he helped out in the shop sometimes. 'But I'll go and get him for you in a minute.'

'I don't want to disturb him if he's busy.'

'He was pretending to do the books last time I looked!' Pete grinned. 'But he'll definitely want to know you're here.'

'Brilliant thanks. Can I order one haddock and chips, one scampi and chips, and two diet cokes while I wait, please?'

'No problem, I'll get one of the girls to bring it over when it's ready.'

'Thanks, Pete.'

Anna and Ella were soon discussing one of their patients who was expecting triplets. There was no way she could be delivered in the midwifery unit or at home with multiples, but she was having some of her check-ups in the community and three babies at once was always a cause for excitement.

'I'm not interrupting, am I?' Brae brought their drinks to the table and Ella shuffled across to the seat nearest the window.

'Of course not. Have you got time to sit down with us for five minutes?' Ella looked up at him as he nodded. 'You know Anna, don't you?'

'Yes, of course. I don't suppose you remember me, though? I'm Morwenna Ayre's brother, Brae. You were her midwife just after I'd come out of the Navy and I was staying with her while I got some renovations done at the shop, so I met you a couple of times.'

'I do remember you actually and I've seen you in here a few times, too. I wanted to say hello, but you've always been rushed off your feet.' Anna returned his smile. Ella had no idea if someone else could feel the chemistry between a couple, but there was definitely something going on, and she was having to clamp her arms against her body to stop herself starting a solo Mexican wave.

'I'd have made time for a chat.' Brae took the seat next to Ella. 'So, what have you two been up to tonight?'

'Drinking wine, talking and waiting for a curry that didn't turn up!' Ella got in first, before Anna had a chance to mention the radio show.

'See, you should always stick to good old reliable fish and chips.' Brae dropped the sort of casual wink that Ella hadn't even known he was capable of.

'I'll definitely do that in future.' Anna reddened and it had nothing to do with the heat of the fryers. If she'd known it would be this easy, Ella would have set this up weeks ago. Now it was time to seal the deal.

'Are you doing anything next Saturday evening? Only Anna and I are going to our friend Penny's engagement party. You remember, you met her at Casa Cantare the night her boyfriend proposed? She's having the party before they move to Aberdeen and we've both been invited to bring along a plus one.'

'I think I could get Pete to cover. So who gets the dubious pleasure of my company?' Brae raised an eyebrow.

'Anna.' Ella's response was emphatic, and she didn't miss the smiles lighting up her friends' faces.

'Brilliant.' Brae was still beaming. 'And what about you?'

'All will be revealed.' She tapped the side of her nose. She'd explained to Brae why Weller had wanted to speak to her, so he knew there was no chance of her bringing her ex. As it was, she'd almost certainly be going alone and that was absolutely fine by her. Revealing to anyone that she and Dan were seeing each other would just make things more difficult when she left. They were making the most of it while it lasted, nothing more. But seeing Brae and Anna hitting it off the way they were, was lovely and the one person she really wanted to tell was Dan.

14

By the week after Penny's engagement party, Brae and Anna were officially a couple and the only people who weren't over the moon for them were Anna's ex and Ruth and Jago Mehenick. Ella hated being responsible for disappointing her parents, but for once it had been worth it to see her lovely friends so happy. When she'd met up with Dan for another takeaway the day after she'd introduced Brae and Anna properly for the first time, he'd been almost as excited as she was about their old friend finally finding someone who might just turn out to be perfect for him.

Things got even better on the Thursday of the following week when she got a text from Weller with some unexpectedly good news.

I hope life in Port Agnes is still making you glow! Had a phone call from Mum last week and my parents have offered a bit of an olive branch. They might not exactly be ready for a Pride march yet, but she said they don't want to lose me. We're taking it slow, one step at a time, but they're coming up to town to have lunch with me and Ste. I wrote to Mum telling her how well you'd taken the news and she said it had got them thinking – if you could accept it, then maybe they could too. Wishing you only good things and you've always got a place to stay with me and Ste if you're ever up in town xx

That's great news. Good luck with your mum and dad and say hi to Ste. Let me know how it goes xx

It was a weird text exchange to have with an ex-fiancé, but it was another blessing that Ella was determined to count. She'd been with Weller for a long time and it would have been sad to wipe all of that out. Now that they were building a friendship it was easier to hold on to the good times and not think of those years as wasted.

Ella had barely put her phone back in her bag when it rang again. She wasn't on call, so she was almost certain it was going to be her mum. But it was Anna.

'Hello?'

'Oh Ella, thank God, where are you?'

'I'm on Paradise Lane, walking back towards the harbour. What's up?'

'A woman has gone into labour with her first baby on the Sisters of Agnes Island, in the old convent.'

'Oh no! Can't one of the hotel's boats bring her back?' Ella could just glimpse the harbour up ahead. The sea was calm for October. Making the short crossing from the island when you were in labour wasn't ideal, but it was a damn sight better than risking giving birth where there were no facilities. Even if it went well, it would mean making the crossing with a newborn baby, or risking doing it on foot when the tide went out. The Sisters of Agnes Island was really just a big rock that was separated from the mainland most of the time, but it was also a bit of tourist draw – a lovely seafood restaurant took up most of the ground floor of the hotel, now housed in the old convent, with panoramic sea views on all sides.

'They've tried to persuade her to make the crossing. She's refused the hotel boat and to be honest I wouldn't have fancied that either, they're not much bigger than rowing boats. The lifeboat crew had a go at convincing her to make the trip with them instead, but she's almost hysterical and absolutely refusing to budge. After that the lifeboat got called out to another job anyway, so one of us is going to have to go over to the island and try to persuade her that getting a boat back is a far better idea than staying put.'

'Why do I get the feeling you're about to tell me I'm the chosen one?' Ella was already running through what she needed to take with her, and whether she'd have to make a stop at the midwifery unit first.

'I know it's your day off, but everyone else is tied up. I've got a lady in labour room two as we speak. The only person who could have gone over instead is Toni, but she's out on home visits and she must be in an area with a mobile signal blind spot, because I can't get hold of her. Once she's free, I'll arrange for her to come and help you out, if you haven't persuaded the mother to get herself back onto the mainland by then. Although obviously that's by far the best outcome.'

'Okay, but there's just one problem. How am I supposed to get over to the island?'

'When the call came through to reception, Lissy's husband, Niall, was here dropping off some thank you presents for you, now that baby Tegen is being seen by the health visitor instead. He offered us the use of his boat and said he'd meet you down by the harbour in fifteen minutes, if you can get there by then? The woman in labour is Natalie Macdonald and she's only thirty-four weeks pregnant.'

'Okay. My bag's at Mum and Dad's and I think it's got everything I need, if I can't persuade the mother to get the boat back with us. But I'll text Toni if I can't and let her know if there's anything I need her to bring.'

'You're a star, Ella, I don't know what we'd do without you.' Anna cleared her throat. 'In fact I wanted to talk to you about that next time I see you. I got an email from Sadie Turner and she's decided not to come back to the unit.'

'Oh, I don't think—' Anna cut Ella off before she could come up with a reason why she wouldn't be able to take over her predecessor's role on a permanent basis.

'I don't need an answer now and I'm definitely not putting any pressure on you, but it would make my year if you decided to stay. I know I'm not supposed to have favourites but, even if it hadn't been your idea for me to go out with Brae, you'd already have had that honour.'

'I'm so glad it's going so well. Brae's a lovely guy.'

'He really is, but don't get me started on that or both our patients will have delivered their babies by themselves!' Anna laughed. 'I'll keep my phone on, so give me a call if there's any news.'

'Will do.' Disconnecting the call, Ella broke into a jog. She had to get back to the house, get changed and meet Niall down by the harbour in less than fifteen minutes. It was at times like this she could have done with Superman's ability to get changed in a phone box. But you could get arrested for stuff like that in Port Agnes and she'd made more than enough headlines already.

* * *

Ella was out of breath by the time she'd run back to the harbour with her bag. She hadn't been to the gym since coming home to Port Agnes, convincing herself that between her job and walking

Daisy, she was keeping as fit as she'd always been. Now she knew it was a lie.

'Where are you, Niall?' Muttering under her breath, she scanned the harbour. Tourists were almost non-existent at this time of year and there seemed to be fewer boats moored up too. Niall should be easy to spot, but she couldn't see him and there might not be a lot of time to waste.

'Ella!' She looked towards where the shout had come from, but it wasn't Niall. Dan was standing on the deck of a small boat, gesturing for her to come over.

'Is Niall with you?' Ella drew level with the boat.

'No. He rushed home to put the cows in so Lissy wouldn't have to do it while he was out, and his back just went. He's had it before, it's something to do with a disc that's protruding more than it should. Anyway, somehow he managed to crawl back to the house and he asked me if I could come down and take you over to the island instead. I've never driven so fast in my life, except maybe on the way back from the airport when Tegen was born!'

'Do you know how to operate this thing?' Stepping off the gangplank she took the hand he offered and the rest of her body completely overreacted to such a light touch. It was no good telling herself she and Dan were keeping things casual when her body was still so determined to do its own thing.

'I can steer a boat.' He laughed at the expression that must have crossed her face. 'All right, I know that doesn't make me sound like an expert, but don't worry, you're in safe hands.'

'Have you operated *this* boat before?' She tried not to look at how weathered the wooden deck looked. She was all for rustic charm, but this was bordering on the rotten and the only boat she'd ever seen Dan use was a rubber dinghy they'd taken down to Ocean Cove when they'd been in sixth form. Even then they'd managed to drift out too far one day when they'd been distracted by the urgency of teenage kisses, and had to jump overboard and swim back to the cove, abandoning the dinghy to its fate. It had probably ended up in Wexford, or maybe even Newfoundland, and none of that did much to reassure her that Dan was the best person to bring Ella or Natalie safely back to the mainland.

'Lissy bought the boat as a wedding present for Niall. Then they realised she was pregnant with Noah and I bought a half share to help them out when they wouldn't let me give them some money to take the pressure off. I took a couple of lessons and got my licence. I take it out more than Niall now, given how often he's away. It's too cold to sit out on deck at this time of year and the boat's a bit of an old tub, but she'll get us there and back, no problem.'

'I'll just have to trust you on that.' There was no time to make alternative arrangements now, anyway. She had no choice but to follow him into the wheelhouse and hope his skills had improved since their dinghy days.

'She's a bit noisy too, so you'll probably want to save your breath until we get to the island.' As Dan started the boat up, the engine began to chug over, and she realised he wasn't joking. If Ella had been forced to describe the sound, she'd have likened it to a lawnmower that had seen better days, but about ten times the volume. She just had to hope the engine had more power than a lawnmower.

As they pulled out of the harbour, she followed Dan's advice and didn't try to talk. The water was a bit choppier than it had been earlier, but the sky was still a deep blue and the waves looked deceptively inviting as a result. Anyone who'd actually taken a dip in Port Agnes during October could categorically say that any comparison with a tropical beach was purely superficial.

The Sisters of Agnes Island rose out of the sea in front of them. It was almost crown-like, and the former convent, that was now a luxury hotel, dominated the centre of the island, looking back across at the town that shared its name.

When Ella was little, and the last remaining nuns had still lived at the convent, she'd spent hours staring across at it, making up stories in her head about what really happened on the island. It was far more fun to imagine that it harboured pirates and their hauls of treasure, or secret tunnels that led down to the mermaids' hiding place, than it was to accept the reality. There'd been rumours at her school about a highwayman who'd met his death on the island after an encounter with the executioner's axe. The story went that he roamed the land from edge to edge at night, in a desperate search to be reunited with his missing head. The idea had terrified and fascinated her in equal measure, but at the time she'd really believed it might be true.

'I think this is as good a place as any to moor up.' Dan shouted above the noise of the engine as he manoeuvred the boat into a small space by the jetty that led onto the island. There were a couple of trips back and forth each day run by the hotel, and you could hire a water taxi in between times if there was one available – which was infrequent in October. When the tide was at its lowest point, which only happened at certain times of the year, it was possible to walk between the island and Port Agnes itself. But there was no way of knowing if that was going to be possible before the baby decided to put in an appearance, even if Natalie could manage it.

'I just hope we can persuade her that a trip back across the water is preferable to taking her chances here.' A headless highwayman might be the stuff of childish imaginings, but Natalie and her baby could be in real danger if she insisted upon staying on the island. It was impossible to predict how any labour would go, but first-time mums always faced unknown territory, especially with a baby that was early.

'Shall I wait here?' Dan looked as though he was hoping for a nod, but she shook her head.

'I might need you.'

'What for? I'm not sure I could get involved in... you know. I helped Lissy deliver a calf once, and seeing a new soul come into the world wasn't the life-affirming experience people claim it to be.'

'Don't worry, I won't be asking you to deliver the baby.' She laughed. 'But I might need your powers of persuasion and, if she can't manage to walk, I might need your help to get her down here. Although you sound distinctly less manly now that I'm picturing you sitting on a bale of straw with your head between your knees at the sight of a cow giving birth!'

'I'll have you know I stayed upright all the way through!' He grinned again. 'Just don't ask Lissy what shade of green I went, or she won't stop laughing for a week.'

'You know I'm going to have to ask her now, don't you?' Raising an eyebrow, she turned towards the path that led up to the old convent. She might be playing it cool, but like Dan she was hoping against hope that they wouldn't have to get involved with an actual delivery. At least not until they were safely back on the mainland.

15

The sound of Natalie Macdonald sobbing drifted along the corridor, long before Ella and Dan reached the conservatory where the mother-to-be was waiting with her husband and the worried-looking hotel manager – whose name was Peiter, according to the badge that also displayed his job title.

'Hi Natalie, I'm Ella, one of the Port Agnes midwives, and this is Dan. He brought me over in his boat. The receptionist told us you were waiting in here.' Ella spoke gently, but she had to raise her voice slightly to be heard above Natalie who was still crying. 'It's going to be okay, I promise.'

'I'm not leaving. Don't try to make me!' Natalie shrugged her husband's hand off her arm. 'It wasn't supposed to be like this. I was booked in at the Portland, but Liam insisted we needed a babymoon and there was no way the baby would come early. It's all his bloody fault.'

'I always thought first babies were late.' Liam looked close to tears himself. 'I shouldn't have risked it though, especially not with Nat having tokophobia.'

'Have you had that diagnosis?' Ella looked at Natalie, and the other woman nodded. If Anna had been aware of it she'd definitely have shared it with Ella, and it put a whole new spin on the challenge facing them.

'I suffer from anxiety and panic attacks anyway, but the bigger my bump got the more terrified I was about giving birth.' Natalie was still crying, but she wasn't actually sobbing in between the words any more, which was progress of a sort.

'What's tokophobia?' Peiter was looking more concerned by the moment, and he was clutching a large bottle of antibacterial gel as if his life depended on it.

'Tokophobia is an extreme fear of giving birth. It's perfectly normal to be anxious about labour and delivery, but tokophobia can end up impacting on a woman's day-to-day life too, making it almost impossible to think about anything else.' Ella crouched down beside Natalie's chair. 'Is that how you're feeling, sweetheart?'

'Uh-huh. I've been having much more severe panic attacks and it's only because of CBT that I can function at all. I'm not working at the moment anyway because I'm a model and obviously not many castings want someone like this.'

'You look more beautiful than ever, darling. I keep telling you that.' Liam put a hand on Natalie's shoulder again, and this time she didn't shrug him off.

'My therapist said I should come on this trip and I used the techniques she showed me to cope with the journey here. But telling myself that nothing bad would happen and that I wasn't going to go into labour this early didn't work out that well, did it?'

'You're doing really well. A lot of people with tokophobia would have gone into a full-blown panic attack by now, so the CBT is probably helping more than you realise.' Ella was grateful that Natalie had managed to keep control of her breathing. If she had a serious panic attack while she was in labour, with none of the support she'd get in the hospital, it could be really dangerous.

Not to mention that she was only thirty-four weeks pregnant and the baby was probably going to need a bit of help too.

'My therapist was supposed to be with me at the hospital to help me through the birth, and they said I could have a C-section if I decided I couldn't go through with a normal delivery. But I wanted to try.'

'Are you having contractions now?'

'It feels more like cramps than what I expected, and they're quite far apart, but I'm not really sure what I'm supposed to feel.'

'I think the first thing I need to do is examine you, Natalie, okay? Then we can take it from there.'

'I'll wait outside.' Dan was already halfway towards the other end of the conservatory, with Peiter hot on his heels.

'You don't need to leave, because we're not going to be able to do the examination here.' Ella could see people walking in the grounds outside, and if she could see them, that meant they could see Natalie. 'Do you think you could manage to get to one of the bedrooms, Natalie?'

'I think so.'

'Her waters broke when we were in the restaurant and I had to virtually carry her in here. She was fighting with me at that point, though.' Liam pulled up his shirtsleeve to reveal a series of angry looking scratches on his arm. 'I know it was only because she was just terrified.'

'I'm sorry.' Natalie had stopped looking like she wanted to throttle her husband and she wasn't crying any more either, but her voice remained strained. 'I was terrified. I still am, but I don't feel quite as hysterical now there's a midwife here. I'm still not getting in a boat, so don't even try to persuade me. I told the lifeboat crew I wasn't going to move and I think I might even have kicked one of them.'

'More than one.' Peiter said. No wonder he was standing as far back from Natalie as he could.

'I've been kicked before, I can take it.' Ella squeezed Natalie's hand. 'Can you stand up?'

'Uh-huh.'

'Great. Let Liam support you then.' Ella got to her feet and took a step back as Natalie stood up. 'Where's the nearest bedroom we can use, Peiter?'

'Room 122 on the first floor is free. I'll go on ahead and open it up for you.' Peiter almost ran out of the conservatory, sensing his chance to escape.

'I don't want Liam in the room while you're looking *down there*.' Natalie managed a half smile. 'He promised to stay at the head end during the birth.'

'How about if Liam and I get a drink and you can text me when you're ready?' Dan looked at Ella as he spoke.

'That's a good idea. If you can both just help me get Natalie up to the room first, that would be great.' There were some women who carried on as though labour was barely affecting them, but Natalie was clearly struggling with the pain levels already. Every woman's pain threshold was different and, having never had a baby herself, Ella was the last person who'd judge anyone for the way they handled labour. It was obvious Natalie was going to need a lot of support and right now that included getting her to the room.

The hotel lift was one of those old-fashioned ones with cage style doors, which had almost certainly been in situ since the building had been a convent. Inside the lift, the space was quite tight for four people especially when one of them was heavily pregnant. Natalie faced forward, leaning on Liam's shoulders and, between them, they took up two-thirds of the space. It left Ella and Dan pressed into one corner of the lift together and, as it juddered to a stop, their hands brushed against each other; the memory of the first time they'd held hands, on the bus back from Three Ports High School, suddenly popping into her head. It had all been so easy back then, they'd just gone with their instincts and trusted that the future would take care of itself.

'Okay, here we go.' The lift doors opened, bringing Ella back to the present. Squeezing through the gap to get out of the lift first, she spotted Peiter standing outside the door of a room about halfway along the corridor. Natalie, who must have been close to six feet tall, had Liam supporting her on one side and Dan on the other. If she was struggling this much just to walk before she was even in full-blown labour, any pain relief that Ella could administer was unlikely to be strong enough to help manage the pain, or the impact that would have on her tokophobia. But if Natalie refused to be moved, that didn't leave many options. Ella just had to hope Toni would get there by then. This was one delivery she didn't fancy facing on her own.

'Can I get you anything before I go?' Peiter handed Ella the key. There were no plastic swipe cards at this hotel. The big black key he'd handed her looked like something a medieval jailer might have used to lock up a traitor to the king.

'We can take it from here, thank you, Peiter. Dan and Liam are going to come back down for a drink once we get Natalie settled on the bed.' Ella stepped inside the room. There was a huge four-poster bed dominating the space and heavily leaded windows which revealed just a glimpse of the sea beyond the hotel grounds. Ella could suddenly understand the appeal a life of solitude that the Covent of the Sisters of Agnes must have offered the young nuns joining the order. In a weird sort of way, she'd almost done the same thing; running home to the gentle safety of Port Agnes when her relationship with Weller had fallen apart. Though she'd felt anything but nun-like as Dan put a hand on her arm after he'd helped Liam lay Natalie down on the bed.

'Just text me or give me a call if you need anything.' Dan's eyes seemed to bore into her soul when he looked at her, another echo of the past. He'd said the same thing to her the day she'd set off back to London, when they'd split up for good after she'd finally realised he was never going to leave Port Agnes to be with her. She'd told him she wouldn't be calling or texting, but he knew where she was if he changed his mind. There must have been a thousand times in that first year when she picked up the phone and so very nearly broken the promise she'd made not to back down and call him.

'I'll let you know if we need anything, don't worry.' Ella smiled at Dan, as Liam bent down to kiss the top of his wife's head. Seconds later, the two men had headed off towards the safety of the bar.

'Have you felt the baby moving since your waters broke?' Ella asked the question as gently as she could, and silently prayed she'd get the answer she was looking for.

'Yes, the movements have been non-stop all day, but every book I've read says that they tend to slow down just before you go into labour.'

'Most of the time, but not always. That much movement is a good sign that everything's all right with the baby, though. I'm going to take a look at you now, Natalie, okay?' Ella took some surgical gloves out of her bag, as the other woman nodded. 'Just try and relax.'

For a moment or two they both fell silent.

'Can you feel the baby's head?'

'No. You've definitely lost your waters, but you aren't in active labour yet and you're not dilating from what I can tell.'

'What does that mean?' Natalie widened her eyes.

'Usually women go into labour when their waters break, but it can take up to twenty-four hours for things to properly start. If you don't go into labour by then you'd usually be induced because the baby's more vulnerable without the amniotic fluid to protect it.' Ella forced a smile that she hoped didn't look as painted on as it felt. 'Do you know what gender your baby is?'

'It's a girl. She's going to be okay, isn't she? She's six weeks early. It's too soon!' The panic was back in Natalie's eyes.

'Any baby born more than three weeks early is technically pre-term, but from thirty-three weeks onwards they usually only need extra care for a very short time.' Ella took a deep breath. 'Even so, it would be much better for you and your little girl if we could get you back on the mainland.'

'I can't. The thought of giving birth on a boat, or even in a helicopter, literally makes me want to throw up.' All the colour had drained from Natalie's face. 'My anxiety gets worse whenever I feel out of control and this feels like the ultimate loss of control.'

'It is, sweetheart, but the prize you get at the end of it really will make it all worthwhile. Every mother I've delivered says the same.' They'd have trouble getting a helicopter to come out and transport Natalie, even if she'd been willing to consider the option and there was somewhere safe it could land. 'If I examine you in half an hour's time and if there's still no sign of any dilation and you aren't having contractions, I promise you won't give birth between here and the mainland. We can have an ambulance waiting at the harbour to take you and Liam straight to the hospital, and they can give you all the help you need. How does that sound?'

'Are there any private maternity hospitals in Cornwall?'

'I don't think so, but the Royal Cornwall Hospital in Truro will look after you and with a diagnosis of tokophobia, you can discuss the option of a C-section if that's already been agreed with your obstetrician.'

'How can you be so sure the baby won't come on the journey?' Natalie was biting her fingernails, even though they were obviously acrylics. Ella had never seen anyone in real life with nails that long.

'Because if you aren't having what looks or feels like contractions, and there's no progress with dilation, there's no way you'll progress that quickly; even if things start to move as soon as we step on the boat. I've looked after women who've had incredibly short labours, but they don't start the way your labour has.'

'And we'd go back on your husband's boat?'

'My husband?' For a moment Ella was nonplussed. 'Do you mean, Dan? We're just friends.'

'I could have sworn, by the way he was looking at you, that you two were together.'

'No, nothing like that.' It wasn't exactly a lie and it wasn't the whole truth, either. But it wasn't important right now. 'Liam seems to be utterly devoted to you.'

'He is. We met when I first started modelling and he was the photographer on the shoot. He says it was love at first sight for him. It takes me a while to trust people, so it took a lot longer for me to use the L word, but I know I'm lucky. Not every man could deal with my anxiety.'

'Plenty of people would say he's the lucky one.' Ella's smile was genuine this time. Natalie was as goddess-like as she'd expect a model to be. She had long, glossy black hair which fell over her shoulders, and striking green eyes. No wonder Liam had fallen in love with her at first sight. It was surprising Dan had even glanced in Ella's direction with someone like Natalie in the room.

'Dan doesn't want to be your friend, you know.' Natalie straightened her clothes and pulled herself up to a sitting position on the bed. 'Men don't look at women they just want to be friends with the way he looked at you.'

'And you worked that out, with everything else you've got on your mind?' Ella raised an eyebrow.

'I've spent every day, since I was fourteen years old, perfecting the look of love and directing it at the camera. I know it when I see it for real.'

'It's complicated. We used to go out years ago, but you can't just turn the clock back, even if I wanted to.' Ella wouldn't normally have opened up to a virtual stranger in the way she had, least of all a patient, but it seemed to be keeping Natalie's mind off the fear of giving birth.

'I've got a feeling he'll do whatever it takes to turn the clock back.' Natalie tapped her temple. 'I'd bet double or quits on my tax bill. You should ask him.'

'I wouldn't know what to say. Anyway, even if you're right, I'll be moving away soon, so there's no future in it.'

'You might not be looking for love, but sometimes it finds you.' Natalie smiled. 'God knows I wasn't planning to settle down when I met Liam and the last thing I wanted was a baby, but look at me now!'

'A few months ago, I was busy planning my wedding to someone else.'

'But you decided he wasn't right for you?'

'Something like that.' Ella instinctively ducked her head, the way she always did when she thought someone might recognise her as the bride whose jilting had gone viral.

'Now you're terrified of Dan rejecting you? That's what it really is, isn't it? All that stuff about not wanting to get into something new, or the timing being wrong, goes out of the window when you meet the right person.'

'It's not—' For a second or two Ella had been about to deny it, but it had taken a stranger to make her admit it. Even to herself. She didn't want to tell anyone how important Dan was to her in case he decided he didn't feel the same after all. She needed to stay in control this time and the only way she could do that was to be the one who decided when to walk away. She wouldn't have admitted it to anyone she was close to, but Natalie was different because she'd never have to see her again after today. So there was no harm in telling her the truth. 'The prospect of being rejected isn't something anyone looks forward to, is it?'

'I've got used to it over years of casting calls as a model, and I don't take it personally any more.'

'I can't imagine you've ever been rejected when you've told someone you've got feelings for them, though.'

'Maybe not, but everyone's scared of something. I'm terrified of having this baby,' Natalie smoothed a hand over her bump, 'just like you're terrified of opening up to Dan. So how about we make a deal?'

'What sort of deal?'

'If I can get on that boat, then you can ask Dan whether he wants more than friendship, or whatever it is you've got right now, as soon as we get to the mainland.'

'What, *straight away*?' Ella furrowed her brow as Natalie nodded, nerves already fluttering in her stomach at the thought.

'Yes, but I'm not promising I'll even make it to the boat, let alone do the crossing. I'll try my CBT techniques and, if I manage it, you've got to keep your side of the bargain.'

'Will you teach me some of those CBT techniques while we're waiting to do the second examination? I think I'm going to need them!' Ella looked at Natalie, who grinned in response. She'd have to use all the positive visualisation she could muster to look Dan in the eye and tell him how she really felt, when she'd only admitted it to herself in the last few minutes. The thought was terrifying, but she had to admit that Natalie was right, it was time to find out one way or the other whether Dan had been any more successful at keeping his feelings in check than she had. Even trying to work out what she was going to say made her heart race, especially as she might end up having an audience to witness it all. She still had no idea how she'd even ended up agreeing to Natalie's suggestion, but she'd cross that bridge if she came to it. There was a much bigger barrier for Natalie to cross before they even reached the mainland. If that didn't happen, she was under no obligation to say anything to

Dan. Suddenly Natalie staying put on the island didn't seem so bad after all.

'I still can't believe I'm doing this!' Natalie gripped the handrail of the boat, as Liam held her mobile phone up in front of her. Dan had suggested checking whether Natalie's therapist was available to FaceTime, to help talk her through the process of getting on the boat. As Ella had expected, there was no sign of Natalie's labour starting when she'd carried out the second examination and the best place for her was definitely a hospital, so they could check on the baby properly. Ella had called ahead to arrange for a midwife from the Royal Cornwall Hospital to be in the ambulance that met them on the other side, just in case Natalie's labour started to progress on the journey to Truro.

'You're doing brilliantly.' Ella wasn't even sure if Natalie had heard her. The therapist was giving some instructions that Ella couldn't make out, and Natalie was tapping a spot on her collarbone and breathing slowly in and out, much like Ella might have advised if she'd actually been in labour. Liam had offered to pay for an Uber to bring the therapist from London to whatever hospital Natalie was taken to and that had seemed to help reassure her. Women with tokophobia needed a clear plan for labour and delivery, and any deviation from that could seem catastrophic. Liam making that promise was the next best thing to sticking with Plan A. All they had to do now was get Natalie across the water, but there was still no guarantee she'd be able to go through with it. They were all squeezed into the small wheelhouse, with Dan at the controls and Natalie and Liam sitting on the small bench behind him. Ella stood to one side in the only space left.

'Are you ready to set off?' Dan turned towards Ella, and for a moment she stood rooted to the spot. Was she ready? Not if she had to keep her promise to Natalie. It didn't really matter, though. Liam and Natalie would have other things on their minds by the time they reached the mainland, and they'd barely even notice that Ella was there.

'I think we're good to go. In fact, it's probably a good idea to get moving as soon as we can, just in case Natalie changes her mind.' Ella glanced at the other woman and then looked back at Dan. 'Good call on FaceTiming the therapist by the way.'

'You were the one who calmed Natalie down. Liam was convinced she'd never agree to get on the boat; but she trusts you.'

'We'd better get back to Port Agnes then, before the baby decides to make a break for it and turns me into a liar.'

'No problem.' Dan smiled and started up the boat, the noise of the engine making it impossible to hear what Natalie's therapist was saying. Whether Natalie could make out the therapist's words or not was anyone's guess, but she had her eyes fixed firmly on the phone screen in any case.

For a few moments all Ella could do was watch Natalie and shoot what she hoped were reassuring smiles in Liam's direction, but then there was a shout that could have been heard above the noise of several boat engines.

'What's the matter?' Ella was crouching at Natalie's side in an instant.

'The call's cut off and now there's no signal. I don't think I can do this without Therese to talk me through it!' Natalie was trying to get to her feet, but Ella took hold of her hand.

'You can do this, sweetheart. It's you who's been doing it all along.' Ella turned towards Liam for backup, but he looked almost as terrified as his wife.

'I need her to tell me what to do!' Natalie's voice was in danger of reaching a pitch only dogs could hear.

'I want you to visualise holding your baby girl in your arms.' Ella knew next to nothing about CBT, but she'd watched a couple of YouTube videos just after the jilting video had gone viral and she'd felt a bit panicky about being recognised. She wasn't confident about any of the tapping techniques, but she'd used positive visualisation to help women through labour before too.

'I can't. All I can think about is what I'm going to have to do to get her here.'

'Do you know what you want to call the baby?'

'We're going to call her Lola May.' It was Liam who answered, as the pace of Natalie's breathing started to quicken.

'That's lovely. Okay, Natalie, I want you to imagine holding Lola in your arms, sitting in the nursery you've set up for her at home.' Ella was taking a punt on the Macdonalds being the sort of people who already had a beautifully decorated nursery ready and waiting. 'What can you see? Give me as many details as you can.' Ella reached out to take hold of Natalie's hand as she spoke.

'I'm sitting in the glider chair we bought for nursing. It's dove grey and white, and the cushions are really soft.'

'Anything else?' Ella kept her voice as steady as she could, but she almost had to shout to be heard over the noise of the boat.

'Lola's making little snuffling noises and she feels heavy in my arms. There's rain beating against the window, but she's content. And so am I.'

'That's great, you're doing so well. Is there anything else?'

'All her Babygros and blankets have been freshly washed and dried and piled up neatly. There's the scent of fabric softener, and the smell of dinner cooking drifting up the stairs. Liam's making it for us and we're all safe at home together.'

'That's how it's going to be, Natalie, you just need to keep that image in your head.' Ella was starting to struggle now; she'd had almost no idea what to do when she'd started talking and she'd already run out of ideas. Looking up at Natalie, who still had her eyes shut, Ella felt some of the tension leave her spine as she caught a glimpse of the outside world. Dan was turning the boat into the mouth of the harbour and the ambulance was already parked on the quayside.

'Are we here?' Natalie's eyes suddenly flew open, but her voice was steady. The realisation that she'd survived the boat journey was enough to keep her relatively calm.

'We are and there's an ambulance waiting with one of the midwives from the Royal Cornwall Hospital. They'll take you there, to assess you and Lola, and decide what's best to do next.' Ella smiled. She must have earned a large G&T after the day she'd had. Although she was still trying to forget the promise she'd made to Natalie.

'I'm not getting in the ambulance.' Natalie had a determined looked on her face and Ella's heart seemed to sink past her feet and straight through the deck of the boat. They'd done the hard bit crossing the water, and she couldn't work out why Natalie was smiling and refusing to move all at the same time.

'It'll be the quickest way to get you to the hospital and you'll be in that nursery, holding Lola in your arms before you know it, just like you pictured.' Ella steadied herself as Dan brought the boat parallel with the quayside.

'I know that. And *I will* get into the ambulance, but not until you've fulfilled your side of the bargain.'

'You aren't serious, are you?' Ella couldn't believe Natalie was going to hold her to it.

'Deadly. Some good has got to come of all this.'

'I can't do it.' Ella shook her head in case Natalie hadn't already got the message, not realising Dan was standing behind her.

'What can't you do?' His voice made her jump.

'Ella wants to ask you something, but she doesn't think she

can.' Natalie screwed up her face. 'And I need her to get on and do it before I start panicking again.'

'You can ask me anything.' Dan gave Ella a serious look and she found herself believing she could; although she'd still rather not have had an audience.

'This,' Ella paused, vaguely aware of Natalie and Liam listening to every word, 'whatever it is that's been going on between us since the Silver of the Sea festival... Is it something you'd want to go somewhere, if I was staying in Port Agnes?'

'Are you thinking about staying then?' Dan hadn't answered her question, but he was smiling in a way that suggested he'd be more than happy if she decided to stay.

'Maybe.' Ella couldn't help returning his smile. 'Anna has asked me if I'll think about it, but I didn't know if you'd want things between us to go anywhere anyway.'

'I don't want things to carry on like this.' Dan hesitated and Ella suddenly found herself wishing that the deck of the boat was as rotten as it had looked, so that she could disappear through the floor. 'I don't want things to carry on the way they have been, because I don't want to have to keep pretending that we aren't seeing each other again. Every time I see Lissy, I open my mouth to tell her what's going on and I have to clamp my mouth shut again. I've always told my sister everything and I don't think I can keep it in much longer.'

'So are you going to get on with it already and stop pretending you don't want to spend every spare minute you have together?' Natalie let Liam help her to her feet as she spoke.

'I don't know about Ella, but I'm definitely not going to argue with a pregnant woman.' Dan laughed.

'I suppose we could give it a try, if you insist.' Ella kept her tone deliberately casual, but the grin on her face kept giving her away.

'Well thank goodness for that! Now someone get me to a

hospital where I can get drugged up to the eyeballs to cope with giving birth.'

Five minutes later, Natalie and Liam were finally safely inside the ambulance and they'd said their goodbyes. Liam had taken Ella's number and promised to message as soon as the baby arrived. Watching the ambulance disappear into the distance, she turned towards Dan, her cheeks going hot as he met her gaze. Now that it was just the two of them standing there, all the old vulnerabilities about confessing how she felt had come flooding back.

'I won't hold you to giving things between us a proper go if you only agreed to keep a pregnant woman happy.' Even as he said the words, she shook her head.

'I didn't need blackmailing.'

'Me neither.' His voice was low as he took a step towards her. 'You were amazing today and Liam was convinced they'd still be stuck on the island if it wasn't for you.'

'You were the one who had the brilliant idea of calling the therapist.'

'Does that make us a team?' He was close enough now for her to reach out and touch him and almost unconsciously she curled her fingers around his – like she'd done so many times in the past – without giving a damn who saw them and worked out that they were back together.

'It looks like we've already perfected the secret handshake that every good team needs.'

'Oi, mate, just give her a kiss and get it over with, will yer?' A man emerging from the pub on the edge of the harbour called out; his voice slurred with drink.

'I think I've had enough of performing for an audience for one day, even if we aren't keeping things secret any more.' Ella forced herself to take a step back, even though every part of her body had been anticipating that kiss.

'Me too, but maybe you could drop your bag home and we could take a walk up to lookout point, just like the old days. If you haven't got any other plans?'

'Nothing that can't wait.' Ella couldn't help still trying to play it a tiny bit cool. Trusting in anything completely again, even her own judgement, wasn't going to happen overnight. For now her biggest worry was how she was going to sneak back into her parents' house and drop off her bag without them seeing her and asking a hundred questions she wasn't quite ready for yet. It really was like being a teenager all over again.

16

'Have we reached this stage in our relationship already?' Dan grinned as Ella reapplied the lipstick he'd just kissed off.

'What stage?' She watched his reflection in the mirror as he stood behind her, the smile still playing around his lips. She'd almost forgotten what the early stages of a relationship felt like; when all you could think about was the other person and when you were going to see them again. It had never been as intense with Weller as it was with Dan.

'The stage where we double date with couple friends.' Dan dropped her a perfect wink, making it clear he didn't really mind.

'It's just so lovely to see Brae and Anna happy and if she hadn't sent me on that call to the Sisters of Agnes Island, I might never have admitted how I felt.'

'It did take a heavily pregnant woman blackmailing you to make you admit you still quite liked me.'

'Are you convinced of that now?' She turned away from the mirror to face him. She was wearing a rust-coloured shirt dress she knew flattered her figure. Dan was constantly telling her how good she looked, he'd been the same back when they were teenagers and she still found it just as hard to accept the compliments as she had back then, but for once she had to admit she looked okay. Maybe even a little bit more than okay.

'I might need a bit more evidence about how you feel.' Dan grinned again and he slid his arms around her.

'I'm not reapplying this lipstick again.'

'Then you'll just have to go naked.' As Dan pressed his lips against hers, she shivered. If they didn't have a dinner date in ten minutes, she'd have been more than willing to comply. As it was, she pulled away from him a few seconds later, but not before he'd done a pretty thorough job of kissing off her lipstick again, so she had to reapply it for a third time. Sometimes it felt as though the ten years between their last kiss and the Silver of the Sea had never happened.

'We've got to go.' Taking his hand, she pulled him towards the door of the bedroom. Jago and Ruth had gone out to visit some friends in Padstow before Dan had even arrived. When she'd finally reintroduced him to her parents, she'd expected her father to be stand-offish at best and mutter something about her getting involved with an emmet again. As it turned out he'd given Dan the sort of effusive welcome Ella could never have anticipated, because Jago had heard on the Parish Council about Dan securing historical building status for Mercer's Row.

The fact that Brae had also told her parents how great he thought Dan was had helped too, as it still seemed to hold more weight with Jago than Ella's opinion. It should have annoyed her, but she was just grateful that everyone seemed to be happy for once. Brae also made sure Ruth and Jago knew that Dan was letting Sophie stay in one of his cottages rent-free, getting one over on Michael Tredinnick after she refused to go back to work for him. The icing on the cake had come when Brae had told them that the reason Dan wasn't staying at the converted stable block at Six Acre Farm was because he'd rented it to a local family, whose house was being repaired after flood damage, for a peppercorn rent.

Ella had hoped her father might consider selling The Old Forge to Dan, too, but his pride would never have let that happen, even if Dan could have paid the price they needed to recoup their investment. To make things even worse, Michael Tredinnick had reported The Old Forge to the local council and the Health and Safety Executive as a dangerous building. If he could persuade them to demolish it, the site would be worth nothing like as much as Jago, Clem and Jack had paid for it. Not even her father's position on the parish council could stand in the way of permission being granted for a small apartment block if they ended up being forced to sell to Michael out of desperation. It was obviously his plan, but he hadn't reckoned on Jago's sheer bloody-mindedness and Ella was terrified that it might end up costing them everything. Her father had already been warned about his blood pressure spiking again and, if The Old Forge got demolished, selling to Dan wouldn't be an option at any price, because he didn't do new builds. When Clem and Jack had begged Jago to reconsider he'd said he might have done if Michael hadn't said the awful things he had about Ella, which made her feel more responsible than ever for the predicament her parents were in.

'Are you okay? You looked miles away.' Dan's voice brought her back to the present and she forced a smile.

'I was just wondering if Anna might have heard from the trust about what sort of contract they'll be able to offer.' It wasn't a lie, the role she got at the unit could make all the difference if her parents finally agreed to accept her support. If she got the job as Anna's deputy, the extra money could really help them and it would seem less of a step down the career ladder. 'Although if we don't get to dinner on time, Anna might decide to withdraw the job offer altogether.'

'I suppose we've got to go then.' Dan's tone was reluctant as he let go of her waist, but he followed her out of the room and down the stairs.

'I don't like you walking behind me like that. You're not looking at how big my bum is, are you?' She turned as they reached the front door.

'You look great, you always do.' Dan took hold of her hand again as they emerged into the darkness of the street. 'But I'd be lying if I said I didn't sneak a look in that general direction.'

'It's okay, I kind of like the fact you want to look after what happened with Weller.'

'Does it still bother you?' Dan's squeezed her hand and she knew she could be honest with him.

'I'm glad. Otherwise I wouldn't have come home.' The glow of the street lamp illuminated the ground in front of them, as they dodged the puddles left behind from the earlier downpour that had been fierce enough to rattle the windows in her bedroom. 'And I wouldn't have had the chance to get to know you all over again either.'

'I must tell Weller how grateful I am to him, too, if I ever get to meet him.'

'I think he'd like that.' Ella smiled to herself. Life could be really weird sometimes. A few weeks before, she'd never have believed she'd be about to sign a contract to stay on in Port Agnes indefinitely.

'Did you get the text from Brae saying that he's got something important to tell us tonight?' He turned towards her when they reached the door of the newly opened restaurant overlooking the harbour.

'No, but now I'm dying to know what it is!'

'We'd better get inside then.' Dan held open the restaurant door and Ella immediately spotted their friends sitting at a table in the window that looked straight out to the water.

'Huh, hmm.' Ella cleared her throat as she and Dan

approached Anna and Brae's table, after the waiter had taken their coats. Their friends certainly seemed to have found something to pass the time. She wouldn't have put Anna down as the sort of person who was comfortable with a public display of affection in a busy restaurant, but judging by the smile on her face, when she finally realised that Ella and Dan were standing in front of them, she was learning to live with it.

'Sorry, we were just...' Anna laughed.

'Uh-huh.' Ella couldn't help smiling too. If she ever decided on a drastic change of job, maybe a career in matchmaking could be on the cards.

'I've ordered a bottle of champagne.' Brae stood up as Ella took her seat. He was still a total gentleman, even if he couldn't drag his eyes away from Anna.

'What's the occasion?' Dan asked, taking the seat opposite Brae.

'Anna's agreed to move in with me.'

'*Already?*' Ella hadn't meant to say the word out loud, but as soon as the thought had popped into her head it had come out of her mouth. 'Sorry, I didn't mean it like that. It's just—'

'Too soon?' Anna shrugged. 'I'd normally be the first person to agree, but all those years with Greg were like wading through treacle trying to get anywhere with our relationship. With Brae it's all happened so quickly, but it's felt like such a natural progression too.'

'You're right and I should know that the length of time people are together isn't any indication of whether a relationship will work or not.' Ella smiled. 'I'm so happy for you both.'

'Me too and the next bottle of champagne is on me.' Dan paused as the waiter brought over a silver bucket, with a bottle of Veuve Clicquot nestled on a bed of ice, filling up their glasses before disappearing again. 'There's a lot to celebrate tonight.'

'Don't tell me you've caught us up already and you've got a big announcement too?' asked Brae, looking distinctly disappointed when Dan shook his head.

'We're a way behind you yet,' Dan caught Ella's eye as he spoke, 'but the fact that Ella has agreed to accept a permanent contract at the unit is more than enough reason to celebrate. I never thought I'd see the day where she'd realise that Port Agnes was enough.'

'You make it sound like I'm committing to it for life.' A sudden frisson of nerves seemed to tighten around Ella's throat. Just because she'd accepted a job, it didn't mean that was it; that she'd gone as far as she was ever going to go in her career. Dan probably hadn't meant it like that, but she couldn't help wondering whether people like Michael Tredinnick would see her decision as just another failure on her part and use that to rub Jago's nose in it. It would have been easier if her parents hadn't told anyone who'd listen about how specialised her work in London had been, but it was too late to take it all back now. The important thing was that she was happy, that's what Dan, Brae and the other midwives had all said to her when she was weighing up the decision, but she couldn't help the nagging feeling that the money her parents had used to set her up in London had been a waste.

'I know better than to try and pin you down to a lifetime commitment to anything, even Port Agnes.' Dan smiled, although there was just the hint of an edge to his voice, but then he squeezed her hand. She was overthinking everything, that was all. She'd woken up the last three nights worrying about the row she'd had with Michael Tredinnick when he'd threatened Sophie with legal action and demanded she pay back her wages for not working her notice after she'd decided she just couldn't face going back there. Ella had happened to be with Sophie when Michael had knocked on the door and she hadn't been able to stop herself from telling him exactly what she thought of him. She couldn't remember all of it afterwards, but she'd definitely used the word bully and there was a possibility she'd used a well-known expletive when he'd managed to make Sophie burst into tears. She might not recall exactly what she'd said to him, but his parting shot was imprinted on her brain.

'You're just like your mother, thinking you're too good for the rest of us, but the Mehenicks will be getting what they deserve this time. When your parents' bakery fails after their debt finally swallows them up, you'd better hope you can use that high horse of yours to transport all their stuff out of Port Agnes. Because they won't be able to show their faces around here, let alone afford to live here, and all of that will be on you.'

'Did you hear what I said, Ella?' Anna's voice broke into her thoughts and she shook her head. There was no point even trying to pretend that she'd heard what her friend had said.

'She keeps doing that today, drifting away somewhere else.' There was no edge to Dan's voice this time. If anything he sounded worried. 'Are you sure you're okay?'

'I'm fine, honestly.' Ella smiled, determined not to let Michael Tredinnick ruin another evening. 'Now pass me a glass of champagne and let's keep the toasts coming!'

'I was just saying that I'm hoping the midwifery unit's relationship curse might finally be lifting for everyone.' Anna topped up Ella's glass. 'Jess seems to think that she and Dom can work things out and he's agreed to go to counselling with her before they get their test results. So they can support each other, whatever happens.'

'That's great. So just Toni and Bobby to sort out then and we've got a full house.' Maybe it was a bit hypocritical for Ella to want Toni and Bobby to get their relationship out in the open, but she had the best of intentions. She knew better than anyone that going public with a relationship put more pressure on it, especially in a place like Port Agnes, and even more so when the couple worked together. But it was obvious that Bobby didn't want to keep things a secret, which was probably why they'd done such a terrible job of managing it. Not having to hide the fact that she was seeing Dan again had been one less thing for Ella to worry about and she was almost certain Toni would feel the same if she could get over whatever it was that was holding her back. Not that Toni was one to share her innermost feelings with the other midwives at the best of times, but she had a heart of gold hidden behind her slightly prickly exterior.

'Okay, I'm going to say this before we get our dinner and I put you all off your food.' Brae smiled, clinking his glass against Anna's. 'Thank you for agreeing to move in with me, my love, and thanks to Ella for finding me someone this far out of my league and somehow persuading her to give me a shot.'

'I didn't need a lot of persuasion.' Anna was smiling too, but then she lowered her glass to the table. 'Isn't that Toni and Bobby coming in together? Their ears must have been burning!'

'What, *together*, together?' Ella tried her best to turn and look without making it too obvious. Anna was right; Toni and Bobby were walking into the restaurant hand in hand. Whatever it was that was stopping them admitting they were together, they really weren't doing a very good job of it.

Gwen, who was partial to a bit of gossip, had told the other midwives that Toni had been due to marry the son of her father's business partner, but something had gone wrong and not even Gwen really knew what it was. Whatever the reason, maybe it was behind Toni and Bobby wanting to keep things low-key. They'd booked annual leave at more or less the same time, with a few days either side to try and throw the rest of the unit off the scent. Ella had happily swapped her planned leave with Toni's when Anna had told her why, but it made her sad that Toni and Bobby felt they had to hide things from the team. Still, it was none of their business. All Ella wanted was for them to be happy and she knew Anna did too.

'Oh no, I feel awful now, they stopped holding hands as soon as they spotted me.' Anna peered past Ella, who had her back to the room and had turned back to face Anna to make it less obvious that she was looking too. 'And now they've walked out. I really hope seeing us hasn't ruined their evening.'

'Are you sure they saw you?' Ella spun around again, but there was no sign of Bobby or Toni.

'Definitely, although they were doing a really good job of pretending not to.'

'Oh God, I feel terrible now, too.' Ella sighed. 'I should have stuck to booking a table in The Jolly Sailor.'

'You do realise not everyone's happiness is your responsibility, don't you?' Dan put his arm around her, and she nodded.

'I know that deep down, but it's another one of my annoying traits.'

'No it isn't, it's another one of the reasons we all love you!' Anna grinned. 'Isn't that right, Dan?'

'Absolutely.' Dan caught Ella's eye. They hadn't said the love word out loud, but Ella had been forced to stop herself more than once. If she said that, there'd be no going back – it came with all the expectation that one of them would change their whole life to be with the other. Maybe it was why Dan hadn't said it either, or maybe he didn't love her. Except when he looked at her, his eyes told a story of their own.

'Dan's right, it's definitely not your fault. They probably just don't want to have their dinner with their boss breathing down their necks!' Brae grinned at Anna and she gave him a nudge in the ribs.

'Hey, I'm a lovely boss, aren't I, Ella?'

'You certainly are.' Ella smiled but she couldn't help worrying that they'd inadvertently ruined Toni and Bobby's evening and, whatever she said to Dan, she already knew she was going to be adding that to her list of things to worry about.

'We should just count ourselves lucky that Anna and Ella are prepared to be seen out in public with us, I suppose.' Dan topped up Brae's glass.

'Oh, believe me, I count myself lucky every day.' Brae reached out for Anna's hand and any shred of doubt Ella might have had about her friends moving too fast, disappeared. If she'd learned anything over the last few months, it was that no one really understood what was going on in someone else's life. And trying to sort out her own was more than enough for Ella to deal with.

* * *

Ella was about to start her lunch in the staffroom after finishing the morning clinic, when her mobile rang.

'Ella Mehenick speaking.'

'Oh Ella, thank goodness, it's Sophie.'

'Is everything okay?' Ella could hear the panic in the girl's voice. The last time Ella had seen her, she'd ended up rowing with Michael Tredinnick when he'd tried to intimidate Sophie into paying back her below-minimum-wage earnings. If he'd been round to Sophie's place again, giving her a hard time, Ella wouldn't be responsible for her actions.

'The baby's not moving.' A sob caught in Sophie's throat. 'I haven't felt anything since yesterday and normally she's bouncing around in there all day long.'

'Okay, sweetheart, where are you?'

'In the car park outside the unit.' Sophie sniffed. 'I didn't want to go anywhere else and I couldn't wait at home. I knew if I saw you that you'd make it all right.'

'Come straight in and I'll meet you in reception.' Ella kept her voice even. She didn't want to promise that everything would be okay, but whatever the outcome, it was up to her to be there. The fact that she was suddenly aware of her own heartbeat had to be put to one side. 'Are you on your own?'

'Yes.' Sophie took a shuddering breath. 'Mum and Dad are driving down here, but I didn't want to wait.'

'I'll see you in one minute.'

Checking for an empty examination room on the way, Ella hurried down the corridor, pushing open the door to the reception area, where she could see Sophie coming through the double doors. The young girl's face was pale, the cheerful mural Dan had painted all along one wall in reception suddenly looking out of place.

'I don't know what I'm going to do if anything has happened to the baby.' Sophie bit her lip, her eyes filling with tears. 'I thought everything was finally going okay now that Dad knows about her and he's okay with it, but now there might not even be a baby!'

'Let's just get you through to the examination room so we can take a look at you. Try not to worry.' Ella wished she could follow her own advice. Nine times out of ten, decreased movements weren't a sign of anything sinister. Sometimes it was just because the woman was busier than usual, or because the baby was lying in a strange position. It was rare for it to mean bad news. But even if it had only ever happened once, it would have been once too often for Ella. She'd faced the worst-case scenario a few times in her career; she just hoped she wouldn't be adding Sophie to that list.

'I tried eating some toast and jam. Normally when I do that she starts doing somersaults straight away, but she's not moving at all.'

'There are lots of reasons you might not have felt anything.' Ella led the way to the treatment room and helped Sophie settle on the examination table. She was just about coming up to thirty-five weeks, and the movements were usually pretty obvious by that stage. Sophie should have been able to feel the baby move on a daily basis.

'It'll be my fault if she's dead.' As Sophie lay down, the tears slid down the side of her face and into her hair.

'Whatever the reason for the baby not moving, it isn't your fault.'

'When I found out I was pregnant I wished her away. I just wanted to wake up the next day and find out it wasn't true. I felt like that until you and Dan helped me tell Mum and Dad. It's only since then that I've let myself start loving her and now she's gone. I should have gone straight home to their place as soon as Dad found out, but I wanted to stay here so you'd still be my midwife.' Sophie's crying intensified and Ella had to try to calm her down so that she could listen for the baby's heartbeat.

'Okay, sweetheart, let's just find out what we're dealing with.' Ella picked up the gel as Sophie lifted up her top, squeezing a little of it onto her belly. The Doppler machine should pick up the heartbeat easily this late in the pregnancy.

'You can't find it, can you?' Sophie tried to sit up.

'I think the baby might have moved into an awkward spot, or it could be the position of the placenta. It's anterior, isn't it?'

'Yes, but it's always been like that, so how come I can't feel her?'

'The placenta grows along with the baby, so maybe its position is getting more significant now.' Ella held her breath as she slid the Doppler across Sophie's stomach, desperately searching for the sound both of them were longing to hear. The silence was deafening.

'She's dead, isn't she?' Sophie's face crumpled again, and she drew her legs up towards her until she was almost in a foetal position herself.

'The Doppler isn't a perfect tool, sweetheart. I think a scan will give a much clearer picture.' Ella was trying not to betray any emotion in her voice, but looking down at Sophie she was struggling. Then something amazing happened; the glorious whoosh, whoosh sound of the baby's heartbeat on the Doppler.

'Is that her?' Sophie's eyes widened, as Ella nodded. 'Oh my God, thank you!'

'The heartbeat sounds really strong, but now we've found out where she's hiding, I'd like to attach the foetal monitor to you for twenty minutes or so, just to make sure there's nothing else going on. I'm also going to request another scan for you, because I think she might be in the transverse position.'

'What does that mean?'

'It means she's lying crossways instead of head down.'

'But she's okay?' Fear was still flickering across Sophie's face.

'Everything sounds perfect.' Ella squeezed Sophie's shoulder. 'Do you want me to give your mum a call while you're attached to the monitor so she knows what's going on?'

'Yes, please. Her number is on my record as the next of kin. I think we might need you to referee anyway.'

'Has something changed at home then? I thought your parents were okay with everything?' Ella began attaching the monitor to Sophie's stomach as she spoke.

'No, Mum and Dad have been great since I told them, but they can't agree on whether I should tell Euan. At first Mum said she'd be okay with whatever I decided and Dad thought I should tell him, but then she admitted they've been rowing about it. It's another reason I still haven't moved back home, even though I know I should, and that it would probably be better for the baby too.'

'Do you know why your mum is worried about you telling Euan?'

'Mum's biological father was never around much when she was a kid. He kept flitting in and out of her life. And, when her stepdad came along, he disappeared altogether for a couple of years. Then he started coming back to the house again and causing trouble. She always says she wishes he hadn't bothered from the start and that it would have been easier. As far as Mum is concerned, unless Euan wants marriage and all that, me and the baby will be better off without him.'

'And how do you feel?' Ella suddenly felt incredibly naïve; she'd been protected by her parents' love and support her whole life. Jess would have known what to say, given that she'd been abandoned by her father too, but ultimately this had to be Sophie's decision.

'I don't know what to do, I just think if things were the other way around, I'd want to know.' Sophie looked up at her. 'What would you do?'

'I can't answer that, because I've never been in a position that's anything like yours. But you're the baby's mother and you have to do what you think is right for her.'

'I'm so glad I've got you as my midwife. I really want to have the baby at the unit, with you there to help me through it.'

'You're definitely set against a hospital delivery then?' Having a first baby in a midwifery unit carried some risk. Not to mention the fact that she was going to need her parents' support more than ever when the baby arrived, so going home to Somerset seemed like the best solution. There was no way of knowing whether Sophie would experience any difficulties or whether she'd be able to manage with the limited amount of pain relief they could administer at the unit, but she seemed determined to try. If the baby was in a transverse position, and she didn't turn before the birth, there was no way Sophie would be having her at the unit anyway. At thirty-five weeks it would be quite late for the baby to turn by herself. There were things they could try, but that was a problem for another day.

'I feel safe here.' Sophie closed her eyes.

'I'm really glad to hear it.' Ella lowered her voice. 'Okay, just keep doing what you're doing and I'll go and give your mum a call and let her know what's going on. The last thing your mum and dad need is to drive down here too fast, because they're in a panic. After that, I'll see if the hospital can fit you in for a scan today and your parents will be able to see the baby if they go in with you.'

'Oh my God, look at that!' Sophie's eyes flew open and she pointed down to her side. It was impossible to tell if it was a foot, the head, or something else pressing up against it, but the baby was suddenly doing everything she could do make her presence felt.

'That's fantastic. Maybe she was just having a lazy day.' Ella grinned.

'I still can't believe I'm managing to grow another human. I was sure I'd mess it all up.' Sophie's face lit up as she traced a hand over the side where the baby's movements had become so obvious.

'You're doing brilliantly and that's why I love this job; pregnancy and childbirth never stops being amazing.'

'Do you want kids of your own?'

'I really do.' Ella smiled again. It was way too early to know whether Dan would figure in that equation, but she could definitely picture him as a dad. When she'd thought about having children with Weller the first picture that had popped into her head was making Jago and Ruth grandparents, but now she could finally picture a family of her own. For a while coming home had felt like running away, and admitting that she'd failed in London, but it was getting harder and harder to imagine ever wanting to leave.

17

Ella had always loved autumn in Port Agnes. The sunsets came early and seemed all the more spectacular for it.

'Do you want to head back to my squat? If I light candles instead of turning on the lights, it almost has a rustic charm!' Dan had his arm around her waist and pulled her closer as they walked back down the narrowest part of the coastal path towards the harbour. Daisy was racing ahead, sniffing every tuft of grass as though her life depended on following whatever scent it was she'd picked up.

'How can anyone refuse an offer like that?' Ella would have been happy to go anywhere with Dan, even if he hadn't been massively exaggerating about the state of his cottage. All of the houses in Mercer's Row had undergone a sympathetic renovation and even though Dan's place had been left until last, it was really beginning to take shape. He'd painted the bedroom, where she and Dan had slept together for the very first time, in the exact same shade of primrose yellow she remembered it being. Maybe it had just been a coincidence, but she didn't think so and it meant a lot that the memories they'd made all those years ago were so significant to him too.

'I could rustle us up my famous pesto pasta? Not everyone can open a jar with the style and finesse I can!'

'Is there no end to Dan Ferguson's talents?' Stopping as they reached the kissing gate, where the narrowest part of the coastal path ended and the final descent into the town began, he pulled her closer towards him.

'I don't know, I was thinking maybe I need a bit more practice with kissing and it would be a shame not to do what the kissing gate tells us to.'

'Well, I wouldn't want to break any Port Agnes by-laws.' Ella leant into him. He'd never needed to improve his technique, even when they were sixteen, but she definitely wasn't going to turn him down. Their faces must have been less than an inch apart when her phone started to ring.

'I could just ignore it.' Ella murmured the words, her hand already almost unconsciously reaching for the phone.

'And you'd never forgive yourself if it was a call from one of your patients who needed you.'

'Thank you.' That was the thing about Dan, he understood what her job meant to her, without her ever having to explain it. Pulling away from him, she answered the call.

'Is that Ella Mehenick?'

'Speaking.'

'Oh, brilliant, this is Margo Kelly, I'm a features writer with the *Three Ports News*.'

'Okay.' Ella furrowed her brow, trying to work out why on earth anyone from the *Three Ports News* would want to speak to her.

'I don't know if you've seen the story in the tabloids about The Undermods celebrating their number one album with the bosses of their record label?'

'I can't say I have.' Ella was already contemplating cutting off the call.

'I don't know if this is going to be difficult for you to hear, but your ex-fiancé was pictured holding hands with his new partner, Ste Jenkins,' Margo cleared her throat, 'and the papers dragged up that video again, the one Jed Harris' fans posted.'

'Surely that's old news now?' Ella looked up at Dan, shaking her head.

'It was, but the journalist who wrote one of the tabloid articles ended by saying how awful Weller's jilted bride must feel about it all. And, being a local paper, we wanted to give you the right to reply.'

'I've got nothing to say.'

'Did you know he was gay?'

'That's nobody else's business.'

'Not even his ex-fiancée's?' Margo was like a dog with a bone. 'Have you forgiven him for what he did to you? It must have been so humiliating.'

'I'm not going to be commenting on my life or Weller's and I'm going to block your number now.' Ella didn't catch what Margo said next and a few button presses later, she'd ended the call and kept her promise to block her.

'What was all that about? Are you okay?' Dan took hold of her hand.

'It was just some woman from the local paper asking if I had any comment on Weller's new relationship. Apparently the success of his latest signing to the label has renewed interest in *the-wedding-that-never-was* and now they want to know how I feel about Weller being with Ste.'

'Some journalists are real vultures. When Mum and Dad died, a couple of photographers kept hanging around at the farm, trying to get pictures of me and Lissy looking suitably heartbroken. They even turned up to the funeral.'

'That must have been horrendous when you were already dealing with so much. How can anyone make their living off other people's misery?'

'It's more common than you'd think, sadly, but don't let it ruin our evening, El. You've still got the culinary delight of pesto pasta in my cosy little squat to look forward to!'

'And Weller thinks he's the one living a life of glamour, just because he produced a number one album!' Ella couldn't admit to how much the call had rattled her – not when Dan had been through far worse when he was still only a kid – even if she did hate the idea of the video becoming Port Agnes' number one topic of conversation again. She'd just have to suck it up and wait for the renewed interest to pass. After all, everything came to an end eventually.

* * *

'Tegen's getting so big.' Ella gently rocked the baby she'd help bring into the world. 'How's Noah enjoying being a big brother?'

'He mostly likes it.' Lissy smiled. 'But sometimes he'll give her a sneaky poke or a pinch when he thinks we're not looking. I think he enjoys days like today, when he's at nursery for a good few hours and he can run around causing havoc without being told to be quiet because of the baby.'

'I'd have loved a sibling, even if it had meant putting up with the occasional pinch.' Ella could remember begging her parents for a brother or sister when she'd still had no idea why it would never happen, and they must have felt awful. When she'd pictured having a family of her own, she'd imagined having at least three children, but with two of her friends facing up to the prospect of infertility, she wasn't taking anything for granted.

'I loved having Dan as a little brother. Although he could be annoying when he had his friends over, before Mum and Dad died. The boys would do all sorts of gross stuff like seeing who could burp the alphabet and giving each other wedgies!'

'Nice! And did he like your friends, or did he give them a hard time too?'

'I think having a big sister was quite handy on that front. Lots of older girls hanging around the place, but he didn't like any of my boyfriends until Niall. It was what convinced me he was a keeper, and I don't know what I'd do without Dan now. Losing Mum and Dad probably made us closer than most siblings.' Lissy grinned. 'Although I've definitely slipped down his list of favourite people a bit.'

'It's been lovely getting to know him again.'

'*Been* lovely?' Lissy raised an eyebrow.

'I just meant...' The truth was Ella wasn't sure what she meant. There were lots of good reasons for staying in Port Agnes and Dan was right at the top of that list, but she'd still spent an hour the day before scrolling through job adverts for Clinical Midwifery Consultants, which had originally been the planned next step in her career. Almost all of the vacancies were in London, where no one cared that she was the girl who got jilted and she'd be as anonymous as anyone else in the city. 'I just don't want to assume that things are going somewhere when they might not be. We're taking it day by day.'

'He talks about you all the time and that's not his usual style, believe me.' Lissy set a bowl of pasta on the table. 'Do you want me to take the baby back while we eat? I thought she might go down before lunch, but no such luck.'

'Midwives spend a lot less of their time cuddling babies than people think.' Ella had been at a home delivery until four in the morning and she could have done with a nap herself. 'So I'm more than happy to hold on to her and you can have a meal where you get to use your knife and fork at the same time for once!'

'No wonder Dan loves you!' Lissy clapped a hand over her mouth as soon as she'd said the words.

'He said that?'

'Oh God, please don't tell him I told you,' Lissy pulled a face, 'or I'll be the one getting a wedgie!'

'I won't say anything, I promise.' Ella couldn't help smiling, even as she tried to work out how she felt. She loved being with Dan, but she had no idea how she'd react if he told her that he loved her, or if she'd feel ready to say it back, even if she already knew it was true. It had been so easy to say when they'd been sixteen, but they'd still ended up breaking each other's hearts. Saying it now would be loaded with expectation about where they went from here and she still wasn't sure they wanted the same things. He might just have been making a throwaway comment anyway; the way Ella did when she talked about loving Cornish yarg, or that pair of suede boots in the window of Sole Mates on the high street.

'Never mind my brother. How's everything else going?' Lissy spooned some pasta onto her plate.

'I'm still loving work and being back in Port Agnes has mostly been great.'

'Mostly?'

Ella had been about to answer, when the sound of the letter box rattling made Lissy's dog bark and the baby flinched in Ella's arms, screwing up her little face for a second before relaxing back towards the edge of sleep.

'Sorry, I'll just check what that is. We're expecting a letter from the council about the change of use we've applied for. Niall has got this bright idea about us getting a few shepherd's huts, so we can both be at the farm full-time if it takes off.' Lissy sighed. 'But in the meantime, it'll just be a lot more work for me. And Dan when he can make the time. It feels a real cheek asking him, but he says he'll be more than willing to do it, if it means I eventually get Niall back here for good.'

Lissy disappeared to pick up the post, as Ella rocked the baby gently; fighting the urge to yawn herself.

'There's nothing from the council, but I'm not sure whether to be disappointed or relieved! It wasn't even the post, just the local paper.' Lissy dropped a copy of the *Three Ports News* on the table and Ella couldn't help looking at the front page just to check that Margo Kelly hadn't come up with some crazy article to resurrect the video. 'But what about you? Have you finally got around to signing your permanent contract at the unit yet?'

'I'll do it by the end of the week.'

'What's holding you back? Something obviously is and I've got a feeling it's the same something that's holding you back from committing to Dan too.' Lissy gave her a knowing look. 'Things are different than they were ten years ago and if you really wanted him to, he'd go anywhere to be with you. You love him too, don't you?'

Ella attempted a shrug. If she said it, then it changed everything. The battle between her head and her heart would be over for good and she just didn't know if she was ready to admit the truth. 'I don't know how he feels.'

'Well I do and all you'd have to do is ask him. Not that you need to, it's written all over his face every time he looks in your direction. And when I watch you with him, I can't believe you don't feel the same way.'

'I do, I always have.' Ella couldn't pretend it was uncertainty about Dan that was holding her back any more, not even to herself. Her heart had won. 'It's just that Mum and Dad paid for me to go to uni in London so that I'd get to do my training in the hospitals there and I'd be able to have the sort of career that would make all that expense worthwhile.'

'Don't you think they just want you to be happy and do whatever it is *you* want to do?'

'I do.' Ella nodded. If only it was that simple. The trouble was she never quite pinned down what it was she wanted, because she was always aiming to achieve the next thing. But maybe Port Agnes would turn out to be what she'd been looking for all along.

* * *

It was starting to get much cooler on Ella's evening walks with Daisy. The windows of some of the shops in the high street had Halloween themed displays and there was a huge loaf in the shape of a witch's hat in the Mehenick's bakery window. It would be strange to spend the run up to Christmas in Port Agnes this year and be able to go to the candlelit Christmas Eve service at St Judes. After she'd had lunch with Lissy, Ella had finally signed the contract that Anna had given her and all she needed to do was drop it into the unit when she was next at work and it would be official – Ella Mehenick was home for good. Whatever it was she'd been looking for all these years didn't mean anything compared to being surrounded by her family and friends, including Dan. There was a wooden sign hanging in the window of Paper and Pottery as she walked past, emblazoned with an oft-used slogan: *Home is Where the Heart is*. It might not have been the most inspirational of quotes, but that didn't make it any less true.

Looping back around the harbour, Ella had to break into a jog to keep up with Daisy. It was past the little dog's dinner time and she was clearly in a hurry to get home.

'All right, girl, I won't keep you waiting any longer.' Ella almost tripped over as Daisy shot between her legs and into the kitchen when she opened the back door of her parents' house. Daisy's food was usually stacked up in individual trays in the larder, but it seemed to have almost run out. She was on her hands and knees reaching to the back of the bottom shelf, when she heard her mother's voice. Ruth was talking to someone, but it took Ella a moment or two to realise it wasn't her father.

'If anyone can persuade him to sell up, it's you, Ruthie.'

'I've tried. We used up all our savings buying our share of The Old Forge, but I didn't realise until the final demands started coming in that Jago had maxed out the overdraft and all our credit cards too. If we don't sell soon we could be in real trouble.'

'Michael Tredinnick has made an offer on the land where I graze half my cattle. If his offer's accepted, and we still refused to sell him The Old Forge, I can kiss goodbye to my business because he'll never agree to continue renting the land to me. There's no way I'll be able to rent another parcel of land like that so close to my farm.'

'I'm sorry, Clem, I wish I could help.' Ruth sounded desperate and Ella was frightened to move in case she knocked a can off the shelf and her mother realised she was in the walk-in larder listening to everything that was going on. Ruth was admitting things to Clem that she'd probably never told Jago and that she certainly hadn't shared with her daughter.

'Why is he so dead set against Michael buying the place? I mean I know he's never liked the man, right since we were back at school. None of us have. But we made a bad investment, the place might have to be demolished, and Michael's the only one who can get us out of it. Sometimes you just have to swallow your pride.'

'I think Jago could have got past all the other stuff, even seeing The Old Forge turned into a block of apartments, if Michael hadn't said those things about Ella.' Ruth gave a shuddering sigh. 'Now she's come back home, he couldn't look her in the face every day knowing she was watching the man who'd revelled in

248 JO BARTLETT

her heartbreak build up the apartment block brick by brick on land that Jago had sold him.'

'So what you're saying, Ruthie, is we can't sell the apartment block to Michael all the time Ella's here? Even if that sends all of us bankrupt.'

'I know it seems crazy, Clem, but Jago's a proud man. You know that better than anyone.'

'Pride won't pay the bills, though, will it?' The words coming out of Clem's mouth sounded as if Michael Tredinnick had put them there himself. Either way, he was right and Ella wasn't going to let anyone lose their business because of her.

18

Ella was trying to sleep. One of the other midwives, who usually worked nights, had been on sick leave for weeks and another long night shift attending a home birth meant Ella hadn't got in until almost six o'clock in the morning. The harbour had already started to come alive by then, with boats being unloaded in the darkness of the quayside. Rain was battering against the window by the time she got upstairs to her bedroom. Plenty of people paid good money to download apps with a similar soundtrack to help them get to sleep, but it wasn't working for Ella. She had too much on her mind.

'Morning, my love, I didn't expect to see you up so early.' Ella's father smiled as she walked into the kitchen just an hour and a half after she'd crept in through the back door after her shift, having already given up trying to sleep. 'I heard you come home while I was putting pasties in the bakery oven. I wouldn't give up midwifery to take up cat burglary if I were you; the quieter you try to be the louder you are! It's like the old days, when you tried to sneak in after a party.'

'I just wish I had the energy for a party these days.' Ella folded herself into her father's arms, as he hugged her close to him. The aroma of baking clung to his clothes: the smell of home. If she went back to London and put enough distance between them to let him sell The Old Forge to Michael Tredinnick without feeling like he'd let her down, she'd really miss all of this. But if she didn't leave, and her father refused to sell The Old Forge, they could lose everything anyway.

'Why aren't you resting now then, my Ysella?'

'My mind won't seem to switch off.' Ella's voice was muffled against his chest and Jago stepped back to look at her.

'You need to start looking after yourself. You look exhausted and you're getting far too skinny.'

'I'm eleven stone, Dad. I'm hardly about to waste away! And I'm tired because I've been doing a run of nights that I'm not used to, and I can't sleep properly in the day. I'm okay, I promise.' She wasn't going to give her father anything else to worry about. He had more than enough on his plate already.

'Me and your mum are here for you whenever you need us, you know that, don't you?' Jago gave her a serious look and she nodded. 'It's good to know you've got someone like Dan on your side too.'

'I thought he was just another emmet?' Ella laughed and her father shook his head.

'He might have been at first, but anyone who works as hard as he has to preserve a piece of Cornish history has earned the right to be called a local. And if he can work that hard to protect an old building, I know he'll do the same for my daughter.'

'I don't need a knight in shining armour, Dad!'

'I know you're a modern woman, but I'm still your dad and I'm allowed to be protective, aren't I?'

'I couldn't stop you being protective if I wanted to.' Ella laid her head on his chest again. As much as she might protest, she was incredibly grateful for her parents' unconditional support. 'But I wish you'd look out for yourself too, especially after what the doctor said about your blood pressure. I know you don't like Michael Tredinnick any more than I do, but I really think selling to him might be the best solution.'

'You'll bury me before I'd agree to sell to that bastard. There's no way any daughter of mine is going to walk around her home town and see a man who insulted her benefit from a deal with her father. I'd rather eat my own head.'

'That's a bit drastic, Dad!'

'Something will turn up anyway. Dan's working on it, he reckons he knows someone who might take it on, even if it ends up needing a complete rebuild.'

'That's great news!' Some of the tension left Ella's spine knowing that Dan was on the case. If anyone could find a solution it was him and the fact that he wanted to help her father after the difficult time he'd given Dan over the years, made her love him all the more. He was selfless, just like he always had been, even when he'd made the decision not to follow her to London. Her father seemed to have forgotten all about his grudge against emmets, too, now that Port Agnes had an enemy within. She didn't care who ended up buying The Old Forge, as long as it got her father, Clem, and Jack out of trouble. She'd never be able to live with the guilt otherwise.

'He's a good sort, that one, and I'll not hear anyone say otherwise. But if I don't get back to work soon, I'll have nothing to serve my customers and I'm already late opening up for the early birds wanting breakfast.' Jago kissed the top of her head. 'Now you go back to bed and get some sleep. Do as your old dad says for once.'

'I'll give it a try.'

'Look what Dan left on the doorstep for you!' Ruth came

through the back door with Daisy's lead in one hand and a huge bouquet of flowers in the other, just as Jago went back into the bakery and Ella was filling the kettle.

'Is there a message?' Taking the flowers from her mother, she pulled out the small white card from the middle of the bouquet.

'London's calling. Answer the call and it might not be such a long fall from your high horse.'

The flowers weren't from Dan and Ella shivered as she read the message again. It might not say who'd sent them, but she knew it was Michael, even if she'd never be able to prove it. Sophie had been cowering in the cottage by the time Ella's row with Michael had reached its peak, so it had only been the two of them who'd witnessed it all.

'What's wrong, my love? You look deathly pale. Was something written on the card?' Her mother's voice was filled with concern, but there was nothing she could do to help and there was no point burdening her with the problem.

'I just feel exhausted all of a sudden, that's all.' Ella dropped the flowers in the sink and stuffed the card into the pocket of her dressing gown. 'I'm going to go up again and try to get some sleep.'

'Okay, love. I'll make you some lunch when you come back down. But try and sleep for as long as you can, you look as if you need it.'

'Thanks, Mum.' Ella gave her a hug, wondering if her mother could feel the hammering of her heart.

Setting the phone down on the bedside table when she got back upstairs, Ella almost fell off the edge of the bed a split second later, as a loud crash thundered through the house. It sounded like it had come from the ground floor. Running down the stairs two at a time she went straight into the kitchen. There was nothing there, but she could hear raised voices coming from the bakery. Forgetting that she was still in her pyjamas and with bare feet, she ran straight through, terrified that Jago's blood pressure had finally got the better of him and sent him crashing to the ground. Relief flooded through her body when she saw him standing in the bakery, despite the fact that there was glass everywhere and a huge hole in the shop window.

'I'm telling you, when that brick came through the window, it missed my head by about half an inch.' A woman, who looked to be in her late sixties was holding on to the arm of a much younger woman to steady herself and there was glass all over the floor.

'There's a nutter on the loose in Port Agnes, no question about it!' Another woman in the queue behind her seemed quite excited by the prospect.

'The good news is no one was hurt.' Ella's father locked eyes with her, he must have suspected exactly what Ella did – Michael Tredinnick was behind it.

'You must have served someone a very bad pasty, Jago, if it's come to this.' The older woman cackled with laughter, but Ella wasn't laughing and her mother looked close to tears. Michael Tredinnick might have started all of this to get back at her father for refusing to sell The Old Forge, but Ella had made things ten times worse by standing up to him after he'd threatened Sophie. The message on his flowers made that clear. If Ella left, that might be enough of a victory for Michael to ease off on the rest, even if her mother and Clem still couldn't persuade Jago to sell The Old Forge to him. She didn't really have a choice. The only question was whether Dan would agree to come with her this time. The thought that he might not made her feel physically sick. It was bad enough that she'd be leaving her friends at the unit and her parents behind, but at least she could take comfort in the fact that she was doing it for her parents' sake. The thought of losing Dan again was like the ground shifting beneath her feet, but asking him to leave would be huge. He had a family he loved every bit as much as she loved her parents, but if she and Dan were going to stay together, one of them was going to have to hurt the people who meant the world to them.

* * *

There were always some patients who Ella developed a closer relationship with than others, and Sophie was definitely one of them. She wanted to tell the younger woman in person that she'd be leaving before the baby arrived, but when Sophie opened the front door, she was wearing a long winter coat with a rucksack on her back, looking like she had somewhere else to be.

'Hi Ella, do you want to come in?'

'No, I just wanted to catch you for a quick chat, but it looks like you're heading off somewhere?'

'I'm going to Truro. I thought about what you said. You know, doing what I think's best for the baby, and I want her to have the chance to know her dad. So I rang Euan and broke the news.'

'How did he take it?'

'Really well, actually, and he told me he missed me.' Sophie blushed. 'He was a bit apprehensive about telling his parents, but they took it better than expected. That's where I'm going now. The three of them have come down for a week or so and they're staying in a hotel in Truro. I'm going to meet them for breakfast and then we're all going to spend the day together so we can get to know each other. We thought it would be best to meet somewhere nearby, with the baby's due date coming up.'

'That's great news!'

'I don't know how it will turn out, but whatever happens, at least I won't have to lie to the baby when she's old enough to understand. I can tell her who her father and his family are, and if they want to have a relationship with her then that's great. If it turns out they don't, I'll just have to do my best to protect her from that. Either way, everything will be out in the open and I won't have to keep looking over my shoulder wondering when the secret is going to come out. I talked it through with Mum first and she realised you were right, we both did. You can't run away from your problems; you've got to face up to them.'

'Did I really say all that?' Ella went hot. She seemed to be making a habit of offering up excellent advice lately, that she couldn't take herself.

'In a roundabout way. You just made me realise that the baby's the most important thing in all of this.' Sophie ran a hand over her bump. 'Are you sure you don't want to come in, I could text Euan and tell him I'm going to be a bit late.'

'No, I just wanted to pop by and let you know that I'm going back to London for a little while to see some old friends.' Ella hated lying, but Sophie was so happy and she didn't want to be the one to rain on her parade. Sophie might be upset for a bit when she realised Ella wouldn't be around for the baby's birth, but she'd get over it and any of the other midwives would do just as good a job. It might even help persuade her to go back to Somerset in time for the birth.

'Just don't stay up there too long, will you? I need you back here for when the baby comes, you're the only midwife I want with me when she decides to put in an appearance.'

'Has everything been okay since your monitoring visit?' Changing the subject was the only way Ella could avoid making Sophie any promises she couldn't keep.

'Yes, she's back to doing somersaults all night long and then kicking me in the bladder just as I'm finally about to drop off to sleep. At my last scan she'd moved back into a head down position. Thank goodness!'

'Ah, the joys of motherhood!' For the first time since she'd made the decision to leave, Ella managed to smile. But she wasn't going to be able to chicken out of telling everyone she was leaving and she still had no idea whether or not she'd be going back to London alone.

19

Ella heard the laughter as she walked along the corridor from the unit's reception.

'You're really going camping in this weather? Have you got a death wish?' Toni was talking to Jess as Ella walked into the staffroom.

'Dom's got this idea into his head that if we camp on the Cerne Abbas Giant, I might finally get pregnant.' Jess didn't look a lot more convinced than Toni. The Cerne Abbas Giant was a huge chalk figure etched into a grassy hill in Dorset and it was a well-known symbol of fertility. 'Apparently if you sleep on the hill where the giant is, you're almost guaranteed to get pregnant!'

'Presumably there has to be some sex involved?' Frankie raised an eyebrow.

'You know what they say?' Gwen was already laughing again. 'If the tent's rocking, don't come a knocking!'

'Dom must be pretty confident, have you seen the size of the giant's bits and pieces?' Anna grinned.

'It's enough to make your eyes water!' Gwen was definitely on form, but all Ella could think about was that this might be the last time she was with them all. She was supposed to be handing her contract in today, but instead she was going to have to try and find the right moment to tell the other midwives that she wouldn't be staying after all.

In the end, it was late morning before she worked up the courage.

'Are you okay, Ella? You haven't seemed yourself all day.' Anna put a hand on her arm, as Ella shook her head.

'I'm really sorry, but I've decided to go back to London.'

'You can't!' Anna widened her eyes. 'I thought you loved it here and the patients and the staff love you too.'

'Oh Anna, I just feel like I'm letting Mum and Dad down. They sacrificed so much so that I could live in London and if I stay here, I might as well have gone to uni in Plymouth in the first place and saved them tens of thousands of pounds.' She couldn't risk telling Anna about Michael Tredinnick. If it got back to Jago that it was part of the reason she was leaving, it would only make things worse. And the truth was there was more to it than that because Michael had been right about one thing; if she stayed in Port Agnes she was always going to feel like a failure and she'd never achieve whatever it was that would make her feel she was enough.

'Have you asked your parents how they feel? I've seen what they're like when they're with you and I honestly can't believe they'd rather you went back to London.'

'They're struggling financially and if I can earn more money I'll be able to help them out.' It was as close as she was going to come to telling anyone other than Dan just how deeply in debt her parents were. And if Michael didn't ease up on his campaign against them, even after Ella left, she might need every extra penny she could get her hands on.

'And what about Dan, are you going to walk away from him

too? He'll want to go with you if you insist on going, I know he will.'

'I'm going to ask him to come. There's no guarantee he'll want to, but it's a chance I'll have to take.' Ella dug her fingernails into the palm of her hands. Lissy had seemed so certain he'd be willing to follow Ella this time, but he had a whole life in Port Agnes and she could hardly blame him if he said no, even if the thought made her eyes sting.

'I can't believe you really want to leave.' Anna's eyes had gone glassy too. 'Finding Brae and having you and Dan to hang out with has made me happier than I can ever remember being. You know you're breaking up the band?'

'Please don't hate me.'

'I could never hate you. I'm just so sad I won't be working with you any more and I'm going to miss you so much.'

'Me too.' The lump in Ella's throat, that had been threatening to choke her, was making it difficult to speak. 'I'll call you when I'm settled back in London and you and Brae can come up whenever you want.'

'Brae is going to miss hanging out with Dan almost as much as I'm going to miss you.' Anna squeezed her hand and all Ella could do was nod. There was a very strong possibility that Brae wouldn't even get the chance to miss Dan and that she'd be the one left missing all three of them instead.

* * *

Dan was carrying lengths of wood into the end cottage on Mercer's Row when Ella went down to see him after work. Part of her had wanted to put if off for a bit longer, but she couldn't risk Anna telling Brae about her decision to leave and it getting back to Dan before she'd had the chance to tell him herself.

'Hello beautiful, I wasn't expecting to see you until later.' Dan turned towards her once he'd put down the wood, after she followed him into the house.

'I know, but I wanted to talk to you.'

'That sounds ominous.' He smiled, but when she didn't mirror his reaction, he frowned instead. 'What's up, Ella? Is it Michael Tredinnick again?'

'He sent me some flowers.'

'I take it they weren't intended as a peace offering?' Dan took hold of her hand, but she struggled to look him in the eyes.

'He more or less said if I leave town, he'll leave Dad alone.'

'And you believe him?' Dan's tone was tight. 'You can't let someone like that dictate your life.'

'He's already put a brick through the bakery window, so I'm worried about what else he might do if I don't.'

'El, why would you leaving town make a difference to Tredinnick anyway?'

'Because I called him out about the way he was treating his staff and because he knows how much mum and dad will miss me if I leave.'

'What about you, won't *you* miss people if you go?'

'Of course, but it doesn't have to be forever... I just need long enough to put all of the rubbish that's gone on this year behind me.'

'And what if I found a buyer for The Old Forge? Someone who'd take it on, even if it does have to be demolished?' Dan kissed her gently on the forehead. 'I know you're worried sick about your parents, El, but I'm so close to getting them a deal. You just have to hold on for a little bit longer and it'll all get sorted, I promise.'

'I don't think I can, Dan, but you could come with me and we could finally have the life in London that we always planned.' Ella's breathing had sped up, but the panic had nothing to do with what Michael Tredinnick might do next. If Dan sorted out the problem with The Old Forge, then she'd have no reason to leave Port Agnes. No reason except for the absolute terror of what staying put might mean. 'You wouldn't have to come with me straight away, I know you've got things to sort out here, but with Niall coming home for good, Lissy won't need you so much and you could finally do more with your art.'

'I love you, Ella, but I don't want to come to London.'

'It doesn't have to be London. I was thinking about applying to one of the universities, maybe even Plymouth, and qualifying to be a lecturer in midwifery. That way we wouldn't be far from Lissy and the children. This isn't like it was when we were eighteen, I know it's not as simple as just upping and leaving.'

'Ella, I've got a business here that I've spent more than a decade building up.' Dan brushed a strand of hair away from her face. 'I know it's been hard coming home and having all the worry about your parents, but we just need to get to the other side of that and you'll wonder why you ever felt so desperate to escape. Even if I wanted to leave Port Agnes, I couldn't just lift the business up and start again elsewhere.'

'Why not? They have properties that need renovating everywhere. Plymouth isn't even that far away and you might still be able to use some of your local contacts.' Ella already felt like she was flogging a dead horse, but Dan hadn't let go of her hand. So there was still a tiny chance he might change his mind.

'And that's what you really want is it, to teach midwifery?' He paused and she finally had to look up at him. 'Is that what you want to do if you go to London?'

'I've applied for a few consultant midwife jobs up there.'

'So *what is it* you want, El?' Dan suddenly sounder exhausted and he'd furrowed his brow as if he was struggling to understand what she was saying. The trouble was, he wasn't the only one who wasn't sure exactly what she meant.

'I don't know. I just feel like I need to do more, *to be more*, than this.'

'And when's that going to change? When is enough ever going to be enough?' Dan sighed. 'If I thought going back to London, or qualifying as a lecturer, would really make you happy, I'd support you all the way.'

'But you wouldn't come with me, would you? I'm still not enough to make you leave Port Agnes.' Tears were clouding her eyes now and Dan was shaking his head.

'It's not that and you know it, but I can't spend my life doing this, El. Searching for something we're never going to find.' He finally let go of her hand. 'I went through all of that with Dad, we all did. He gave up his job as a stockbroker because he wanted to teach, and then after he became a headteacher he decided he wanted to run a smallholding in Cornwall. When that didn't fulfil him in the way he thought it would either, he decided he wanted to train to be a pilot and run a private charter. He wanted us to up sticks and move to the highlands so he could operate flights out to the islands. He spent every penny we had on the plane that he and Mum ended up dying in. It was why we struggled so much with the farm afterwards, even their life insurance didn't cover the debt.'

'This is nothing like that.' Even as Ella protested, she had a horrible feeling Dan knew her better than she knew herself. But if she admitted it, she'd have to stop striving for the next thing and the thing after that, and she had no idea who that version of her would be.

'It feels the same to me, Ella. Mum spent her whole life following Dad from dream to dream and she ended up paying for it with her life, because every time he got what he supposedly wanted, it turned out not to be what he wanted at all. I'd do anything to make you happy, Ella, but until you work out what that is, you can't ask me to give up everything else.'

'If I don't do something more with my life, I'll be letting Mum and Dad down.'

'Stop making that your excuse for not working out what it is *you* want.' There was a muscle going in Dan's cheek now. 'You've spent your whole life trying to live up to impossible expectations, but the only one who has them for you is you. Do you really think your mum and dad fought so hard to have a child just so they could boast about the job you do, or how much you earn? They love you for *who* you are, Ella, not *what* you are, and so do I. But none of that matters if you don't feel the same way about yourself.'

'I can't do this, I can't stay here.' He didn't understand, no one did. Her parents might not care if she failed, but she couldn't let them down. She had to make up for all the other children they'd tried so hard to have – she'd forgotten how to do anything else – even if that meant saying goodbye to Dan.

'Just stay and talk to me. We can work this out. I'll call my friend and see if he's ready to move forward with The Old Forge.' He tried to take hold of her hand again, but she pulled away.

'If you won't come with me, then we're back where we were when we were eighteen years old.'

'El, don't do this.'

'It's too late.' Turning away from him, she ran out of the cottage before she could hear what he said next. She was terrified he might be right and that she was never going to be able to stop striving for the thing that would finally convince her she was worth something. She didn't want to be that person, but she had no idea how to be anything else.

Dan was still calling her name and, when she looked over her shoulder, he was running after her. She had to get back to the bakery before he caught up with her and made her admit he was right. It was easier to keep running, just like it always had been. Darting into the road without looking, she only caught sight of the white transit van in the split second before it hit her. It was one thing she couldn't outrun and, as the first wave of pain engulfed her, everything went black.

20

If this was heaven, Ella was going to complain to the advertising standards agency. It smelt of school dinners and the clouds weren't anywhere nearly as fluffy as she'd expected them to be. She tried to open her eyes, but it felt as if they'd been glued together and she had the worst headache in history. Worse even than when she was sixteen and she'd got so drunk at a friend's birthday party – on the illicit vodka someone had smuggled in – that she'd woken up in the garden shed. She'd had her head wedged between a lawnmower and a folding deckchair. And, Amy, her best friend from school, was curled up next to the strimmer. It had been enough to put her off vodka for life, but the pain she had in her head now made that feel like nothing.

An involuntary whimper escaped from her lips as Ella tried to open her eyes again.

'Ella, can you hear me?' For a moment or two the face of the person leaning over her swam in front of her eyes, as she finally managed to prise them open. Whoever it was, they were just a series of blurry shapes. 'It's me, Anna.'

'Anna?' The name came out as a croak.

'Oh, thank God. I'm so glad you're okay! I can't believe your mum and dad missed it, they've been here for the best part of two days waiting for you to wake up properly.'

'Are they okay?' It was still difficult to get the words out and Ella couldn't tell if she was slurring or not.

'They're fine, at least they will be now. I literally had to force them to go and get a cup of coffee while I sat with you. They'll be over the moon that you're back with us.' Anna squeezed her hand and it took all the energy Ella had to return the gesture.

'What happened?'

'You got hit by a transit van that was coming out of the fish market. Luckily it hadn't had a chance to pick up much speed. Otherwise...'

'I could be dead?'

'There's a chance.' Anna squeezed her hand again. 'But Dan was there and he dragged you out of the road, just in time to stop another car coming in the other direction from hitting you too.'

'Did it hit him?' Nausea rose in her throat; if Dan had been injured it would all be her fault.

'He got you both out of the way in time, but he was terrified that your injuries might be worse because he'd moved you.'

'Where is he?' Every word was an effort and Ella didn't have any energy to spare. It was hard enough trying to process the information Anna had already given her.

'I don't know. He stayed here the whole of the first night, in the waiting room, until the doctors were sure you were going to be okay, but I haven't been able to get hold of him since. Brae drove up to Six Acre Farm in case he was up there, because Lissy hadn't seen him either.'

'I need to speak to him, if it's not too late, and tell him he was right.' Ella forced the words out, but she wasn't sure if Anna even heard over the sound of the door to her room being flung open.

'Oh Ysella, you're okay!' Jago crossed the room in two huge

strides and kissed Ella's forehead more gently than she could ever remember, with Ruth just behind him.

'I'm so sorry. I love you both so much...' Ella's throat was burning with emotion. She'd nearly left them forever, without even having the chance to say goodbye. She knew for certain now that she couldn't leave, no matter what the cost. She had to find another way.

'Oh darling, we love you so much, too.' Ruth moved to her other side, next to Anna. But when Ella tried to turn her head it made her wince. 'Don't move, my love, you've got severe concussion and you need to take it really slowly.'

'Will I get better?' Ella could wiggle her fingers and toes, which had to be a good sign. But she was starting to wonder if she'd ever be able to string more than a few words together.

'You will, darling, but you can't rush things.' Her mother stroked her hand and Ella closed her eyes again. She had a million questions, but she couldn't find the words to ask any of them. All she wanted was to see Dan and tell him she finally understood what he'd been saying, but her eyes just wouldn't stay open.

It was four more days before Ella even began to feel like she was getting back to normal. The hospital had finally said she could leave, but she had to take it easy and get lots of rest. When she got home, her mother had turned into the matron from a nineteen fifties hospital drama. She was as strict about lights out time as she was about Ella finishing every mouthful of the chicken soup she'd made. There were enough flowers in her bedroom to give the average high street florist a run for their money. There was a bouquet from the team at work, a separate one from Anna and Brae, roses from Lissy, a huge orchid from Weller and Ste, which looked capable of swallowing a small dog whole, and a bright red poinsettia from Sophie.

One person who hadn't added to the floral collection, or the deluge of get well cards and texts, was Dan. She could hardly blame him. She tried to make him choose between her and his family twice over, and the truth was she hadn't wanted to leave Port Agnes any more than he had. It had taken a near-death experience to make her realise it, but everything she'd ever wanted was here.

'What do you fancy for your dinner tonight?' Ella's mother straightened her covers and tucked the duvet into the mattress so tightly she was going to need the skills of Houdini to escape.

'Am I allowed to come downstairs?'

'I think you should rest up here for one more day.' Ruth's tone didn't offer scope for argument.

'I suppose I should. Seeing as Dad almost gave himself a hernia carrying that thing up the stairs.' Ella gestured towards the Hitachi TV, which was about a foot deep with a metal coat hanger replacing the original aerial. Her parents didn't seem to realise that she could stream Netflix on her phone, but they meant well and she appreciated that more than ever.

'How about my famous chicken kebabs?' Her mother smiled. It was a step up from chicken soup. Ruth clearly thought she was getting a bit better if she was finally being allowed solid food. As far as Ella knew she hadn't loosened any teeth in the accident, but her mum was clearly erring on the side of caution.

'That sounds great, Mum, and thank you.'

'For what?'

'Everything.' Ella looked up at her mother. 'You're not disappointed in me, are you?'

'Why on earth would you say that?' Ruth sat on the edge of her bed, smoothing Ella's hair away from her forehead like she had whenever Ella had been unwell as a child.

'Because I messed everything up. I made things worse for Dad with The Old Forge, by rowing with Michael Tredinnick. I handed my notice in at the unit and told Dan I was leaving when I didn't really want to leave at all. I know I should be making the most of the opportunities I've got when you never got the chance, and after you and Dad sacrificed so much to give me the chances you never had. You worked yourselves into the ground to do it and Dad's blood pressure went through the roof. I feel like all I've given you in return is more worry.'

'Oh darling, your dad's blood pressure has got far more to do with a short temper and a passion for pasties, which he's got an endless supply of, than anything else. Least of all you. Having you and watching you grow into the amazing young woman you are was the best thing we've ever done. You don't know how many times over the years me and your dad wanted you to come home, but we promised each other we'd try not to show just how desperate we were to have you back in Port Agnes and maybe we ended up doing too good job of it.'

'I just wanted to make you proud and now I haven't even got a job.'

'You've only ever made us proud, my love, and Anna's already said she didn't know how to even begin trying to replace you. So the job's there if you want it.'

'I do. I really do.'

'That's honestly the best news I've had in a long time, my love. Just promise me you're not going to try and get up and start rushing about before you're ready. You gave us quite a scare!'

'I'm not going anywhere, and not just because you've tucked this bed in so tightly that I'm losing the feeling in my legs.' Ella grinned. 'I really am glad I came home, Mum.'

'Not as glad as I am, darling.' Ruth blew her a kiss as she got to the door. 'I'll bring the kebabs up in about half an hour, try to get some rest.'

Ella nodded, but her brain wasn't playing ball. Every time she shut her eyes her mind started churning things over. She might have one less worry now that she knew she still had a job to go to, but even her mum hadn't been able to reassure her that Michael Tredinnick might not still do his worst. As for Dan, there was still no word from him and she had to stop herself from trying to contact him again. She'd already left a text, a WhatsApp and a voicemail with no response, and she didn't want to become one of those stalking stories for Lissy to tell the next girlfriend. She'd blown things with Dan for a second time and some things just couldn't be fixed.

* * *

With sleep continuing to elude Ella, she put on yet another episode of *Friends*. She was halfway through rewatching the entire ten seasons on Netflix already and she'd only been home two days. It was like a comfort blanket. If that – and Ruth Mehenick's famous chicken kebabs – didn't make everything right in the world, then nothing would.

One of the good things about watching a programme you'd watched so many times before was that it didn't require too much concentration, which almost inevitably meant that Ella would be scrolling through her phone at the same time.

Hey you!
I'm so glad you're on the mend. I didn't think your Mum and Dad would ever talk to me again, but they've been really good sending me updates on your progress and Ste sends his love too. We wanted you to be one of the first to know that we've got engaged!!! Thank God things are getting better with Mum and Dad all the time, but I'm still not sure they'd have been up for a wedding and I didn't want it to be

too much like last time. So we're looking at a secluded beach, where
we can do the whole thing in our budgie smugglers!

I'm so happy and I want you to be happy too, Ella, no one deserves it
more. You can do it, if you just stop trying so bloody hard! I've found
my Prince Charming and you will too.

Love always, Weller and Ste xxxx

Ella wasn't sure how she was supposed to feel about the fact that
her ex-fiancé was now engaged to someone else, but by the time
she'd reached the end of the email, she'd realised she was smiling.
She and Weller had spent years together, both of them pretending
to be someone they weren't. It had taken far more bravery for Weller
to admit the truth, but it was Ella who'd needed to be hit by a van to
knock some sense into her. It shouldn't have taken a near-death
experience to make her realise what was really important, but even
slow learners like her could catch up in the end.

Half an hour later, she was still half-watching Friends and the
last thing she'd expected was a knock on the bedroom door;
usually her parents just barged in. The memory of being caught
by her dad when she was seventeen – kissing Dan, as they both
lay fully clothed on the bed – still made her skin prickle. Her
father had chased Dan halfway to the Port Kara road and it had
been the last time he'd been allowed to cross the threshold, at
least until very recently. So why her mum had suddenly taken to
knocking on the door was a mystery.

'Come in.'

'Your order, madam.' Dan stood in the doorway holding a tray,
with a tea towel over one arm, doing his best impression of a
room service waiter and, for a moment or two, Ella lost the ability
to speak. Even when she did, her voice came out with a strangely
high pitch.

'What are you doing here?'

'That wasn't quite the welcome I was hoping for.' Dan grinned. 'Can I put this tray somewhere before your dinner ends up on the floor? There's a reason I was sacked from Pizza Express, TGI Friday's and Zizzi when we were in sixth form. No wonder I ended up in the building trade, I was born to knock walls down.'

'Over there is fine, thanks.' Ella pulled herself up on the pillows, trying to smooth out her hair while Dan had his back to her. He was in her room acting like nothing had happened, but the last time he'd seen her, he was giving her every painful home truth she hadn't been ready to hear.

'I've been wanting to come and see you, but when you were first at the hospital it was family only and Anna only got in because she pretended to be your sister. And then...' Dan turned to look at her. 'And then I didn't know if you'd even want to see me, Ella. I'm so sorry.'

'What for? From what everyone told me, I might not even be here if it wasn't for you.'

'You wouldn't have ended up running in front of that van in the first place if I hadn't said all those things to you.' Dan moved towards her and sat on the end of the bed, forcing Ella to clamp her hands down by her sides.

'Everything you said was true.'

'It wasn't, it was just after everything that happened with my Dad—' Ella cut him off before he could try to apologise again. He needed to know he had nothing to be sorry for.

'You were right. I've spent my whole life trying to be perfect. Ever since I was eight and I found the memory box Mum had kept from her fertility treatment and she told me how many times they'd tried to have a baby and how special I was.' Ella pulled a face. 'But I never felt special enough and they deserved the best. So I tried hard at school and I chose a career that I knew would make them proud and then I tried even harder at that. But I forgot to do the one thing they wanted me to do, the only thing they really wanted for me, and that was to be happy.' Unclamping her arm from her side, she finally reached out a hand towards him. 'I was always happiest when I was in Port Agnes with you.'

'The moment I saw that van coming towards you and I knew I wasn't going to be able to get to you in time to stop it, I realised that nothing else mattered and I swore to God if you made it through I'd do whatever it took to never let you go again.' Dan traced a finger across the palm of her hand. 'I've spent the last few days making plans so that if you still wanted to leave Port Agnes I'd be ready to come with you. I can get sub-contractors to finish the Mercer's Row project and I've organised extra cover at the farm in case Lissy and Niall need it. I even had a follow-up from a call I made to the ACAS helpline to say a certain caravan park might not be treating its employees properly.'

'You didn't!'

'I did and it turned out that was the least of it. When they investigated there were thirty illegal workers employed by Tredinnick's building firm and none of them were even getting the minimum wage. They were working in unsafe conditions and the staff accommodation failed on almost every health and safety principle going. Even if Michael doesn't end up with a prison sentence, he'll be paying so many fines he won't have the spare capital to try and buy The Old Forge.'

'You're amazing, but I hope you don't end up having to pay the price for making an enemy out of the Tredinnicks.'

'I don't think they've got too many friends left in town, so I won't lose any sleep over that.'

'Do you think someone else might offer to buy The Old Forge.' It was so ungrateful of Ella to ask for anything more, but she wasn't going to be able to stop worrying until her parents had finally paid off their debts.

'There have been a few different people expressing an interest and it'll sort itself out. You just need to have faith for a tiny bit longer.'

'If you say it's going to happen then I believe you, because you've already worked miracles. I don't know how I can ever repay you.'

'How about promising me you won't just run off again next time we hit a bump in the road, and that whatever it is, we'll work through it together? I've let myself fall in love with you all over again Ysella Mehenick and I don't want to risk waking up and finding you've done a moonlight flit. So if you ever decide you want to leave Port Agnes, we'll find a way to make that work. Together.'

'I never wanted to leave. I love Port Agnes and the most important people in my life are all here.'

'The stable block at Six Acre Farm is technically on the boundaries of Port Agnes and Port Tremellien and I'm due to move back in when the flood damage to the Carmichaels' place has been repaired, so I'm not sure where that leaves me?' Dan grinned and her stomach flipped, the way it always did when he smiled at her like that.

'I think that still qualifies.'

'Well if it doesn't, I think I might be able to get into that select group soon anyway.' Dan's eyes met hers. 'I've been thinking about moving permanently into the end cottage on Mercer's Row. We'd practically be neighbours and you know exactly why that place means so much to me...'

'I can't believe you'll be living just a few doors up. It's a good job Dad doesn't think of you as an emmet any more, or you might have ended up being the one with a brick through your window.'

'He seemed pretty pleased when I told him just now. He even suggested we go for a beer at The Jolly Sailor together later to celebrate the news.' Dan grinned again. 'So it seems I've won over Jago Mehenick. The question is, can I win over his daughter?'

'I can think of worse people to have as neighbours. There's Michael Tredinnick for a start!' It was Ella's turn to grin as he tried and failed to look offended.

'It's a start, but I was hoping we might not be neighbours for long anyway.'

She looked up at him and he suddenly looked incredibly nervous. 'I was hoping I might be able to persuade you to move those few doors up the road too, eventually.'

'I wasn't expecting you to say that.' Ella couldn't keep the smile off her face, despite her attempts to play it cool. It was all she'd ever wanted when she'd still been scrawling Dan's name on the back of her exercise books at school. But there was still a tiny bit of her that couldn't believe it might not all be snatched away again, she just needed a moment to let it all sink in.

'It's okay, I don't need an answer now. But Port Agnes felt like home to me from the moment I moved here, and nowhere more so than Mercer's Row. I can't imagine ever wanting to leave.' Dan lowered his voice. 'Unless it's with you.'

'Don't you think it's too soon for you to know that for sure?' They'd only been back in each other's lives for a few months after all those years apart, but even as she tried to protest she knew it wasn't true. She was as certain of anything she'd ever been in her life that she wanted to be with Dan and she'd had more than enough of chasing after things that were never going to make her happy when all she had to do was say yes.

'It's not too soon for me. I love you Ysella Mehenick. I've loved you since we were sixteen.'

'I love you too, Dan.' In the end, the words had just slipped out, before she'd had the chance to debate whether or not she should say them. If something was as natural as that – like breathing in and out – it had to be right. Looking at him as he smiled in response, she felt a surge of pure joy. The sort it's impossible to feel unless everything in life is just the way you want it.

'In that case I'm even luckier than I realised.' Dan leant into her, closing the gap between them and she lifted her head from the pillows to kiss him. Fate had led her back to Port Agnes when she'd desperately needed to come home, but the last thing she'd expected was to fall in love with Dan Ferguson all over again. It wasn't just Dan, though, she'd fallen in love with her home town again too, and the new life she'd built there. As Dan kissed her again nothing could spoil the moment, not even the threat of Ruth or Jago bursting in, and catching them kissing, just like when they were seventeen. She was exactly where she was meant to be.

The green man, whose face was swathed in bandages so that only his eyes and mouth were visible, held his arms out, doing a convincing impression of a zombie and Ella waved her wand in front of him, stopping him in his tracks.

'Dan Ferguson, you might be some weird mixture of a mummy and Frankenstein's monster, but if you get green face paint all over this costume, I'll show you what scary really is!' Ella laughed, as he playfully tried to make a grab for her all the same. 'And anyway, it's taken the best part of an hour to bandage you up, I'm not about to start all over again.'

'Do we really have to go this Halloween party? I never thought I'd find a witch quite this irresistible – well not since my crush on Sabrina the Teenage Witch when I was about ten years old. But those fishnets...'

'I'll turn you into a toad.' Ella blew him a kiss, despite the threat. 'Tempting as it is to stay home, I promised Anna and Brae we'd be at the party and I don't want to let them down.'

'Neither do I. But can you at least put on a false nose and paint one of your teeth black? It's the only chance I've got of resisting you. Whatever this costume might suggest, I'm only human.' Dan took hold of her hand and she forgot all about the prospect of getting covered in green face paint.

In the end, they'd had to run hand in hand to the party from their cottage on Mercer's Row, a good half an hour after it had started. There were two more witches in the garden of Anna and Brae's house, one of whom was puffing on a vape, while the other drank beer straight from the bottle.

Inside the house there were ghosts, nuns, several Count Draculas and even a zombie version of The Beatles. It took a few minutes to track down Anna and Brae, who were in their front room, dressed as Superman and Wonder Woman. They were dancing with a group of others to the 'Time Warp', including Jess and Dom, who seemed to be working things out despite the strain that infertility had put on their marriage. It was so nice to see everyone looking so happy.

'Oh, thanks for coming!' Anna stopped midway into stepping to the right and threw her arms around Ella.

'I'm sorry we're late.' Her apology was lost as the others shouted out the chorus of 'Time Warp' and danced around them as if they weren't even there.

'Now you're here, we've got something to tell you.' Brae looked towards Anna as he spoke, and she nodded.

'Not here, though. It's too noisy.' Anna smiled. 'We'll go out to the conservatory. I don't think there's anyone out there.'

Dan took hold of Ella's hand again as they followed their friends out towards the back of the house away from the hub of the party.

'We're going to be making an announcement later, but we wanted you to hear it first.' Anna didn't waste any time when they reached the quiet of the conservatory and Brae wrapped his arms around her waist; risking a static shock from all the polyester in their costumes.

'You're not moving away, are you?' It was selfish of Ella to ask, but everything was so perfect as it was, she couldn't bear to think of a single thing changing. Anna was her boss and her best friend, and Anna's relationship with Brae made Ella almost as happy as her own life with Dan. She loved her job, and spending so much time with her parents, as well as all the other friends she'd made since being back in Port Agnes. Ella had even become a godmother to Sophie and Euan's little girl, Robyn, whom Ella had delivered safely before Sophie had finally moved back in with her parents. Sophie and Euan were making a go of things, dividing their time between Scotland and Somerset, and Sophie came back to Port Agnes to visit as often as she could.

Ella and Dan had moved into the end cottage of Mercer's Row about a month after the accident. After Sophie had left the cottage at the other end, he'd rented it out to a local couple for far less than the going rate, much to Jago's delight. The middle two cottages had been turned into holiday lets, but Jago could hardly complain about that either, since he'd used the money he'd recouped from The Old Forge to buy one of them and get a regular income that would be all the more welcome when he and Ruth retired. Dan's friend, who'd been interested in The Old Forge, had turned out to be the vicar from St Jude's and Dan had helped him get listed building status for the building, as well as securing church, community and lottery funding to buy it. The building had been turned into a community centre, with everything from computer lessons for pensioners, to a soft play centre for local pre-schoolers.

When Dan had asked Ella if she was disappointed that she'd never get to live at The Old Forge, she'd honestly been able to say that there was nothing she wanted that she didn't already have. Michael Tredinnick had escaped with a suspended sentence and a series of crippling fines. Within months Tredinnick Farm and the caravan park had been up for sale and word had it that

Michael was moving to the Costa del Sol – with the rest of the criminals, as Jago had so eloquently put it.

'As if Brae would ever agree to leave his beloved fish and chip shop, let alone Port Agnes!' Anna gave her boyfriend a playful nudge as she spoke, snapping Ella out of her reverie.

'I would if you wanted me to.'

'Well, luckily for you, I don't.' For a moment Anna seemed to have forgotten that Ella and Dan were even there. 'Sorry, we're wittering on, but what we really want to tell you is that we're getting married in July. I know we've not been together for all that long, but we've been talking about this for months.'

'Really? That's brilliant!' Ella smiled at her friends, hoping with all her heart that this would be the start of a new chapter for them. Anna had confided that she'd been trying for a baby with Brae ever since they'd moved in together. With a wedding to think about, maybe they'd stress a bit less about conceiving and it would all fall into place.

'Congratulations!' Dan shook Brae's hand. 'Have you set a date?'

'The sixth of July, it would have been my parents' anniversary if they'd still been here.' Anna blew out her cheeks. 'I start to hyperventilate when I think about organising a wedding without my mum, but I'm sure it'll be fine.'

'I don't give a damn about the details, as long as I get to marry Anna.' Brae shrugged and Ella couldn't help smiling again. They really were perfectly matched.

'Well if there's anything we can do to help, just let us know.' Dan exchanged a look with Ella and she nodded.

'I was going to say the same. I've been involved in organising a wedding, so I'm more than happy to help, as long as you don't think I'm a jinx!'

'That's why we needed to tell you first, because I wanted to ask Ella if she'll be my maid of honour and Brae's got something he wants to ask Dan.'

'I'd love to!' Ella cut across Brae, before the poor man even had the chance to speak. 'Sorry, I'm just so thrilled you asked me.'

'Who else would we ask, when it's down to you that we're even together?' Anna gave her a hug.

'My question might seem a bit less obvious.' Brae shuffled from foot to foot. 'But I wanted to ask if you'd be my best man, Dan. I know we'd barely seen each other since school until we met up again last year, but with the fish and chip shop I don't get to socialise that often and my cousin, Pete, has already booked to go to Las Vegas for his birthday in July...'

'I'd be honoured.' Dan went to shake his hand again, but Brae pulled him into a hug making all of them laugh.

'I think we need to have dinner together next week to do some initial planning.' Ella was already checking off a mental list of what needed to be done. Anna might not have any family around her, but she had the next best thing.

'That sounds like a great idea, but maybe we should get back to the party before everyone starts to wonder where we are. I'm so glad you're both on board, it means I don't have to feel like I'm doing this all on my own.' Anna linked her arm through Ella's, as a security light in the garden suddenly came on, and a couple dressed as pirates sprang apart.

'Isn't that Toni?' Ella peered into the garden, but the couple had already darted out of sight.

'I think so and if I'm not mistaken, she was being more than friendly with Bobby when they triggered the security light. It doesn't matter how hard they try to insist they're just friends, or why they've tried to keep the pretence up for so long, they give the game away every time they're in the same room. Even if they're nowhere near each other.' Anna sighed. 'I've got no idea why they're so determined to try and hide it. I can't imagine people being anything but happy for them.'

'I hope they find a way to work it out.' Ella caught Dan's eye and he held out his hand. 'If they're trying to keep it secret until they can find the right time to tell everyone, they might find it's already passed them by.'

'They'll work it out. The four of us worked it out okay in the end, didn't we? Even if I'd already been in love with Ella for fourteen years by the time she finally moved in.'

'Dan's right and, if I can muddle through, anyone can.' Brae laughed as Anna nudged him again.

'Is that what I am, a case of muddling through?'

'You're my whole world and I'm going to stand up in front of everyone and tell them that. Even if there's a good chance of me falling over my words.' Brae wrapped his arms around Anna again, as Ella leant into Dan. Things had a way of working themselves out and Port Agnes looked after its own. In the past year, life had changed beyond all recognition for two of its midwives; but there were babies waiting to be born and other midwives whose stories had only just begun. For tonight, though, Ella was going to celebrate and trust in the knowledge that Port Agnes would take care of tomorrow.

ACKNOWLEDGMENTS

Thank you to all the readers who choose to spend their time reading my books and especially those who go to the effort of leaving a review, it means more than you will ever know and I feel so privileged to be doing the job I love.

I hope you have enjoyed the first of The Cornish Midwives novels. I am not a midwife, sadly, but I have done my best to ensure that the medical details are as accurate as possible. I am very lucky that one of my close friends, Beverley Hills, is a brilliant midwife and I will be dedicating one of the future books in this series to her. However, if you are also one of the UK's wonderful midwives, providing such fantastic support for new and expectant mums, I hope you'll forgive any details which draw on poetic licence to fit the plot.

My thanks also go to the team at Boldwood Books for their help, especially my amazing editor, Emily Ruston, for whipping this book into shape! I have already learned so much from you, Emily. Thanks too to my wonderful copy editor, Cari, and proofreader, Shirley, for all your hard work on this first book in The Cornish Midwives series.

I can't sign off without thanking my writing tribe, The Write Romantics, and all the other authors who I am lucky enough to call friends.

Finally, as always, the biggest thank you goes to my family – Lloyd, Anna and Harry - for their support, patience, love and belief.

MORE FROM JO BARTLETT

We hope you enjoyed reading *The Cornish Midwife*. If you did, please leave a review.

If you'd like to gift a copy, this book is also available as an ebook, digital audio download and audiobook CD.

Sign up to Jo Bartlett's mailing list for news, competitions and updates on future books.

http://bit.ly/JoBartlettNewsletter

ABOUT THE AUTHOR

Jo Bartlett is the bestselling author of nineteen women's fiction titles. She fits her writing in between her two day jobs as an educational consultant and university lecturer and lives with her family and three dogs on the Kent coast.

Visit Jo's Website: www.jobartlettauthor.com

 twitter.com/J_B_Writer
 facebook.com/JoBartlettAuthor
 instagram.com/jo_bartlett123

ABOUT BOLDWOOD BOOKS

Boldwood Books is a fiction publishing company seeking out the best stories from around the world.

Find out more at www.boldwoodbooks.com

Sign up to the Book and Tonic newsletter for news, offers and competitions from Boldwood Books!

http://www.bit.ly/bookandtonic

We'd love to hear from you, follow us on social media:

facebook.com/BookandTonic

twitter.com/BoldwoodBooks

instagram.com/BookandTonic

Printed in Great Britain
by Amazon